KAY MAREE

Contents

Inked Temptation
Book One
Inked Series

All rights reserved

Copyright © 2018 by Kay Maree

Cover and Interior Images © Depositphotos
Editing – Susan Horsnell & Word Writer Pro
Cover and Formatting – Susan Horsnell

Published By:

Susan Horsnell T/A Cocky Romance Publishing

A.B.N. 57 357 599 847

Dedication

Aleisha Maree and Kirstymarie, you ladies push me daily and I couldn't have finished this book without your constant love, support and encouragement.

I fight for strength, to breath and to earn my wings every day and no matter what time it is, I know you girls have my back.

So, I dedicate Ally & Xavier's story to you two beautiful souls and I hope you push for strength, for breath and for the wings you need in life to make your souls complete.

Love you girls hard.

Friends for life. xx

Social Links

Facebook - https://www.facebook.com/kay.maree.334
Twitter - https://twitter.com/MisKay85
Website -
https://kaymareesmutlover.wixsite.com/contemporary-
romance

Acknowledgements

First a huge thank you to my family - without your love and support I wouldn't be where I am today.

Secondly, I want to thank my beautiful editor Susan Horsnell. You are amazing, special, kind and so much more. You always go above and beyond to help me and there are never enough thank yous in the world to repay what you do for me.

To my Beta girls, you ladies are amazing and encouraging and no matter what I throw at you, you eat it up and still ask for more. I love you crazy girls, keep being you and never let anyone dull your sparkle.

Leanna, Cynthia, Amanda, Tania, Annmarie, Kristine, Erica, Zoe, Ianeta & Julie.

To all my Readers -thank you so much for taking a chance on my book babies. I hope they touch your lives just as much as they touch mine. You guys are amazing keep being you, fight over book boyfriends, keep stalking the Authors you love, but also remember to raise your face to the sun and feel the heat flush against your skin, Dance in the rain just to remind yourself you're alive. It's the simple moments in life which keep us pushing forward. Fight for strength, love and the happily ever after you deserve.

Love you all, you guys make my heart full.

Kay Maree xx

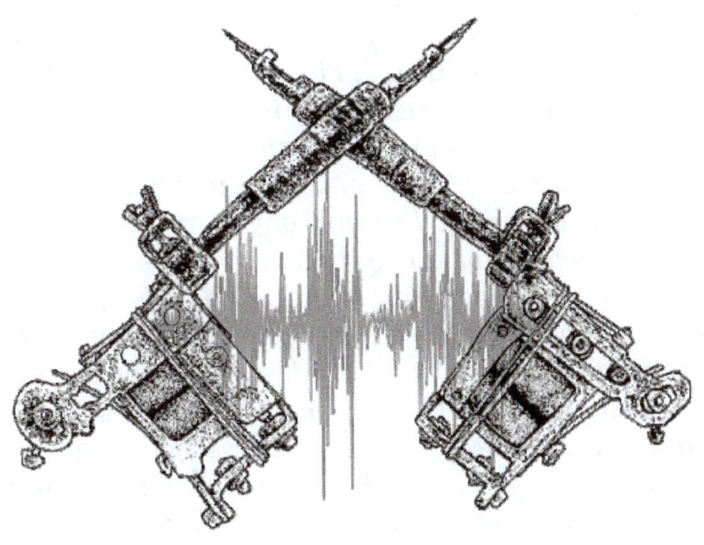

THE PAST

"Morning Button," my father calls out as I make my way into the

kitchen. I find him flipping pancakes like a pro.

"Morning Dad." I cross to where he is standing at the stove, wrap my arms around his waist and he bends down to kiss the top of my head.

"How did you sleep?"

Releasing my hold, I head to the fridge and grab the orange juice before moving to the small dining table.

I turn to smile at him. "Great, did Mom get away okay this morning?" Mum was heading to Queensland for a couple of days with a few of her friends.

"Yep."

I look over my shoulder to see him nodding and peering through the kitchen window with a faraway look on his face. I know they've been having troubles lately, I hear them arguing at night when they think I'm sleeping. My parents never argue in front of me and I know it's mostly because my father won't allow it. He doesn't want me seeing their animosity toward each other. But, I'm eighteen now, not a little girl anymore. I'm aware they've been having problems for a long time and as much as I love my parents, my mother is far from maternal. I've heard her a few times, late at night, telling my father the only reason she had me was because of him. It hurts a little less each time she says it. I guess I've become used to the way she is, I can't change her so, I try not to let it worry me. My father loves me dearly and only ever wants me to be happy, I just wish he would realize, I want him to be happy too. Whether it's with my mother, or on his own, everybody deserves to be happy. Especially my dad.

"Ally!" Dad's shout breaks into my thoughts.

Shaking my head, I make my way towards the cupboard to grab some glasses.

"Sorry, dad."

"You looked like you were off with the pixies." He laughs and shakes his head at me as he plates up the mouthwatering pancakes.

"Is everything ok, Button?" Concern is clear in his voice and I hate that I have worried him.

I smile at his pet name for me. He used to call me Button Nose, but when I turned fourteen. I told him I was getting too old for it. So, he shortened it to Button and won't budge. I won't ever admit it, but I kind of like it.

"Yeah everything is perfect, I was just..." I don't get to finish my sentence when the doorbell sounds

"I'll grab the door, here pop these on the table" I hand him the glasses and hurry towards the front door. I glance at the clock on the wall as I pass, it's 8:30 am. I wonder who would be calling this early on a Saturday morning. Pulling the door open, I'm surprised to find my ex-boyfriend, Luke, standing before me.

We broke up about two months ago. He was too intense and borderline crazy for me to handle. Not the good kind of crazy, more like he enjoyed pushing the limits by inflicting pain type of crazy. We were only together for about four months before his true colors surfaced.

I feel a chill descend over me and realize I'm shaking. My chest tightens. What is he doing here? He should be in jail. Oh God, why is he here?

"Luke....." I manage to get out in a shaky voice before severe pain erupts across my belly.

I look down and my eyes widen at the sight of a huge knife protruding from my belly. A river of blood soaks my shirt. I stumble backwards, trip on the hallway rug and crash to the ground as everything around me becomes a blur. I hear my father shouting in the background while things are smashing in the distance. I taste the salt of my tears. My eyes flutter shut. Pain and blood flash behind my eyelids before darkness pulls me under.

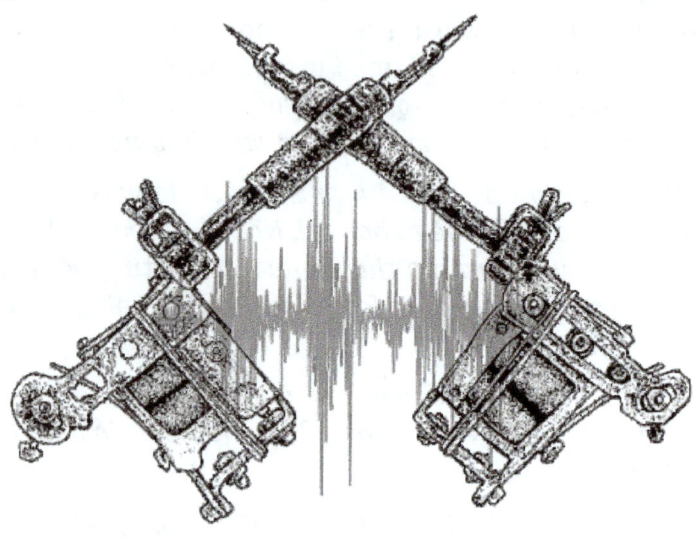

CHAPTER ONE

Ally

I wake with a start....heart pounding.... sweat pouring down my face. My hand shakes as I reach out and grab the glass of water from my bedside table. Holding the glass to rest against my forehead, I hope the coolness will calm me down and slow my racing heart.

Reaching out with my free hand, I grab my phone and swipe the alarm off. I'm not in the mood right now for my alarm tone - *Brave* by *Sara Bareilles.* I have had it as my alarm tone since it was released, hoping it would push me forward each day. But, today I don't feel the need to push forward. I guess for the next week, this is a feeling which will haunt me. It's been four years since the nightmare of *that* day happened and it still feels like yesterday.

I remember so clearly, waking up in the hospital and being told my father was dead. Then, being told I had been asleep for 6 days.

I had expected to see my mother sitting beside my bed, but I should have known better. The selfish cow only ever thought about herself so, why did I think losing her husband and nearly losing her daughter would change anything? Shaking the thoughts free, I push to my feet and head towards the bathroom, needing a shower to clean myself of the recurring nightmare.

Have you ever looked at your reflection in the mirror and wondered how you ended up the way you have and not in a good way? I do this every morning, wonder where I went wrong. Was it the moment my father was taken away from me or, was it what happened afterwards when my mother put it all on me? Every day I feel like I'm stumbling through the dark and no matter what I do, I can't seem to shake free and pull myself into the light. Pushing the feeling to the back of my mind, I blow out a deep breath.

Thinking of my mother, I better go and see her today. I don't live at home anymore. When I was released from the hospital, I couldn't go back to where dad had died. So, I used the money I had saved and moved to a one-bedroom apartment near Merewether beach. It's nothing flash, it's actually not much more than the size of a shoebox, but it works for me and it's cheap. It's not like I have a lot of stuff.

Reaching up, I take the towel off my head and watch as auburn hair falls to my shoulders. I shiver as a few water droplets slide down my back. After quickly drying off, I throw on a pair of black yoga pants and a brown tank top before sitting on the side of my queen size bed and pulling my sneakers on. I already feel my stomach roil at the mere thought of having to see *that* woman. I hate going there. Not only does she still live in the same house, but every time I visit, she gives me another reason why everything which happened four years ago is my fault.

I can still hear her voice in my head from the last time I called in... *"What good are you? I wish I'd never had you."*

I shake my head as I make my way towards the front door. I try to visit at least once a week on a Saturday because I know my dad would have wanted me to and I guess I believe I deserve the ugly words she throws at me.

Looking up at the yellow painted two-story house, it looks so picture perfect with it's green lawn and white picket fence, you would never guess at the ugliness which happened that day. Pushing my shoulders back, I swing open the gate and make my way up the path towards the front door. I reach out and grip the door handle. My hand shakes as visions from that day assault my mind once again. The yelling, the pain and then nothing but darkness. As I open the door, I squeeze my eyes shut to stop the tears from falling. After a moment, I open my eyes and allow them to adjust to the dimly lit hallway. It's like I have walked into a cave with only a few lamps scattered around the place emitting a soft glow. The curtains are drawn closed. Trying to ignore the state of the house, I head towards the living room where I hear the television. I suck in a deep breath as the stench of stale cigarette hits my nose, causing my stomach to roil. It smells like an ashtray in here. This is nothing like the home I grew up in.

"Hi, mother." I speak as nicely as I can.

Turning to face me from her recliner, I notice her bloodshot eyes and know today's visit is going to be a bad one. I straighten my back in readiness for the verbal blow I know will come. I move forward and start picking up the empty bottles of alcohol strewn on the floor as well as the overflowing ashtray beside her. I keep my eyes on what I'm doing so I don't have to see the hate and disgust in her eyes. I don't need to see them to know that's the look she is giving me. I can feel them boring into me as I move around the room.

"Why you?" Her speech is slurred.

My stomach twists and my heart feels heavy in my chest knowing exactly what she means by those words. *Why did I survive and not my father?* I don't answer because, I don't know the answer. It's also the same question I ask myself every day.

"I'm talking to you, you little bitch," she spits out.

I still don't say anything.

"You're such a fucking spoilt brat!"

I suck in a breath when I hear her moving around behind me and cringe, knowing what's about to come.

"You think you're so fucking special!"

She pushes me and I try to keep my balance, but it's no use and before I know what's happening, I hit the ground hard. Rolling onto my back, I wince as pain shoots up my side. I try to keep the pained look off my face because I know it will only give her more ammunition to use against me.

"Don't touch me," I bite out in a voice I can only hope comes out stronger than I'm feeling. Not backing down, I look her dead in the eyes. Something flashes across her face but it was so quick, I don't get time to work out what it was.

"You're not worth it," she spits before turning and making her way towards the stairs leading up to the second floor.

I don't bother helping her when she wobbles and has to use the wall for support. Instead, I wait to hear her reach the top, quickly clean up the mess I can see and get the hell out of here.

I know my reality, I know what my life has become. I don't have any friends which is why all I do is work and go home. I can't let anybody in because nobody deserves to deal with the failure I have become.

I struggle to catch my breath and hear my heart echoing in my ears. I need air. I need to be somewhere which centers me. I need out of this house, out of this nightmare which has become my constant companion.

I just want to breath and live without this weight always holding me down.

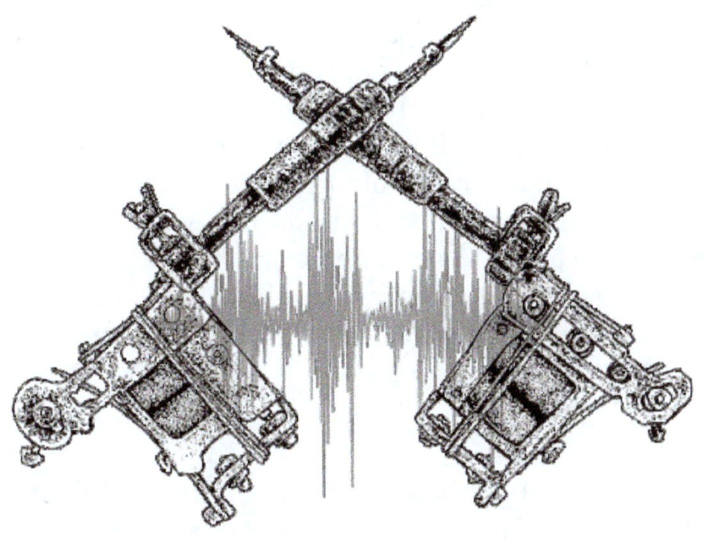

CHAPTER TWO

Xavier

The breath catches in my throat as I watch the way her head tilts back while she soaks in the warmth of the day. Her hair falls down her back in waves, the ends kissing the sand. I bite back a groan as the urge to grip those silky auburn strands in my hands overwhelms me. Fuck, it's been like this for weeks.

I can still remember the first time I saw her. One glance and it was as if I'd been sucker punched in the stomach. I couldn't catch my breath. I'd sat on an old wooden bench seat overlooking Merewether beach after grabbing some lunch from one of the cafes nearby. I had just lifted the coffee to my lips when I spotted her. She was walking along the sand, the water rushed over her feet and she bent down to pick up a shell. As she lifted it to her eyes, the sun shone around her. It was as if everything else disappeared and it was just her and me, the smell of salt in the air.

Her long auburn hair fluttered around her, lifted by the soft sea breeze. Her curvy hips swayed as she walked, but it was the look on her face which took me off guard and had everything in me standing to attention. I wanted to wrap my arms around her and keep her safe, but instead I stayed rooted to the spot and watched as she made her way along the sand. I couldn't take my eyes from her. She seemed so lost and far away. From the first day I saw her, I wanted to go to her, claim her. It was like a force was pulling me to her, but the faraway look in her eyes, the pain, held me back. So, instead, every day I sit on the same bench, eat my lunch and wait for her to come.

Pushing through the glass doors of Xtreme Ink on Darby street, I soak in the familiar atmosphere which always surrounds me. I know, no matter what happens, this place is where I belong.

I bought Xtreme Ink a few years back. No matter what shit is thrown my way, I know this place settles me. I look around at the bare brick walls which have copper pipes running along them. Black framed photos, showcasing peoples tattoos in each of them, hang from the pipes. Copper pendant lights hang above each one highlighting the images below. I soak it all in, from the charcoal tiles on the floor to the roof with its bare wooden beams left open and on display. A huge copper fan spins slowly, circulating and cooling the air. It resembles an old warehouse but is a smaller version. It doesn't matter what happens outside this place because being in here centers me.

I pass by the huge, black leather lounge which sits along one wall and the sleek black desk in the waiting area before heading towards the hallway which leads to a small kitchen at the back of the shop. I need a coffee.

My best friend, Beau strolls out of the kitchen and gives me a chin lift. I hired him not long after I bought the place. He looks like a mean bastard with his dark hair and sharp blue eyes. He stands an inch shorter than my 6'4" and is covered in tattoos. We have known each other since we were kids and nothing gets past him, including my bad mood.

"What's happening, mate?" he calls out as I storm past him, not interested in stopping to talk.

I grunt in reply not in the fucking mood for his candy ass today. I should have known better than to think he'd leave me the fuck alone when he starts following me into the kitchen.

"X what's up, man?" He leans against the bench as I make my coffee, eyes boring into me.

Erica, another one of my tattoo artists walks in wearing a large pair of black sunglasses. She looks pale, pasty, like she has been hugging the toilet bowl all night.

"You sick?" I ask her while attempting to ignore Beau.

I can feel his eyes still on me, but don't want to get into shit right now. Especially before my morning coffee. How could I even begin to explain what the fuck is going on with me when I don't even know? Fuck! I'm no fucking saint. I've had my fair share of women but this woman does something to me and I've been trapped in some kind of fucking bubble ever since.

From the first time I laid eyes on her, nobody has come up to scratch and my cock has no interest in anybody else. I haven't even said two words to this woman. One fucking look! One fucking look was all it took. I may as well cut my balls off and give them to her.

Erica speaks, snapping me back to the present. I need to have my head fucking examined, this zoning out shit is not fucking helping.

"I think I had too much to drink last night." She groans, flops into a seat at the small table in the middle of the room and lowers her head to the table. Her mousy blonde hair fans out around her.

"You good to go today or not?" I snap.

Fuck, that's all I need today, to have to find someone to cover her shift. I may have no choice but to call in Justin even though he's worked the past seven days straight and I know he needs a day off. We're usually pretty quiet on a Thursday, but for some reason, I'm fully booked and so is Beau. We can't take walk ins today which is why I asked Erica to come in, she could cover anyone who comes in.

"What's up your ass?" she hisses out.

I look over my shoulder in time to see her wince at the loudness of her own voice. Fuck, it's going to be a long day. I shake my head and turn back to focus on the coffee. I have no intention of talking about it. I'm a private person, I don't share much, even with Beau.

"Nothing," I finally manage to grunt.

Fuck! I need to get my shit together. Running my hand down the side of my face, I feel the rough stubble from not shaving, there's a few days growth. Fuck, I can't even be bothered to shave. I blow out a deep breath, pick up my coffee and head towards the door. I'm done with this shit today and it's not even 9 am yet.

"I think some pussy has him all fucked up." Beau laughs from behind me.

I feel my muscles tense and lock when he says the word pussy. I'm used to him being a man whore and the shit which comes out of his mouth, but for some reason, possessiveness grips me when he calls my mystery girl – *pussy*. Before I have a chance to call him on it, Erica pipes up.

"You're fucking disgusting sometimes, Beau."

"What the fuck ever, you love my ass," he fires back, still chuckling.

I shake my head and head towards my station while Erica continues giving him shit. It's the same shit, just a different day with them. They need to fuck each other and get it out of their system, even I can feel the tension between the two of them.

After a couple of mouthfuls of coffee, I start to feel a little better. After placing the coffee down on my desk, I reach over and flick on the power of the sound system which is built into the wall. The first bars of *Enter Sandman* by *Metallica* blasts from the speakers. Grabbing plastic wrap, I go about preparing my station before my first client arrives.

Leaning back in my chair, I stretch the aching muscles in my back after finishing a huge piece of a dragon on the guy's back. It's fucking stunning, but I felt like I was going crossed eyed while making sure not to fuck up the intricate detail on the damn thing. Rolling my head back on my shoulders, I push to my feet. I'm in desperate need of another coffee.

"Thanks man, it's fucking awesome." Jeff, my client, studies the tatt in the large mirror on the wall. This is his third visit to get this piece done. I'm stoked it turned out great and he likes it.

"No probs, man. Go and see Erica out the front, she'll fix you up." I nod towards the front desk where Erica is busy doing some paperwork.

"Sure, maybe I'll finally get that date I've been after." He smiles before sauntering towards the front, his shirt still off.

I turn to look at Beau when he growls low in his throat. He doesn't notice me, he's totally focused on Jeff and I swear I hear him mumble – *like fuck.*

I shake my head and look through the cut-out window which lets us see the waiting area out front. A chuckle leaves me when Jeff leans over the desk and runs a finger down the side of Erica's face. I laugh harder when Beau jumps to his feet and rushes out to the front.

"Erica, I can fix him up, go grab yourself a coffee," Beau barks out.

I don't hear her reply as I head down the hall, but I have confidence in Erica's ability to handle herself....and Beau.

I flick the kettle on and glance up at the clock. It's almost 2pm. Another hour and I'll take my lunch break. Hopefully, I'll get to see my girl. Fuck, I run a hand down the side of my face. How the shit did she become my girl?

"What the fuck is Beau's problem?" Erica snarls as she steps into the kitchen.

I'm amazed she has to ask. Beau has had a hard on for her ever since he first saw her, but his usual come ons haven't worked on her at all. I shrug, not giving the game away, this shit is funny to watch.

"Fucking men," she grumbles as she moves towards the fridge.

"Your father just walked in as Jeff left," she says over her shoulder.

She speaks just as the man himself walks through the door.

"Son," he smiles while looking around.

"Dad, is everything okay? Do you want a coffee?"

"Everything is fine. Can't I just stop by to see my son?" He chuckles "Coffee would be good.".

I go about fixing another cup as he takes a seat at the table.

"What's happening, dad?" I ask as I pour milk into the cups.

"I'll just be out front, I'll call out when your next appointment turns up."

"Thanks Erica." I continue stirring the coffees.

Dad stops by probably once a week to chat and I don't mind. My father is my fucking hero. He used to be a firefighter and had always wanted me to be one. The day I came home and told him I wanted to be a tattoo artist, I thought he'd lose his shit but he has supported me since the beginning. He even sends his old fire buddies to see me as well as the new recruits. He still trains the new guys but doesn't work in the field anymore, not since my mom got sick.

"How's mom doing?" I feel a lump form in my throat every time I think of her.

"Good, she misses you." He nods and looks down at his cup when I place it in front of him.

I notice how much older he seems to look today. He's a big man with dark hair and green eyes, I look just like him except, I have more tattoos than he does. I notice his hair has a few more grays spread throughout and the dark circles under his eyes seem to be blacker. I know he finds it hard to sleep. My mother is his soulmate and knowing he can't do shit to help her, guts him.

One night over drinks, he had a little too much and told me how much it fucks with his head. He hates knowing there is nothing he can do to stop this fucking disease from taking her mind. It must be hard as shit for the love of your life not to know who you are after so long. My parents have been together since they left high school. My father said, from the moment he set eyes on my mum, he knew she was the one for him.

I clear my throat and try to concentrate on the conversation instead of thinking about all the other shit. It makes me think of the situation I find myself in with my mystery girl and now is not the time to be thinking of her.

"I saw her on Monday."

"Yeah, the nurse told me. She also said it was a bad day."

I nod, it was a bad day. I doubt she remembers I was even there. What the fuck, I doubt she even knew who I was! My mother was diagnosed with Alzheimer's Disease last year and shit has been hard on all of us. It fucking sucks to watch such a strong woman slowly forgetting things, especially her family, those she loves most of all.

"I'll come over after I finish work." I watch as a small smile graces my father's lips. I know he needs me now more than ever.

"Good, I'll grab something on the way home and we can have dinner together."

"Sounds good, dad."

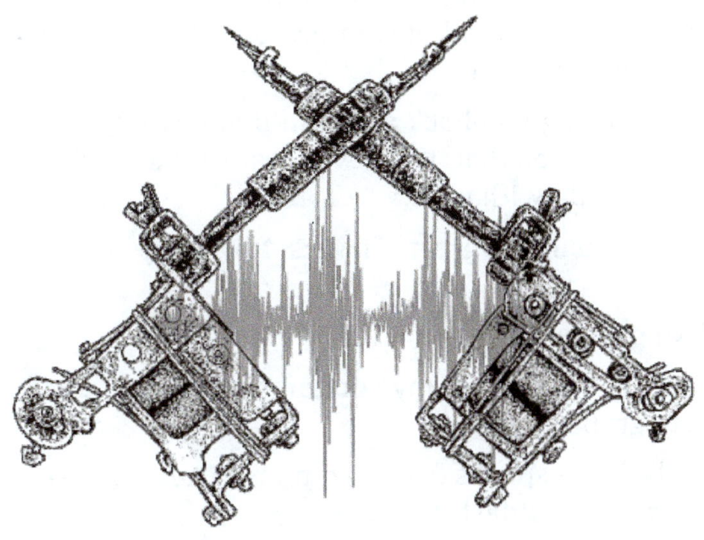

CHAPTER THREE

Ally

"I'm going to take my lunch break now." I look up at the clock to see it reads ten minutes to three. I always have a late lunch break, something about the afternoon sun has an effect on me.

Cynthia looks up from the trolley of returned books she is stacking back onto the shelves. I work in the local library where I have been for a few years. There is something about working here which grounds me. I know it may sound weird, but the history and love stories which lie between the pages of the books lining the shelves, lets me get lost in a different world, even if it's only for a brief time.

"Okay." She shrugs her shoulders, her voice snapping me out of my head.

I like Cynthia, but it's not like we're friends. She doesn't talk much either. It's kind of comfortable, she seems to always be in her own world also.

"I can bring you back a muffin if you want," I smile. I'm not sure why I asked that. I've never really talked to her before, unless it had to do with work

"That would be great. Thanks, Ally." She smiles back at me.

"No problem."

Feeling a bit out of my comfort zone, I turn and head to the desk to grab my bag.

"Ally?" She speaks from behind me causing me to startle and my heart to beat faster

Shit, get it together, Ally! I take a few deep breaths before turning around to face her. I notice the wide-eyed look she is giving me.

"Sorry," she apologizes.

"It's fine, I just didn't expect you to be there." I shake my head at my over-reaction.

"I just thought you might want to grab a coffee after work today?"

My first instinct is to tell her no, but when I look into her eyes again, I see a touch of sadness there. Something inside me shifts and maybe a coffee wouldn't be so bad. I know she recently moved here from Queensland and she doesn't really know anybody. What harm could come from one coffee?

"Sure, sounds like a great idea." I feel my stomach twist at the idea of allowing anybody in, but I can't keep shutting people out. A friend is probably exactly what I need. It doesn't mean I have to give her my life story. A huge smile spreads across her face and it makes me happy to see she's excited to have coffee with me.

"We'll work out the details when you get back from your break."

"Sounds great." I head out the door as a feeling of lightness washes over me.

Taking the concrete steps down to the sand, I reach the bottom and slip off my ballet flats. Holding them in my hand, I scrunch my toes in the soft warm sand and let the feeling of calmness flow through me. Leaning my head back, I close my eyes and let the warm summer sun soak into every pore while I breathe the salt air in. I always feel at peace at the beach, I'm not sure if it's the air, the sound of the waves crashing against the rocks or a combination of everything. I always remember the times my father brought me to the beach when I was young. We'd build sandcastles, explore the rock pools and swim in the rolling waves. It was like nothing could touch us while we were here, everything in the world settled and calmed. My father was always a happy man, but when we were near the water he seemed relaxed and carefree.

"I miss you dad," I whisper into the slight breeze as it floats around me.

I feel closer to him when I'm here. Bending down I pick up a shell which is buried in the sand, Lifting it to eye level, I watch as the sun bounces off the water droplets which drip from the edge. My hair is lifted by the breeze and dances around me. That's when I feel it and my skin prickles. It's as if someone is watching me, it's the same feeling every time I come down here.

I look over my shoulder and see a man sitting on one of the old wooden benches. I can't make him out, he's too far away, but I can tell by the way the hairs on my arm stand on end, it's the same man I see every time I come here.

Dropping the shell, I rub my arms as goosebumps breakout across my skin. Turning back to the water, I try to shake off the strange feeling which has settled in the pit of my stomach. I take a few steps forward and let the cool water rush over my toes, calming me. After a few moments, I look down at my watch and notice I have been out here for almost forty-five minutes. Shit, I need to get back to work. I can't believe how time flies when I'm here.

Turning, I make my way back up the beach towards the stairs. Once I get to the top I rinse the sand off my feet and head back to the library. I'll stop at a local cafe along the way and grab two muffins and coffees for Cynthia and me to have for afternoon tea. Swinging my shoes in one hand, giving my feet time to dry, I get the strange feeling of eyes on me again. I glance over my shoulder, but nobody is there. Shaking it off, I keep going I don't want to be late.

A few more hours of work pass and it's finally time to head home. I'm grabbing my bag when Cynthia walks over to the desk to grab her stuff.

"Are you still wanting to grab a coffee?" I hear the hope in her voice and feel bad that she thought it was such a hardship on me.

"Of course, on my way back from lunch I spotted a little cafe called *The 3 Monkeys.* I haven't been there before and it's just down the road."

"That sounds perfect." She reaches past me and grabs her belongings.

"Thank God, it's Friday." She laughs and I nod, agreeing with her.

"What would you usually do on a Friday night?" Cynthia asks as we head out the door.

I try to think what a normal Friday night for me is like and guess I'm a little ashamed to admit, I don't really do much.

"I usually just stay at home, get take out and curl up in bed with my Kindle."

"Damn, this friendship might work after all!" She giggles and I laugh at her reaction

"Why, what do you do?"

"Pretty much what you said, but with a side of wine."

"Well, I don't drink." I shrug, not sure what to say and not ready to give her a reason as to why I don't drink.

"Well, I can drink enough for the two of us, no worries at all." She laughs and I laugh again. She has a laugh which makes you join in and it also makes me feel lighter. I never really took much notice of her before, but she is really pretty. She has a pixie little face with black framed glasses which showcase honey colored eyes and beautiful shoulder length dark brown hair.

Strolling down the street towards the café, we pass a few businesses which have closed up for the day. We stop to look into a couple of windows to see what they have and I notice a beautiful lace dress which is absolutely stunning.

As we continue to walk, we chat about random things such as what we like to eat and so on. When we near a tattoo shop, Cynthia looks at me and then at the front door of the shop. I keep walking, not interested in going in there. Needles scare the shit out of me and I couldn't imagine allowing someone to push one into my skin unless it was a medical emergency. I couldn't think of anything worse.

"Hey, wait up!"

I look back and realize how far ahead I am.

"I'm guessing you don't like tattoos." She's panting a little after having to run to catch up.

"Oh, I love tattoos. I think there are some amazing artworks, it's the needle part I have an issue with." I laugh nervously.

"It doesn't hurt as bad as people think."

"You have a tattoo?" I sound surprised. She doesn't seem like the type of person who would have one, but then again, I don't really know her.

"I have a few actually. In places where I can cover them up if I need to and some in places where I don't have to watch." She slides her watch aside and shows me a gorgeous, colorful butterfly.

"Oh wow, that's beautiful." I grab her hand to take a closer look the wings which are scattered with oranges and reds with pink mixed in.

"Yeah, I got it when I was eighteen. I have more, but I don't think taking my shirt off in public would be a good idea."

"Um yeah, probably not," I laugh with her.

"Come on let's have that coffee and maybe I can talk you into getting one for yourself one day,"

"Hmm, I don't see that happening so don't hold your breath."

She links her arm through mine and we laugh as we head to the cafe a couple of stores down.

"You would be amazed at how freeing it can be. If you find something you really like, that you could deal with for the rest of your life. Having it on me, I can look at it and remember a specific time in my life that I never want to forget or, simply having a quote written on me which builds me up when I'm having a bad day." She looks at me and I notice a touch of sadness in her eyes.

It grips something in me, I know exactly what she means.

She shakes her head as if erasing her thoughts "Does that sound weird to you?"

"No, it makes perfect sense."

I nod, completely agreeing with her. I get it. I get what she means and maybe, just maybe, it might be what can help me too.

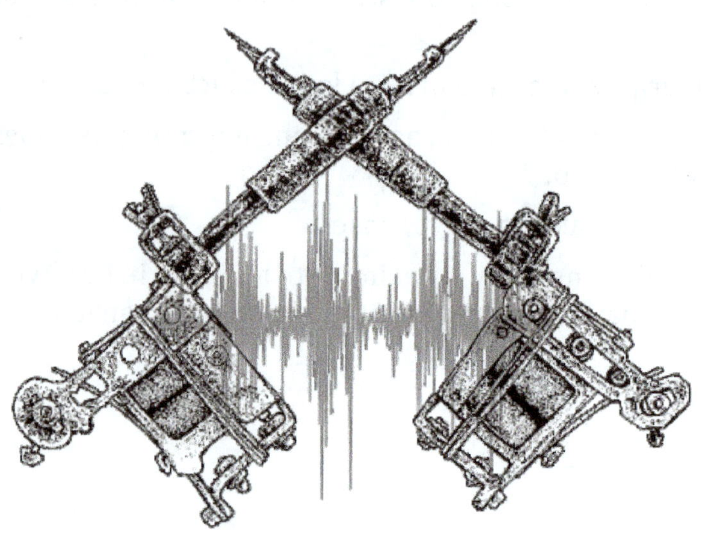

CHAPTER FOUR

Ally

It's been just over a week since I had coffee with Cynthia and our conversation has been running on a loop through my head ever since. I have thought constantly about tattoos and the way they mark certain moments in time. I guess it's the reason why I find myself standing in front of the tattoo shop we passed by last week. I'm contemplating whether or not I should just suck it up and walk in there. I know what I want, but I have to swallow my fear so I can sit in a chair and have a needle stuck into me......*over and over again!*

"Ah, screw it, you only live once," I mumble to myself as I push through the glass doors and step inside. Cold air from the air conditioning, which must be cranked up high, assaults me and it's welcomed. Outdoors is as hot as Hell. I wipe away the small droplets of sweat which had formed across my brows on the walk here and take a look around the small waiting area.

Music wafts from the speakers overhead, I'm not sure of the song, but it has a good beat. I turn slightly and take in the large area – leather couches, magazines with images of tattoos laid out on a couple of small tables. Everything is neat and clean including the charcoal colored flooring. Overhead is a huge copper fan and I focus on it for a few moments. It spins slowly and is stunning in it's raw simplicity. Bare brick walls with horizontal copper piping resembles an industrial warehouse, but there is warmth to this place. I bypass one of the huge leather couches to where photographs have been carefully hung from the pipes on one wall. So many beautiful pieces of art are showcased and I can't resist the urge to run my fingertip over the cool glass, following the intricate lines of a beautiful Tree of Life image. It's been placed over the ribs on the side of a body. I'm totally captivated and don't realize someone is standing behind me until they speak.

"Can I help you, Miss?" The deep voice makes me jump in fright and the gravelly pitch zaps through me.

I take a moment to compose myself before turning to come face to face....no, make that face to chest with a man who has to be at least a couple of feet taller than me. *Well, damn!* I take a step backwards and rake my eyes over the man. Jeans pull tight across his obviously muscled thighs, stretching them in a mouthwatering way. They're matched with a black *Henley* which I swear must have been painted on. It's rolled up to his elbows which shows off ink covered forearms that would have anyone drooling. His shoulders top layers of muscle and are broad. When my eyes lift to his face, I suck in a deep breath. His gaze is focused on my mouth, the look of hunger is like he wants to devour me. My belly flip flops out of control. When he swipes his tongue over his plump bottom lip, it takes all my control to suppress a moan. Heat radiates through every cell in my body and suddenly I find myself every bit as hungry for him.

Without realizing what I'm doing, I take a step forward. Then, another. I have an overwhelming urge to run my fingers over his five o'clock shadow and raise my hand. The moment I snap back to reality, I wave the hand around the reception area. I know I appear flustered while trying to put together my words.

"I...um...ah...tattoo. Shit!" I blow out a deep breath and step back, needing to put some distance between us so I can regain my sanity. Being so close to the man has me screwed up and I don't know which way is up.

I suck in another deep breath and try again.

"I was after a tattoo. Do I need to make an appointment?"

I peer up and become fixated on his gorgeous blue eyes. They remind me of the ocean. Amusement at my discomfort is obvious which causes embarrassment to hike up a notch. I feel the heat creep up my neck and drop my eyes to study the floor. He chuckles and I try to shake off the effect the deep sound has on me.

"Miss....?"

I snap my head up, oops...he doesn't yet know my name. I jut my arm towards him. "Ally." I don't usually shake hands, I don't meet enough people so, I'm hoping I'm doing it right. Dad always said to use my manners and shake hands when introducing myself to someone new.

He looks down at my hand and I'm worried he isn't going to shake it. A few seconds pass and then he slides his hand into mine. My body tenses with the contact and electricity fires through every cell.

His eyes lock on mine. "Xavier, but my friends call me, X."

I release my hand while trying to figure out why my body reacted the way it did. Then, like a fool, words tumble from me before I can think of what I'm saying.

"Am I your friend?"

I feel like slapping myself upside the head. What the hell is wrong with my brain to mouth filter today? He must think I'm the biggest fucking idiot around.

He opens his mouth to speak when the music from above seems to get louder. *So What* by *Pink* blasts through the speakers and I can hear other voices speaking over the top of the loud music.

"Excuse me for a sec." Xavier moves to the reception desk and twists a knob which has the music lowering.

"Touch it and I swear I'll fucking stab you." It's the voice of an angry woman.

"Seriously?" A man bellows back.

"Try it, Beau. I'm warning you. Try it and see what happens to your nuts."

I look through an opening which shows the tattoo stations in the back and bite my lip to keep from laughing. This has to be the weirdest friggin' day I've ever had.

A gorgeous woman with blonde hair and covered in tattoos stands holding what looks like a pen. She has pulled back over her shoulder like it's a knife. I watch as the man in front of her stands with his arms raised. He has a stupid smirk on his face as he tries not to laugh at her.

"It's not funny! Pink is awesome. Leave my fucking music alone!" Anger seems to be coming off her in waves.

"Come on Peaches," he croons.

"Don't fucking call me that!" She's angry, but I swear I see her lip twitch.

"I thought you loved me?" He dissolves in laughter which seems to diffuse some of the anger.

"Loving you is like a papercut....it stings at first, but then you get the fuck over it."

"Fuck you're cute, but your also psycho, Peaches." He shakes his head and laughs as he strides towards a door and disappears into a hallway.

I turn my attention back to Xavier, wondering if this day can get any stranger.

Xavier laughs, I'm not sure if it's at what just happened or at me. Either way, it doesn't matter, I'm here for a tattoo, nothing else.

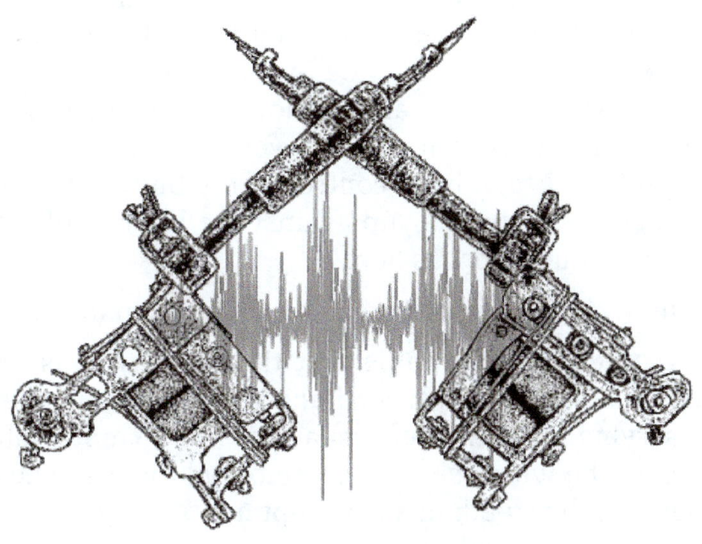

CHAPTER FIVE

Xavier

I couldn't believe my fucking eyes when I walked into the reception area and my mystery girl was standing mere feet away from me. I had to grab my chest as my heartbeat picked up and thumped in my ears. I thought I was fucking dreaming.

Stepping up behind her, I had to keep a few feet between us because fuck knows what I would have done if I got too close to her. The minute I spoke, I heard how low and gravely my voice sounded, but I couldn't help it. There was an onslaught of emotions swirling inside me and that was before she even spoke. I can't even begin to explain the effect her voice had on me.....fuck. Every fucking nerve ending in my body finished at my cock and I couldn't control a damn thing.

I have never been so hard, to the point of pain, in my life.

When she lifted her hand to shake mine, all I could think about was how many times I'd wished I could touch her. She made me feel like a nervous fifteen-year-old kid instead of the twenty-six-year old man I am. I know she wondered why I hesitated before slipping my hand over hers, but I needed to steady myself and take back control of my body. Otherwise, I was in danger of taking her up against the brick wall and not giving a fuck about who was here.

Finally, I had a name for the beautiful woman.

I grunted out my name, but the moment was broken when the music blared overhead and the dipshits in the back started carrying on with their usual bullshit. I stood watching Ally's face as she witnessed the commotion, the way she drew her lip between her teeth in an attempt not to laugh.

I focused on blocking out Erica and Beau and seized the opportunity to take in every curve and dip of Ally's body. My fingers twitched at my sides, I wanted so badly to run them through the long auburn locks which hung down her back in soft waves. I folded my arms across my chest and leaned against the reception desk to prevent myself from doing something stupid which would send her running. I tried to act cool, like I didn't have a care in the world, while all the time, world war fucking three was going on inside me.

I wanted to reach out and pull her into my arms, feel every delicious curve rubbing against me. I bit back a groan at the sight of her in tight black jeans, molded perfectly to her body and the white tank top which almost matched her milky skin.

"Xavier?"

I snap my eyes to Ally's when she speaks my name. She has an expression on her face like she's been trying to get my attention for a few minutes. I realize Erica and Beau aren't arguing any more.

"Shit, sorry." I shake my head. I might even shake some fucking sense into it.

"I was asking if I need to make an appointment?"

"For what?"

"For the tattoo I came in here for." She giggles at me and it's like hearing the best song ever played. Fuck, a tattoo. She wants a tattoo. I need to get my head back in the game. Looking her up and down, I wonder what it would be like to tattoo her perfect skin, to be able to touch her. My already hard as fuck cock jumps with excitement.

"No, I have time. I can fit you in right now if you want, honey."

I snap my head around at the sound of Erica's voice. She's standing in the doorway, which leads back to the tattoo area and she's looking straight at Ally.

"I've got this Erica," I grunt. I don't want her touching my girl.

If anybody is going to tattoo her, it's going to be fucking me.

"It's okay X, I've got this. Go to lunch." Erica smiles at me before looking back to Ally.

I struggle to hold back my anger because I was heading to lunch, but that was before my mystery girl appeared on my turf.

"*Erica*," I say through clenched teeth. "I've got it."

She tilts her head and gives me a funny look, I raise an eyebrow at her.

"Between you and Beau today, I don't know what the hell is going on." She shakes her head, turns to head back to the kitchen and grumbles under her breath as she leaves.

"I can come back if it doesn't suit." Ally's voice comes from beside me and draws my attention back to her.

"No, it's fine." I reassure her

"'But..."

"Come on, I'll take you to my station and get you set up. What do you have in mind?" My voice still sounds husky despite trying to act normally as I head towards the doorway which leads through to the back. I cast a glance over my shoulder to make sure she's following me. I blow out the breath I hadn't realized I was holding when she follows.

When we reach my station, which is set up ready, I indicate the black leather adjustable Inkbed for her to sit down. I take my seat on the swiveling stool and wait for her to get comfortable. I notice the way her hands shake as she positions her bag on her lap.

Reaching over, I place my hand over hers. A small gasp escapes her slightly parted lips and she lifts her eyes to mine. Being so close, I note for the first time how green her eyes are and the golden hue which surrounds the irises. My heart thumps and skips a beat. Shit, I'm back to reacting like a fucking fifteen-year-old again. I remove my hand, sit back and wait for her to find whatever it is she's rummaging in her bag for.

"Are you nervous?" I ask quietly.

She gives a forced laugh. "Am I that obvious? I'm sorry, I've never done this before and needles scare the shit out of me. My friend, she has a few and well...." She drifts off and I try not to smile at her rambling.

"Shit, rambling. Sorry." She huffs out a breath and blows at the hair which has fallen in front of her face.

"It's fine. Are you sure you want to do this? Once I start, there's no going back."

"Yeah, I'm sure. I'm just nervous." She locks her eyes on mine and I can see the nervousness there, but I can also see the determination to do this.

After a moment of silence, I clear my throat. "So, what is it you want?"

She pulls a piece of paper from her bag and holds it towards me. The moment I unfold it, I know what it is.

"A sound wave?" I know I sound puzzled.

"Um... yeah, it's a voice wave." She gnaws on her bottom lip.

I study the paper and return my gaze back to her eyes, they are glassy with tears. Pain swims in their depths and it does some shit to my chest. I hate that she is feeling pain, I want to take it away. Whatever this is, it must mean a lot to her. I nod before standing and scanning the drawing into the computer. Once ready, I hit print and wait for the image to be printed onto the transfer paper before sitting again.

"Where would you like it?" I take the image from the tray and grab the scissors to cut around the image. When she doesn't answer, I turn back to where she was sitting. All coherent thought flees on a gust of breath and I grip onto my table to prevent me from falling off my fucking chair.

Ally has taken her shirt off and is lying on the bed beside me. In her tight as fuck jeans and a tan sports bra, it's like every one of my fucking fantasies is coming to life right before me.

"Can I please have it on my ribs? I was going to get it on my wrist but after seeing the Tree of Life Tattoo out the front, I've changed my mind." She closes her eyes and lets her breath out slowly. I take a moment to allow my eyes to track every inch of smooth, perfect skin. I squeeze my free hand into a fist against my thigh, resisting the urge to claim her right now. I take a few deep breaths to settle myself and watch as she lays her shirt across her stomach.

Was that a scar near her belly button?

I look back at her face, her eyes are still closed but a look ghosts over her features which makes her seem fragile and delicate.

"That's fine," I manage to choke out. I pull on a pair of gloves and grab the razor to begin prepping her side. Once done, I pick up the design and get ready to place it.

"Where on your ribs would you like it?"

"Um, just below the elastic of my sports top." She points out the area.

"Across or straight down?"

"Across, please."

"I need you to lie on your side facing away from me."

She rolls onto her side so her back is to me and I run my eyes over her body again. I'm drawn by the dip which leads to the curve of her hip and then to her ass which is shaped like an upside-down heart. My pulse kicks up at the thought of turning it pink with the palm of my hand.

Fuck, I need to get my shit under control. I lay the transfer over the area where she wants the tattoo and apply the ink.

"How's that?"

She lifts her arm above her head and I notice the way her breasts move in the sports bra. I lick my lips and imagine sucking a tight, hard nipple into my mouth. Maybe even applying pressure with my teeth. I wonder how her skin would taste and swallow down the groan at the image which plays out in my head. Her voice washes over me, breaking me from my thoughts.

"That's perfect, thank you."

I nod my head, worried my voice may betray what I'm thinking. Re-adjusting my painfully hard cock, I reach over, grab my tattoo gun and get to work while the scent of the sweetest apples I have ever smelt surrounds me, causing my head to buzz.

CHAPTER SIX

Ally

After what feels like forever, but was probably only an hour or so, the tattoo is finished and the excruciating, painful torture is at an end. I can finally get off this bloody bed, not that it wasn't comfortable, it was until he started with the needle. As soon as it began to buzz, my whole body tensed. I relaxed slightly when Xavier began talking to me and asking me questions about random stuff but tensed again when he asked me about my family. It's not that I meant to be rude, but how do I explain that I'm the reason my father was murdered? Now, my mother is a drunk who hates my guts and wishes I was dead instead of her husband. Nope, somehow I don't think that kind of shit would have been easy to explain and I don't need this sexy as sin man's pity. I think it's best if we just avoid that conversation.

I stand on shaky legs and head to a mirror fixed on the wall, careful to keep my shirt in place where it covers my stomach. I position myself side on and lift my arm to check out what has caused me so much pain. Tears spring to my eyes. "I love it, Xavier."

"I'm glad you like it." His husky voice smooths over me like silk over steel and I shiver. I can't explain the reaction I seem to have to this man, I need to get out of this room.

I turn away from the mirror, my back to Xavier and hurriedly pull my shirt on. Moving back to the table, I grab my bag and wait while he snaps his gloves off. He then follows me out to the reception area, his warm palm at the base of my spine guiding me. I try to smother the hitch of my breath when shivers race through me and goosebumps prickle my skin.

I struggle to hide my reaction and quickly head to the numerous photo frames, again letting the beautiful tattoos draw me in.

How can a voice, both gravelly and smooth and the simplest of touches from this man have such an overwhelming affect on me? The only reasonable explanation I can come up with is....I must be losing my damn mind. I have never had anyone make me feel or react this way. I need to pull myself together, the last thing I need now, or ever, is a man in my life. Particularly this man. He has the ability to shred my already paper-thin heart and nothing would be able to fix it once he was done.

I take a few steps closer to the brick wall and study the intricate detail in each photo. I still can't believe how breathtaking they are.

I feel Xavier, rather than see him, come up behind me. I concentrate on controlling my body's reaction to his heat I feel, shimmering behind me. Swallowing several times, I try to direct saliva into my parched mouth so I can speak. Before I get the chance, his voice washes over me again.

"I need you to fill out a client form, please."

When I turn, he lifts a hand and runs it through his dark hair. My fingers itch to do the same. I watch as the flex of the muscles in his arm has me practically drooling. I nod, words have deserted me, take the form and pen from his outstretched hand and move to the reception desk where I begin filling it out.

"Sorry, I should have had you do it before you had the tattoo."

I look over my shoulder to where he stands behind me, his eyes move over my body before lifting and locking with mine. He shrugs his shoulders, knowing he's been caught checking me out. He's not the least bit apologetic and something about his attitude has my body humming again.

"It's okay." My voice sounds shaky and scratchy – way to hide the reaction I'm having to him.

I turn my attention back to the card and hurriedly fill in the details before placing the pen on the desk. Shifting the bag on my shoulder, I spin around and offer my hand again.

"Thank you," I mumble while preparing myself for his touch again.

"Do you want to grab dinner with me, tonight?" he asks as his palm connects with mine.

Snapping my eyes up to his, I get lost in the ocean blue orbs and it takes me a moment to formulate an answer. His thumb rubs small circles across the top of my hand and he reaches out with his free hand to run fingertips across my cheek. I suck my lower lip between my teeth when I feel myself trembling. Seconds feel like hours as they pass while I'm lost in his touch. Then, flashes of the last time I allowed someone to touch me have me snapping back to the present. I try to think of a way to say no to his invitation when all the while my body is screaming for me to say yes.

"Um…." I'm struggling with what to say when the front door opens and our attention is drawn to a couple who enter.

I pull me hand back fast and step back as if I've been caught doing something I shouldn't. Xavier gives me a confused glance before turning toward the man he obviously knows.

"Justin." Xavier lifts his chin in that way men have of saying hello.

I study Justin and notice how handsome he is. He looks like a surfer; his dirty blonde colored hair is up in a man bun so I'm guessing it's long. The sides are shaved shorter. His arms are covered in tattoos, he's broad shouldered and almost as tall as Xavier. When I turn my head towards Xavier, I note his attention is focused on the woman at Justin's side.

"Cass, what are you doing here?" He sounds annoyed with the woman.

"X, baby, I missed you." The woman's voice is sickly sweet. She looks at me like I'm a piece of trash from the street. An ugly sneer forms on her heavily caked-on made up face.

Oh, shit! Did Xavier really just ask me out when it's clear he has a girlfriend? Typical. What a fucking jerk. I run my eyes over the length of her. She's tall and skinny, nothing like my five feet two with curves. Her dark brown hair has blonde streaks and dances on her shoulders. I grudgingly admit, she's gorgeous. I need to leave. Now! I don't want, or need, the drama this moment could develop into.

"I need to get going." I drop my head and hurry towards the door.

"Ally!" X calls out.

When I glance back, the woman moves to him and wraps her arms around him; pushing her body up against his. My stomach twists with a bite of jealousy and I'm angry with myself. I have absolutely no reason to be jealous. I don't even know the damn guy. He's just a guy who tattooed me. A temptation I don't want or need. A temptation I cannot allow into my life.

Without a backwards glance, I push through the glass door and make a beeline for my apartment. It's only ten minutes away, but as each step leads me further away from Xtreme Ink and him, it gets harder to breathe.

I stop and grab two coffees from the café on my way into work on Monday morning. I'm feeling guilty that I ignored messages from Cynthia on Saturday night, she wanted us to catch up. After the tattoo on Friday and visiting my mother on Saturday morning, I was in no mood to spend time with anyone.

Mother had been in her usual good form, throwing insult after insult at me. It all served to reaffirm what I already knew. So, I returned home, ordered takeout and snuggled into bed to read *The Hurricane* by *R.J. Prescott* before falling asleep and dreaming about finding a love like in the book.

I push through the solid wood door and take a deep breath, allowing the smell of old books assault my senses.

Cynthia looks over from the desk where she is checking in books and smiles when she sees it's me. Striding over, I place the cups on the desk and push one towards her.

"I'm sorry about Saturday, I wasn't feeling a hundred percent." Not the truth, but not really a lie. She doesn't need to know all about the crap in my life.

She waves a dismissive hand in the air and hums when she sips at the coffee.

"This makes up for it," she laughs. "I can't believe it's Monday already."

"I know, the week flew by," I groan which causes Cynthia to laugh again. "What did you end up doing?" I move behind the desk and stash my bag.

"Not a lot. JT and I had a movie night on Saturday and yesterday I took him to the pool."

JT is her six-year-old son. I haven't met him, but he sounds like a good kid.

"Aw, damn. That would have been great, sorry I missed it." I pick up a stack of books which need to be placed back on the shelves.

"I'm taking him to the park after work this arvo, would you like to come with us? We can have coffee and check out the single dads while he plays." She wiggles her eyebrows and smiles.

I smile for the first time in days and nod. "Sounds like a great idea, count me in." I head to the stacks to put books away.

Xavier's ruggedly handsome face with his ocean blue eyes flashes before my eyes. Not for the first time since I've met him. There is something about the man which drew me in. As quickly as he enters my mind, I push him aside, reminding myself, he's taken. I would never be the woman who chases after someone else's man. I return the books in my arms to their rightful places and notice a trolley stacked high with others needing to be put away. It should keep me busy for a while and my mind off other things.

After placing the last book where it belongs, I glance at the clock on the wall to find it's time for my lunch break. I head back to the desk and grab my bag.

"Do you want anything?" I ask Cynthia.

She looks up from the computer, a devilish smile curls her lips.

"How about we be naughty and have something sickeningly sweet?"

"Hmm, how naughty are we talking? Donuts? Cheesecake? Or, chocolate mud cake drizzled with chocolate sauce?" I try not to laugh or moan as I speak.

"Definitely the mud cake."

"Sounds like a damn good idea to me." Laughing, I hoist the strap of my bag onto my shoulder and head for the door.

I make my way to Darby Street, cross to the opposite side of the road so I don't have to walk past Xtreme Ink and make my way to the beach. Tilting my head back, I look up to the grey sky and hope it doesn't rain.

When I reach the beach, I slip off my shoes, step onto the cool sand and breathe in the salty, sea air. I stride to the water's edge and as the water rushes over my feet, a peacefulness settles within me. I stare off in the distance and watch ships as they sail past before watching small waves roll into shore.

A familiar feeling of being watched has the hairs on the back of my neck standing on end and I look to where old wooden bench seats line the promenade. A man is near one of the benches. The same man who is always here and seems to be watching me. This time he's standing and making no secret of the fact he is looking straight at me. My eyes are drawn to him and a familiar warmth settles in my stomach.

Keeping his eyes on me, he starts towards me carrying something. He takes the concrete steps two at a time and doesn't bother removing his shoes as he takes measured strides towards me. As he nears, I note the two travel cups in his hands

He comes to a stop before me, hands me a cup and without thinking, I accept it. We continue staring at each other. My heart seems to lodge in my throat and then that gravelly voice washes over me.

"I thought you'd like that." He nods to the cup in my hand.

"Xavier, what are you doing here?"

"You're welcome." He chuckles before taking a sip from his cup.

"I'm sorry, thank you."

"You never answered me the other day." He speaks simply, as if I didn't see another woman's arms wrapped around him.

I know I sound angry when I speak.

"You seemed to have your arms full and I don't fool around with guys who already have girlfriends." I turn and head back up the beach, kicking myself for how jealous I sounded. I hear him come up behind me, but don't pay him any attention.

"Jealous, Sweetness?"

"Nope. I don't know you well enough to be jealous and I don't get jealous." I hate the fact my words sound like a lie even to my ears. *Friggin' hell, what the hell is this guy doing to me?* I hurriedly make my way up the steps and head for work.

"Ally, have dinner with me!" he calls out.

Is this guy for real, did he not hear what I just said? I don't bother to answer. What's the point, he doesn't appear to listen to me.

"She isn't my girlfriend and means nothing to me."

My foot pauses on the top step when he speaks and the warm feeling returns on hearing he's single. It doesn't change anything though, I can't go out with him.

"It doesn't change anything." My head is lowered, my voice soft. I'm not even sure he hears me.

"It sure fucking does," he growls.

I jump and spin around, not realizing he was directly behind me until he spoke. How the shit does someone as big as him move so fucking quick and so quietly.

"How does it?" I challenge him. I look up and wish I hadn't. His eyes capture mine and his earthy scent mixed with the salt air has my head spinning. He hasn't shaved since I last saw him and the growth on his chin is longer. My fingers itch to run through it. Damn him for being too friggin' sexy for his own good.

"Tell me you feel it too." He leans forward and cups my jaw, sending shivers racing down my spine.

His voice is deep, his touch soft, gentle.

"It doesn't mean anything," I whisper before turning away, forcing his hand to drop down.

I will myself to walk away. *He's a temptation you don't need* plays on a loop in my head. But, I take one last look into those deep blue orbs and see a million emotions playing in them. A small thrill shoots through me, knowing I can affect him in the same way he affects me.

Walk away, Ally. Turn and walk away. Now!

"I'm sorry." I increase the pace of my escape and don't stop to wash my feet as I usually would.

"I'll prove you wrong, Sweetness," he calls out to my back.

Something inside me grabs onto those words and I hope that one day he will indeed prove me wrong.

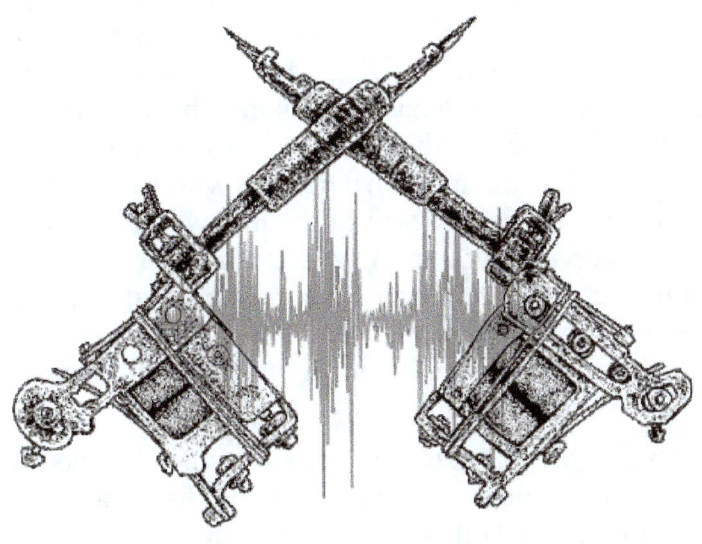

CHAPTER SEVEN

Xavier

I stood watching her like every other time but couldn't stand back anymore. I knew from the moment I left Xtreme Ink what would happen. I felt like shit intruding on her quiet moment but I needed to get close to her again. I haven't been able to get the feel of her soft skin out of my head for days. The minute her eyes connected with mine, I couldn't resist the pull which hung in the air. It was so strong, I felt it clawing down my back.

As I took the steps down to the sand one at a time I could see the rise and fall of her chest and heard the hitch in her breath as I came to a stop in front of her. It's the sound I have dreamt about for the past couple of nights. I have imagined what she would sound like once I'm buried to the fucking hilt.

It was like we were caught in the moment and something different settled around us.

I latched onto my lip with my teeth to stop a smirk curling my lips when I heard a hint of jealousy in her voice because she thought I had a girlfriend. It kind of pissed me off at the same time because she has no reason to be jealous. The only one I want, and can think about, is her. Now the lines are drawn and the gauntlet has been thrown down. I won't stop till I smash her walls to smithereens. I will find some way to prove to her that this... whatever is going on, means something. I never back down from a challenge. When I want something, I go after it. Nothing stops me and this will be no different. I won't stop until I have her under me, screaming my name to the heavens and she realises she is mine.

"X-man you ready to go?" Justin's voice breaks into my thoughts. I swing around in my chair to find him standing in the doorway with his wetsuit on and holding his surfboard.

"Yeah man, give me a minute to pack this shit up." Nodding, he turns and heads towards the front of the shop.

Running my hands down my face, I blow out a deep breath and pack up my station. Once sorted, I push to my feet and stretch out my back. When I came back from lunch, Justin took one look at my troubled expression and told me we were going to hit the waves after work this arvo. I agreed, thinking a surf might take my mind away from all this shit which is going on. Truthfully, all I want to do is head home.

Racing out to my truck, I grab my boardshorts and head back inside to get changed. After throwing a singlet shirt on, I head back out to the front of the shop where Justin is talking with Beau.

"You coming, mate?" I ask Beau.

"Not today. I have some shit I have to sort out." He runs a hand through his hair, he looks frustrated.

I shrug. "Fair enough. Justin, let's get going before it gets too dark, it looks like it's gonna rain." I push open the front door not bothering to look back and head towards the beach.

"Hey, wait up!"

Without stopping, I turn back and watch as Justin has to jog to catch up.

"What's the fucking rush?" he grunts as he makes it to my side.

I don't say anything, I just keep walking.

"Fuck man, do you want to talk about it?"

That gives me pause for a minute, it's unlike Justin to want to talk about shit. He's the most closed off fucker I have ever met. I know he had a shit childhood but I don't know much more about him. He's like a safe and never wants to talk about shit. Erica calls him a grumpy ass because for as long as we have all known each other, he never smiles. The only places he seems content and at peace is in the waves or when he's working. Apart from those times, he's a brooding asshole. Someone fucked this guy up pretty bad in the past, is my guess.

Erica tells him all the time that he needs to get laid and maybe that will cheer his ass up. That's the weird thing though, the whole time I've known him, I have never seen him with a woman.

I shake my head to indicate I'm not interested in talking about it, I wouldn't even know where to begin anyways.

"Fair enough," he accepts.

We walk the rest of the way in silence.

Something draws my attention and the hairs on the back of my neck stand on end as I'm about to take the steps down to the beach. I turn to look back to the park across the road and watch my woman take a seat at a table. She has a coffee in her hand and is laughing with a woman I haven't seen before. Something grips in my chest when a man walks over to where they are. Before I can think about what I'm doing, I sprint across the road. I have only one goal in mind....to get this fucker away from my woman.

Justin calls out from behind me but I ignore him. I zero in on the man as he reaches out to touch her, she recoils at his touch.

"Don't fucking touch her, you piece of shit!" I snarl.

"X-man, what the fuck?" Justin yells out again.

"Give me a fucking minute," I call to him.

At the sound of my voice, two piercing green eyes stare straight at me. They widen with recognition as I get closer. I notice the light flush hitting her cheeks as she takes me in from head to toe, it has the effect of settling some of the beast in me. The man looks at me curiously and decides to turn and walk away. *Smart man,* I think.

"Who is that hunk of man meat?" her friend asks.

My lip curls up and a chuckle rises in my throat. I watch as Ally swallows hard before licking her lips. The action causes my cock to jerk in my shorts. Fuck, what would it feel like to have her mouth wrapped around me, her tongue lick every bit of cum from me. Growling low in my throat, I try to get rid of the image before I lose all control.

"Sweetness," I breath out as I stop in front of her. Reaching out, I grab her hand, bring it to my mouth and brush my lips across her soft skin.

"X.. I mean, Xavier."

I hear the tremor in her voice and smile, I know she felt what I do to her.

"What are you doing here?" She narrows her eyes.

"I was heading for a swim." I nod over to the beach.

"Hi, I'm Cynthia." Her friend holds her hand out to me.

I don't want to let go of Ally but know it's rude if I don't shake her hand. I reach over and put my hand in hers, before I can say anything I hear Justin come up behind me.

"X-man, the sun…" he stops mid-sentence and after a few moments of silence, I look beside me.

"Fuck me," he growls.

I watch as something passes over his face, it's as if he's looking at a ghost. I'm about ready to punch his bloody face in for staring at my woman, but then I realise his soul focus is on Cynthia. I look back and forth between the two of them and wonder what the fuck is going on. Cynthia sucks in a deep breath. I look back at Ally and raise an eyebrow, wondering if she knows what the fuck is happening. She shrugs and gives a small shake of her head, she's obviously as confused as me. The silence is broken suddenly when a boy calls out "Mummy" from the playground.

"Shit," Cynthia hisses. She gets to her feet and runs her hands down the black pencil skirt she is wearing before taking a few steps away.

"My Queen," Justin murmurs.

I watch as Cynthia's shoulders stiffen and she stops. Her shoulders rise and fall like she's struggling to breathe before she turns around with a pissed off look on her face.

"Don't you *ever* fucking call me that. The last time I let you call me by that name, I fell at your feet. I wanted nothing more than to be that special person in your life. It was a fucking lie back then, just like it is now. I'm not your fucking anything and I'm not wasting anymore fucking tears on you."

With that said, she turns when a boy of about five or six years old runs to her and hugs her legs. She sweeps him into her arms and whispers something in his ear. He nods before Cynthia turns back to Ally and mouths, "I'm sorry I have to go." I don't miss how glassy her eyes are.

After a few moments of silence, Justin snaps out of his head and springs into action. He drops his board to the ground with a thud before racing over to the parking lot, screaming out her name. By the time he reaches where her car was parked, she is already pulling out of the car park.

"Fuck!" he yells.

I hear the pain in his voice. He watches her car turn the corner and runs both hands through his hair before turning back to where I stand with Ally. He grabs his board off the ground and heads towards the tattoo shop.

"Justin!" I call out but he doesn't say shit, he just keeps on walking.

"Fuck!" I spit.

He looked like he was ready to kill someone and I wonder again what the fuck is going on. I should probably go and see if he's okay, but knowing him, he won't say shit until he's ready. I would just be wasting my breath.

"I better get going," Ally mumbles breaking into my train of thought.

The rain which has been threatening all day, begins falling lightly.

"Let me give you a lift," I say.

"It's okay, I don't live far away. I'm good to walk."

She leans over and grabs her bag off the seat, but I'm not taking no for an answer. I grab her hand and entwine her fingers with mine.

This time I *tell* her, "I'll give you a lift." Not waiting for an excuse, I head back towards the shop with her hand firmly gripped in mine.

"Xavier, where are you taking me?"

"My truck is back at the shop. We'll grab it then, I'm taking you to dinner."

"Um.. excuse me?" She tries to pull her hand free, but I'm not letting go.

"You need to eat," I say simply, not giving an inch.

After a few seconds I feel her hand soften in mine. "Fine, but only because I'm hungry and I don't feel like two-minute noodles."

Laughing, I squeeze her hand, bring it to my lips and brushing a kiss over her knuckles. I love the feeling of having her close to me. When I look down, I don't miss the smirk which kisses her lips before she turns her face away from me. I feel a slight tremor race through her hand.

We take our seats at The Dockyard along Honeysuckle. We decided to sit outside so we can take in the view. There is only one fucking view I need, but I'm getting the feeling, Ally likes to be outside. After placing our order and she huffed and puffed about the fact I wouldn't let her pay, I made sure she was comfortable before taking my seat. I immediately realise, I don't like the table distance between us so, getting to my feet I move to the same side as Ally and seat myself next to her.

"What was wrong with the other seat?" She squeals when I reach under her chair and pull it so it's butted up to mine, there is now no room between us.

Satisfied I smile at her, not bothering to answer her question.

"How's the tattoo?" I ask before taking a sip of my beer.

She looks at me for a moment, seeming lost in thought before she blushes and turns to look out at the harbour. The sun is low in the sky and I'm thankful for daylight savings as the sun bounces around her.

"It's good. Don't get me wrong, it hurt like a bitch but I love the outcome and I think it might be addictive." I hear the smile in her voice as she speaks.

"I know exactly what you mean." I chuckle and look over all my ink. "If you ever want any more, let me know. I enjoyed popping your cherry." I finish speaking as she lifts her coke to her mouth and takes a mouthful.

She chokes on the liquid when I say *cherry* which has me chuckling. I pat her back to help her catch her breath and after a few minutes she gasps. "What?!" He eyes are wide and I have to bite back a smile as the blush I have come to know and love creeps up her neck.

"Ink babe. Your Ink cherry."

"Right." She nods but her attention is on her finger as she runs it across the wood grain on the table. Needing her eyes back on mine, I reach over with my free hand and run my fingertips under her chin before lowering them. I start to apologize but can't get the words out. I'm lost in the depths of her green eyes and the gold hue which surrounds her irises making them sparkle.

Fuck, being this close to Ally and smelling her sweet apple scent is driving me fucking crazy. I lick my lips and watch her lips part. When I look back to her eyes, they seem brighter, hungrier. I look over the curve of her small nose and note the small smattering of freckles across it. The natural sight turns me on even more. When I return my gaze to her lips, I realise how much closer we are as we lean into each other.

I take a deep breath and let it out slowly. A quiet moan leaves her and if we hadn't been so close, I wouldn't have heard it. She licks her lips again and my control is splintering by the second. Fuck it, I need a taste. As I begin to close the inch between us, the waitress comes over and places our meals on the table.

Ally jumps back like she just touched fire and got burnt. I can't help the irritation I feel at the interruption.

"Fuck," I growl low.

Looking towards the waitress, I nod and say a quick, thanks. I don't miss the way she eyes me up and down. I hear Ally mumble something and she cuts her eyes to the chick who's still standing and staring at me.

"Thanks," I grunt again.

I hope the waitress gets the message. I'm dismissing the chick and finally, she seems to snap out of whatever fantasy she was living in long enough to nod before walking away.

"She was cute." Ally mumbles as she picks up her knife and fork.

"Not interested. There is only one woman I want and she's sitting right next to me." I don't mean to sound so gruff, but fuck, I'm hard as stone. Having her so close to me and not being able to touch her is pissing me right the fuck off.

"Xavier...."

I hold up my hand to stop her from speaking because I have a feeling I know what she is going to say.

"Sweetness, you could dangle one hundred women in front of me right out of the pages of Playboy and none of them would ever compare to you. You are going to test my patience and control, but I know in the end when I finally crack you open it will be worth it. And trust me when I say, you will be mine."

I hold her eyes with mine, not letting her look away. I see the moment she hears the truth in my words and lets out a breath she must have been holding. I wink to break the tension which seems to have fallen around us. I pick up my burger and take a bite before I clear this whole fucking table and take a bite out of her. Eyeing her out of the corner of my eye I watch as she cuts a piece of her chicken schnitzel and takes a mouthful.

Throughout dinner, the conversation is more laid back. I learn she works at the library down the road from my shop and that's where she met Cynthia. I tell her about the shop and explain, I don't really do much else except for hitting the beach with Beau and Justin. I tell her about when my dad used to be a firefighter and how he gave it up when my mum got sick. I watch as she takes all my words onboard and how her eyes glass over when I talk about my mum. My heart does some flip flop shit again. When I ask her about her family, she seems to close down. I don't push but fuck if I'll let it go. This is only the first date in the million we are yet to share, I'll find out sooner or later.

By the time we finish eating, it's almost 8 o'clock. The sun has set and I probably should take her home. As if on cue, she places her hand across her mouth and yawns which makes me chuckle. Strands of her hair fall in front of her face with the action. Reaching over, I tuck it behind her ear. Not being able to stop myself, I run the tips of my fingers down the side of her face. My fingertips caress her soft cheek and she gasps. She looks up at me from beneath the veil of her thick lashes and as a shy smile curves her plump lips, I find myself wanting to bite them.

"We should go." Her breathing is slightly erratic, almost as if she's fighting her emotions. After a moment, she pulls back and my hand drops.

I blow out a deep breath and wait as she gets to her feet. I run my hands down my thighs, willing my cock to settle down. It's no fucking use. Gritting my teeth, I push to my feet and adjust myself as discreetly as possible before wrapping my arm around her waist. I refuse to allow her to get too far away from me.

Her body tenses at my touch, but she softens and moulds against my side. I smile, lean over and inhale the sweet scent of her hair as I plant a light kiss to her scalp. I then lead her back to my truck

CHAPTER EIGHT

Ally

Leaning my back against the stacks in the library, I blow out a deep breath. Reaching up, I run my fingers over my lips. They feel like fire ants are marching across them from Xavier's kiss last night. I swear when I came into work today they were still puffy and tingling. Leaning my head back against the shelves, I close my eyes and recall everything that was said during dinner and when he dropped me home.....

Xavier's arm wraps around my waist and I tense at the contact. His fingers trace small circles into my hip and I can't help melting into his touch. It feels so right and it's like I'm where I am supposed to be. I resist the urge to close my eyes at the sensation for two reasons - one we're walking and I don't want to trip over and two - I still don't know what this is or even what it means. I have never felt so shy and uncertain in my life and it scares the shit out of me.

What would happen if I let this man in? I'm not stupid, I know there are no certainties in life, but damn - having this temptation constantly in my face is starting to weaken my resolve to stay away from him. The way he was speaking to me while we were eating, wanting to crack me open so I could be his.... Damn I wish those words didn't give me goosebumps and I sure as hell didn't expect the flutter of hope in my heart.

Coming to a stop at Xavier's truck, I come out of my head. I feel the weight of Xavier's hand against my lower back and hate to admit that it feels good. Reaching forward, X opens the door for me and a smile curves my lips at the gesture. I don't think anyone has ever opened doors or, waited for me to sit before them. It feels nice. I feel special.

Damn why does everything feel so good with him?

"Come on, Sweetness, let's get you home." X holds the door open and grasps me with his free hand so I don't fall while trying to get into his truck. The bloody thing is huge but, I like it. It suits him.

"Thank you." I smile up at him while fastening my seatbelt. Before he closes the door, he throws another one of his winks at me and a smile curls the side of his lips. Like the last time he smiled at me, I watch a small dimple pop. Even though it's hard to see through his five o'clock shadow, I know it's there. I find for the millionth time today that I have to suppress a moan.

Trying my hardest to stay quiet, I suck my bottom lip into my mouth, look down and pick at my nails. I hear the door being pushed shut and closing my eyes, I take a deep breath in. My body comes alive as his fresh, clean intoxicating scent runs through every cell in my body.

Shit. Shit. Shit. I need to get it together.

When he slides into the truck, I open my eyes and stare at his profile.

"You're a temptation I shouldn't want," I blurt out before slapping a hand over my mouth. I can't believe I said that out loud.

Reaching over, he rests his warm hand on my thigh and I swear a tingling sensation sears through my skirt.

"Sweetness, you are the embodiment of temptation and I can't wait for you to accept how mine you really are because when you do, we're going to set the world on fire."

I stare at him wide eyed, not sure exactly what to say. Do men actually talk like this or is Xavier a different kind of man who I've been completely blinded to. Everything he's saying should scare the shit out of me or, even piss me off. But it doesn't, it has the opposite affect and I'm not sure what I should do with that little revelation. I guess I'll pin it in the corner of my brain to reassess later when I no longer have his smell invading every one of my senses or his deep voice wafting around me, causing my head to spin.

I glance through the passenger side window to get my bearings before turning back to face front and explain where I live. I'm not sure how I feel about him knowing where I live, but it's late and I really don't want to walk. I guess I'll have to trust that he won't abuse the power of knowing my address.

He eases the truck into the curb in front of my building, I release the seatbelt and reach forward to open my door but Xavier is already there. Damn, how the hell does he move so fast? I didn't even hear him get out of the car. I note the flutter in my heart has returned.

"Thank you," I whisper as he takes my hand and helps me to step out onto the path. I think he'll now let go of my hand, but he doesn't. Instead, he maneuvers me out of the way, shuts the door and I hear the beep of the locks engage. He turns and guides me to the front door of my building. We pause at the glass entry *door. I'm not sure if I should ask him up, but I think better of it. I need distance so I can get my head on straight.*

"Thank you for dinner, it was lovely." I look up at him through my eyelashes, notice the hungry look in his eyes and my stomach does somersaults.

Wrapping his arms around my waist, he pulls me into his hard chest and I feel every hard ridge of muscle through his singlet shirt. He sucks in a deep breath when my hands land on his shoulders and I flex my fingers. My nails bite into the hard muscle causing him to growl low in his throat, it vibrates straight through me causing my nipples to harden and heat to pool low in my belly.

Holy shit, what is this man doing to me? His hand cups my jaw, drawing my face up to his. Without thinking, I close my eyes and lean into his touch.

"So fucking hot," he growls.

Opening my eyes to lock with his, I see the moment his control snaps and his lips land on mine. I thought it would be hard, demanding, it's anything but. It's agonizingly slow and controlled to the point where I can't help myself and run my tongue along the seam of his lips, craving a taste.

He opens his mouth on a growl and runs his tongue along mine. A slow moan escapes this time and it's like fuel to a fire. I'm pushed up against the concrete wall of my building and X lifts my leg, locking my knee into place by his hip. His other hand grips my hair, tangling his fingers in the strands at the top of my head. In this position, he holds all the control. It should freak me out, but it doesn't. Instead, I claw at his back, taking everything he wants to give me as he pushes forward. The hard ridge of his cock pushes against my aching clit and I moan again.

Xavier groans greedily, sucking down every noise I make. After a moment, he pulls back, his breathing heavy. I concentrate on catching my breath as he rests his forehead against mine.

"Fuck Sweetness, I need to stop. I'm about two seconds away from stripping you bare and taking what's mine." His voice is raspy and he breathes in short gasps.

My mind starts to spin at his words. Licking my lips, I see if I can still taste him and hum at the tingling sensation running through them.

"Inside now babe, before I change my mind."

I nod and he eases my leg back to the ground where I struggle to regain my balance as my legs won't stop shaking. Shit, he has literally kissed me legless. I always thought that was some fiction crap only written in romance novels.

Damn.......

Turning towards the glass door, I grab the keys from my bag. When X's hand closes over mine, I realise how much I'm shaking.

"Let me Sweetness" putting the key in the lock he pops the lock and pushes the glass door open handing back my keys he leans down and pecks my lips before spinning me around and giving my ass a slap. "See you tomorrow, Sweetness."

I nod and take a few steps away. I turn at the sound of his voice and find him slouched against the still open door, lust flashing in his eyes. I grip the banister to the stairs, my entire body feels like it's melting and if I don't hang on, I'll end up a puddle on the damn floor.

He straightens up and crosses his arms over his chest. "Next time you kiss me like that, babe, I don't care where we are - I will have your ass naked and bent over the nearest flat surface, feeding my cock into you so hard and fast you'll be begging for more."

The click of the lock on the door echoes around the small entryway as he walks away. I suck in a shaky breath.

"Ally!"

I snap out of my memories from last night when I notice Cynthia in front of me laughing.

"What?" I turn my face away, knowing I must resemble a tomato. I can feel the heat coming off me in waves from the memories.

"I've been calling your name for the last five minutes," she huffs playfully.

"I'm sorry, I was caught up in my head." I place the book I was holding onto the shelf behind me.

"I could tell. I wanted to let you know it's three o'clock and time for lunch. Be warned, when you get back I'm going to insist you give me all the details to whatever has had you drifting in and out of your head today and causing those creamy white cheeks of yours to turn bright red." Cynthia laughs when I duck my head, feeling embarrassed to be caught out.

"You don't have to tell me if you don't want to," she reassures me.

I nod, not knowing what to say.

She smiles and heads back to the desk but not before I notice it's the forced smile she has been giving me all day. I hate that she feels she needs to hide from me. I guess we all have our stories to tell and when she's ready, I hope she'll open up and tell me hers. I hope one day, I'll feel confident enough to open up to her.

Sighing, I push the trolley back to the desk and grab my bag, Cynthia is reading some paperwork. She's barely said anything today and I might not know her very well, but I do know it's not normal.

"Do you want me to grab you anything on my way back?"

Cynthia doesn't even glance up from the papers in front of her. "No thanks." She shakes her head.

"You sure?"

"Yeah, I'm good thanks." She still doesn't look up from what she's doing.

"Okay," I mumble as I throw my bag over my shoulder and head for the door. I'm worried about her but I don't know what to say. I'm sure if she wanted to talk, she'd say something.

I'm not paying attention as I push through the door and smack straight into a hard chest. A pair of hands steady me which is lucky, otherwise I would have ended up on my ass.

"Shit, I'm so sorry." When I finally look up, I come face to face with a smiling Sean. He's a regular here, he comes in a couple of times a week. I think he has a thing for Nina, a girl who comes in at the same times he does. I don't think their being here at the same time is an accident. I see the way he watches her and I'm pretty sure she knows as well.

"I'm so sorry, Sean, I wasn't paying attention." I shake my head and laugh but when he opens his mouth to respond, a deep growl from behind cuts him off.

"You wanna get your hands off my woman?"

X's deep voice slides over me and my traitorous body hums in approval. I wanna kick my own ass for the way it responds on just hearing his voice and then what he's said dawns on me

"I'm not...." I'm start to say until Sean drops his hands and takes a step back.

I note the angry look of possessiveness in X's eyes and think better of saying anything when he holds his hand up to stop me talking. What in the actual fuck! I swore to myself I would never allow anybody to treat me like a doormat again.

"Xavier, I'm not your fucking woman!" I slam my hands on my hips.

Without taking his eyes off Sean, he speaks in a low gravelly tone which has my nipples hardening.

Damn him!

"I thought I made myself quiet clear last night, Sweetness." He lifts an eyebrow in question.

I open my mouth to tell him I hadn't agreed to be his, even though I think it may be a wasted effort when Sean speaks first.

"Sorry man." He turns to face X with his arms raised.

"Sean," X says.

"X-man. Shit mate, I didn't realise she was yours, but she ran into me and almost fell. I only reached out so she wouldn't hurt herself." He rubs the back of his neck, looking a little anxious.

"Bloody men," I grumble.

Not caring about the pair of them as X walks over to shake Sean's hand, I have no interest in what the hell they are saying and take it as my cue to leave.

"Ally!" X calls out but I don't stop.

I pick up my pace and keep walking.

I hear his footsteps behind me and don't say a word when he wraps his arm around my waist and pulls me into his side. Instead, I try not to melt into him as we keep heading towards the beach. I hear him breathe me in before he plants a kiss to the top of my head. A smile curves my lips at the action.

"It's been a long day, Sweetness and I couldn't wait to see you."

"Xavier, you can't just show up at my work and start beating your chest claiming I'm yours cause another man..."

"Like fuck, I can't," he growls. We reach the beach and he stops dead in his tracks pulling me to a stop with him. I tilt my head back to look into his face. "I've been craving your touch all day and the minute I get you in my sights, I find another fucker has his hands on you."

"He's a friend," I defend but I'm not sure why.

"I get that but your touch...." He pauses, blows out a deep breath and runs one hand through his hair. Bringing it down, he cups my cheek in the palm of his hand and I lean into the warmth of his touch. Locking eyes with him, it's like he's fighting for control but I see the moment he lets go and he leans down and brushes his lips over mine. I feel the warmth of his breath whisper over my cheek when he pulls back and starts speaking again. His voice has become deeper and my blood pumps faster through my veins as delicious tingles run up and down my spine

"Your touch is like Braille and I'm a blind man reading everything for the first time and it's just for me. Every time you touch me, it imprints on me even more. It's like you're writing our memories into my skin and I don't want to share that with anyone." He growls out the last part and I suck in a deep breath.

Oh, damn this man.

Releasing my breath, I stay quiet, not sure how I should respond. It seems to be a common problem I have when I'm around him. He just keeps knocking me for six and I'm not sure how much longer I can fight these feelings.

Closing my eyes, I tilt my face towards the sky and breath in the mixture of salt air and Xavier's intoxicating scent, letting it simmer through me. I feel the light breeze move past me and swirl in my hair. I try to centre myself to this moment in time. I never want to forget the words he has just spoken to me. They were the most romantic words I've ever had said to me. I let them work through every cell in my body until they reach my heart and for the first time in what feels like forever, my heart doesn't feel paper thin.

Feeling the lightest touch to my cheek, I open my eyes and I'm trapped in the ocean blue depths of his eyes. They shine as the sun bounces off them, so clear and full of emotion.

"You don't know how gorgeous you are, do you?" His husky words throw me off kilter yet again.

I shake my head in response.

"Good."

He slides his fingers over my cheek to my throat and I feel the weight of his hand as his thumb moves in slow circles over my pulse point. I shiver under the possessive hold. It's not tight, just enough to know he's in control. I melt into his touch.

Licking my lips, I watch as he tracks the movement with his eyes and the deep rumble of his low growl vibrates through me. My body is pressed hard against his.

"Why?" I gasp as heat pools low in my belly and my clit starts to ache. I squeeze my legs together to ease the ache, but it's no use I'm lost to every feeling this man creates inside me.

"Because all you have to do is walk past a man and he can't take his fucking eyes off you, babe." He wraps his free arm around my waist and slides his hand to my ass, giving it a squeeze.

I bite back the moan which is desperate to escape and try to break the sudden tension that has settled thick in the air around us before I break every single rule I have ever made myself and climb his sinful body like a tree.

"Walk on the sand with me," I whisper while looking up into his eyes.

Bending over, he brushes his lips over mine. I lick my lips to transfer his taste onto my tongue. He pulls back and nods. Releasing his hold from around my neck, he keeps his arm wrapped around my waist and we head down the concrete steps to the sand.

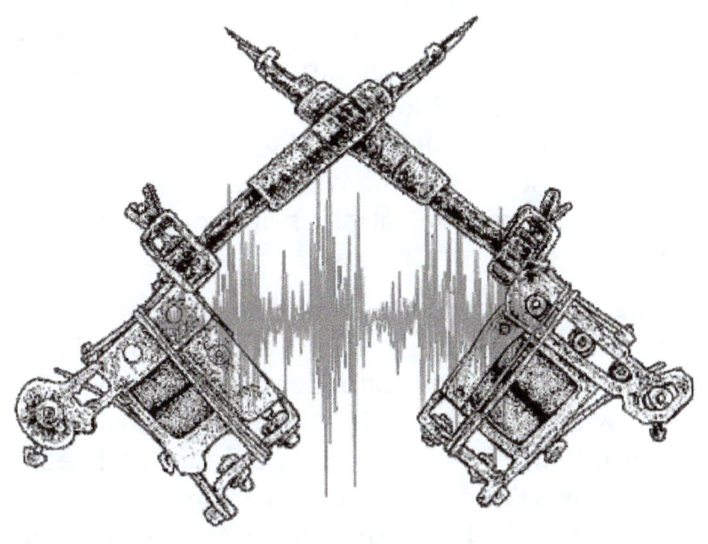

CHAPTER NINE

Ally

As I stir the life out of my coffee, I stare through the kitchen window. Dark clouds roll in, taking over the beautiful clear blue sky I'd woken up to an hour ago. Even with the crappy weather, I smile when I think about the week which has passed. It's been a crazy whirlwind that I never pictured happening to me.

After the beach incident on Tuesday, Xavier met me at work every day and we walked down to the beach. Sometimes we talked about our day - small things you know, nothing too heavy. But, yesterday, no words were spoken as we walked along the beach and soaked everything in. I know no matter what, he always had his arm around me or was holding my hand. It's like he couldn't be near me without some form of contact. I'm starting to crave his touch as much as he seems to need mine.

When I finished work, he was there to take me to dinner. As each day passes, it becomes harder to tell him no. Last night we didn't have dinner together although he wanted me with him. Having dinner with him is one thing, having it with his parents is a completely different ball game which I don't think I'm ready for. So instead, he ended up texting me all night when he should have been concentrating on spending more time with his mother.

Taking a sip of my coffee, I look at the clock on the wall above the fridge. I watch as the second-hand ticks away, reminding me I need to leave shortly to go and see my mother. My stomach twists at the thought and my heart beats louder in my ears. I'm not sure I want to burst the bubble I seem to be living in these days. I'm hoping today is a good day and I can get in out of there unscathed so I can come home and get everything ready for tonight. Xavier is coming over and I'm planning on cooking him dinner. The stubborn man refuses to allow me to pay when we go out so, this is my way of saying thank you. A thrill runs through me just thinking about having him in my space tonight. Again, I hope I'm making the right decision about him because I don't think I can fight this attraction any longer.

I stand staring up at the two-story house which brings back the nightmares from years ago. Taking a deep breath, I make my way towards the front door and push it open I hold my breath to reduce the stale smell and pick up the empty alcohol bottles lining the hallway as I make my way towards the sound of the television that's blaring in the lounge room. I expect to see my mother sitting in her chair but it's empty. I look around the dimly lit, smoky room but she's not here. Maybe she's upstairs or has gone out.

I ignore the fact she's not here and continue picking up bottles and emptying the ash tray beside her recliner. I don't hear her come downstairs as I head for the back door to take out the rubbish.

"Ally, is that you?" Her voice is slurred and I have to bite back the irritation I feel at hearing it. Pushing everything back to the recesses of my mind, I call back as I open the back door.

"I'm just taking the rubbish out."

I listen for a response but hear nothing. I do what needs to be done before heading back inside. When I reach the kitchen, I'm faced with dishes piled up over the benches and sink. I shake my head, it's always the same. Fuck knows how long they've been sitting there, probably since the last time I was here.

I run the water and as I open the cupboard under the sink to grab the washing detergent, I hear her stumble into the kitchen. I cringe when she knocks over one of the chairs at the dining table, but quickly wipe the disgusted look off my face before I look over at her. No point giving her any reason to start her shit today. *Just do as you planned, Ally get in and out as quick as you can.* I keep repeating the words to myself as I start to wash the numerous cups lining the bench.

"Why the fuck are you so happy?" She snarls and I look up from what I'm doing.

"What do you mean?"

"You're fucking humming." She spits out the words like humming is the worst thing in the world.

Just a little bit longer, Ally. Take a deep breath and let it out slowly. Do not show this woman any emotion.

"I w-wasn't," I stammer, annoyed with myself for allowing her to intimidate me.

"Don't fucking lie to me, you bitch!"

"I..I..I…." I stumble over the words, not sure what to say so I eventually shut my mouth. Then, without thinking I blurt, "I

75

met someone." I slam my mouth shut. I can't believe I told her. I wait for the nasty shit to fall from her mouth and I'm surprised when it's dead silent. Glancing over my shoulder, I watch as a million emotions flash over her face before an ugly sneer settles in place.

"You little slut as if any man would be interested in a selfish little bitch like you!"

There is so much malice and hate in her voice and I cringe at the power she has to hurt me deeply. No matter how many times I tell myself that her words mean nothing to me, it's all a lie. I feel a bite of pain slide up my arm and wince. Looking down I notice I have picked up a knife by the blade and squeezed my hand around it.

"Shit!" Dropping the knife, I move towards the roll of paper towel attached to the wall near the fridge. I tear off several sheets and quickly wrap it around my hand to stop the blood, but it's no use, the blood soaks the paper and crimson droplets hit the floor. My mother continues her vicious taunts, my eyes mist over and although I close them to stop myself crying, tears slide freely down my cheeks. She goes on and on, her voice rising with every sentence.....

"No one could ever love someone like you."

"You're in dreamland if you think you're worth anything at all!"

"Such a selfish cow!"

I can't take it anymore and let out a scream which rocks me to my core. There are so many things racing through my head and I can't stop the words as they pour out of my mouth.

"Shut up! Shut up! Just shut the fuck up!" My breathing is short, coming in pants and even though I try hard to get more air into my lungs, I'm struggling.

"You are nothing!" I scream but don't stop there "You think I don't live this nightmare every fucking day or every fucking time I come here? But, instead of us dealing with this together and helping each other, you waste your time on getting so drunk you're lucky if you make it upstairs. You're a waste of space and I deserve better." I throw everything I have into my words, hoping she can feel the hate I have for her. Taking up the space between us quicker than I thought possible in her state, she gets up into my face and shoves me into the wall. My back hits the paper roll attached to the wall and breaks away. I'm amazed at her strength.

"You're a weak and worthless, bitch. What have you done in your life that was so great? Don't you dare judge me, you took away my only reason for living. Don't you dare fucking come here and wave in my face how happy you are. That shit is a dream. This..." She waves one hand around. ".... is your reality and you need to get that through your thick fucking head. Nobody could ever love somebody like you." She spits and it washes over my face, the stench of her alcohol laden breath makes my stomach roll.

I push her away in anger. "Get out of my face and don't ever touch me again. You're the worthless one. Even when dad was alive you never gave him what he needed." As the words leave my mouth, I feel the sting to the side of my face as she hits me. I raise my injured hand to rest against the tingling, burning pain of my cheek. I watch as she turns, stumbles over her feet but catches herself on the bench then, straightens and makes her way towards the lounge room.

Tears are coming fast and furious now, I can't deal with this anymore. I'm done. I send a prayer up to my dad and tell him I'm sorry because I will never come back to this house again. This is not my home, it hasn't been for a very long time and personally, I don't give a shit what she does with her life. I hope this house of horrors burns to the fucking ground.

CHAPTER TEN

Xavier

I park the car and re-read the text message. Ally informed me about an hour ago that dinner was off and she couldn't see me again. If she thinks she can blow me off with a text message she has another thing coming. I deserve to know why she has done a complete one eighty on me since last night.

I run a frustrated hand through my hair and squeeze the back of my neck, trying to ease some of the tension which has settled there. Last night at dinner was fucking hard as shit. It seems mum is worse every time I visit and it's taking its toll on my dad. The only thing which helped me shut my brain off and get some sleep was knowing I would see my girl today.

Slamming my palm against the steering wheel of my truck it feels like everything is falling to fucking pieces. This past week with Ally has been one of the best I have had in a very long time and I'm not going to let her walk away without putting up a fight. With that settled in my mind, I climb from my truck and make my way up the path until I reach the front door. I study the intercom panel next to the glass doors and try to work out which apartment is hers. Out of a choice of thirty buzzers, I see an A. Stevens and an A. Malone. That's not bad odds. I push A. Malone first and wait anxiously for an answer. A smile breaks over my face when I hear her voice, but I frown at the sadness which coats her words.

"Hello," she murmurs.

"Sweetness, let me in." I try not to sound too demanding.

"Xavier?"

"Yeah, babe. Open up, we need to talk."

"X I-I don't th-think that's a good idea." She stammers and I swear I hear tears in her voice causing my heart to twist in my chest.

When I look through the glass door and see a girl coming down the stairs, I decide I'm sick of standing outside waiting, checking the apartment number next to Ally's name and wait for the chick to open the door.

I take the stairs two at a time, hurrying up to the fourth floor. When I find apartment 4b, I pause to compose myself before I break the fucking door down. Placing both palms against the wooden door frame, I let my head fall forward and take a few deep breaths. Rolling my head on my shoulders to loosen the tension, I try to calm down. Then, I hear what sounds like quiet sobs coming from the other side of the door and my control snaps. Knocking lightly, so as not to scare her, I wait a few seconds before knocking again. I'm worried she won't open the door, but I hear the shuffle of feet and a sniff before she speaks.

"Mr. Samson, I'm fine you don't need..." she trials off when she opens the door and finds me standing outside.

I'm not sure who this Mr. Samson is, but I'll deal with that later. Right now, I need to soak her in from head to toe. I take in her donut covered pajama pants and have to bite my lip so I don't laugh at how cute they look. A white singlet top is stretched tight across her chest and I bite back a growl when I notice her nipples are hard.

"Xavier," she chokes out.

I snap my eyes to hers and grip the door frame harder, hearing it crack under my weight. What the fuck! Why the fuck does she have a black eye? And, there is a cut on her cheek bone which has been taped up. When I study her closer, I see her hand is also bandaged.

"Who the fuck did this to you?" Anger laces my voice and I feel it prickle my senses. My muscles lock, ready to kill the motherfucker who hurt my girl.

Without a word, she throws herself at me and without thinking about it, I catch her. I wrap my arms around her and feel her body shuddering as she cries into my neck. Lifting her into my arms, I step into her apartment and kick the door closed behind me. I head straight for the lounge and sit with her held close to my chest. She curls into a ball in my lap and I rub my hand over her back in a soothing motion. I lower my head and breath in her sweet scent before planting a kiss on her forehead, reassuring her I'm here and I'm not going anywhere.

I'm not sure how long we sit quietly with me rubbing her back, but eventually her crying stopped and her breathing slowed. At one point I thought she might have fallen asleep, but then I felt her fingers running lightly over my chest. I had to shift her position when I felt myself getting hard as stone, it was becoming uncomfortable. Lowering my face into the top of her hair, I grit my teeth and allow her scent to soothe some of the ache in my balls. It only makes it worse.

"How was dinner and your mum?" she murmurs softly.

"Sweetness, I'll tell you all you want to know about last night, but first you're going to tell me who did this to you and why you thought you could blow me off in a message." I place my hand over hers on my chest, stilling her movement because I don't know how much more I can take.

Leaning back a little, she stares up at me gnawing on her bottom lip. The sight of her bloodshot eyes just about kills me. She attempts to stand, but I hold her a little tighter, not wanting to lose this connection.

"I need to go to the bathroom."

Reluctantly I let her go. "Okay, Sweetness, go clean yourself up. How about I order us some food and we can relax for the night"

"I.. um.. was supposed to…"

I lift my hand and her words fall away. I know what she was going to say - she wanted to cook for me and like hell if I'm letting her lift a finger tonight.

"All I wanna hear out of that gorgeous mouth of yours is - pizza or Chinese" I get to my feet and wrap my arms around her and because I can't help myself, I plant another kiss to her forehead.

"But….."

I place a finger over her lips, "No buts, babe."

A shy smile washes over her lips and my heart beats a little faster at the sight. Knowing I put it there allows some of the rage boiling inside me to settle a little.

"Chinese, please." She murmurs before pulling away from me and heading towards a hallway.

Grabbing the phone from my pocket, I search for the closest Chinese place which delivers. Finding one close by, I hit the call now button, place my phone to my ear and wait for it to connect. While I wait, I look around and take in the small space. She doesn't have a lot, but when I see a bookshelf lining one wall, my curiosity spikes. Crossing the room, I study the titles on the spines. Taking one from the shelf, I flip it around and read what the book is about. My eyebrows shoot up when I realise my girl must have a dirty side if this book is any indication.

"Good afternoon, you have reached the Tucker Hut. How can I help you?"

A man's voice in my ear snaps me back to what I should be doing and I place the book back on the shelf, making a mental note of the title for later - *Paid For by Alexa Riley*, and place our order. I'm not sure what Ally is going to feel like eating so, I order one of nearly everything on the menu. After disconnecting the call, I head into the kitchen and sort through her cupboards for plates, cutlery and cups. After I grab everything, I set the table and look at my watch. I'm starting to worry because Ally still hasn't come out of the bathroom. Turning I look through the kitchen window and notice the rain has started to fall.

Fuck. I don't want to push her but I need to know who hurt her. From the first moment I saw her, I knew there was something in her past, a backstory. I don't give a shit what it is, we will deal with it together. I'm not letting her push me away just because she is scared. To be honest, the thought of losing her scares the shit out of me.

"Xavier, you didn't have to set the table, I could have done that."

Her voice breaks into my thoughts and I swing around from the window to find her standing in the door of the hallway.

"Dinner should be here soon." I no sooner say the words than a buzzer echoes through the apartment. "Why don't you get comfortable and I'll get that."

Ally starts to turn away. "Let me grab my purse."

"I've got it babe, relax and let me handle this."

She huffs at my words but does as I ask and takes a seat at the table. I smile to myself as I walk towards the door and press the button to let the delivery person in.

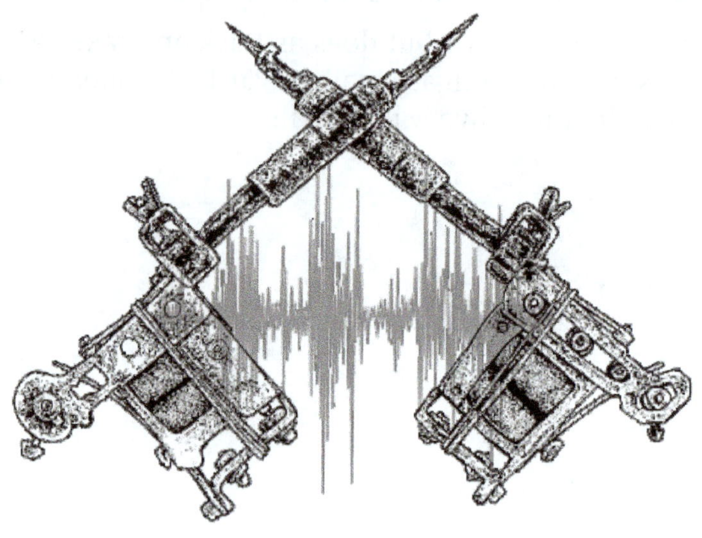

CHAPTER ELEVEN

Ally

I watch Xavier head to the door to let the delivery guy in and take in the rise and fall of his ass as he moves. The Henley shirt, grey instead of black for a change, is molded to every perfect inch of his chest. I shake my head, I have enough shit going on without drooling over this man.

I should have known when I sent him the message earlier that it wouldn't keep him away and he'd turn up on my doorstep. I was deluding myself by thinking it could have been so easy.

When I first heard the knocking, I thought it was my neighbor at the door. He would have been worried about the state I was in when he saw me arrive home earlier. But, when I threw the door open and found Xavier there, my first instinct was to throw myself into his arms. I didn't know I needed him until he was there. I want to kick my own ass under the table for falling for this guy but how could I not when he's always around.

I glance at the table and smile, underneath all that hard is a really sweet guy although I wouldn't tell him that.

"Babe!"

I snap my eyes to Xavier and see he has placed the food on the table, the delivery guy is already gone. That will teach me for getting lost in my thoughts.

"Sorry, what did you say?"

He chuckles and starts pulling food from one of the bags. "I asked what you felt like eating." He indicates the containers and I notice, he must have ordered everything on the bloody menu.

"Holy crap, Babe. Did you order everything they had? That's a lot of food." Lifting my eyes, I notice the megawatt smile plastered on his face and raise an eyebrow, wondering what he's so happy about.

"You called me…Babe."

"I did?" I scrunch up my face, knowing I did. "Well, it's your fault." I sound like a five-year-old petulant child instead of a twenty-two-year-old adult but fall short of poking my tongue out.

He laughs, a deep laugh which ricochets through every nerve in my body.

"How so?"

He raises an eyebrow as he takes a seat beside me.

"You're always around these days and keep saying it to me. I picked it up from you." Even to my ears I sound lame.

Leaning over, he brushes his lips over mine before whispering against my mouth. "Get used to it."

He leans back in his chair and I suck my bottom lip into my mouth, savoring the taste of mint, X and coffee. I think it's my new favorite flavor.

"C'mon, babe, let's eat."

I nod and reach over to grab the honey chicken and fried rice, but Xavier grabs them first and moves them from my reach. I'm about to kick him in the leg but then he starts scooping the food onto my plate and I smile.

"Damn, the look you just gave me, I thought I would die," he laughs.

"I thought you weren't going to let me have any food." I take the first mouthful and hum around the spoon.

"Never, babe. I just wanted to help because of your hand."

I glance down at the bandage on my hand and realize, for the past twenty minutes, what happened this morning has been completely forgotten. I know he'll want to talk about it when we finish eating and my stomach turns over at the thought.

I feel the lightest touch under my chin and he turns my face up to his before leaning forward and kissing the tip of my nose. The five o'clock shadow across the top of his lip tickles.

"Don't stress, babe. Eat."

I look back to my plate. My appetite has vanished but I try to eat anyway.

While cleaning up after dinner, I realise how easy it is to be around Xavier. I worry if what I have to tell him will scare him away, but I guess it's a risk I'm willing to take. I know there are no certainties in life so I'll just have to bite the bullet and tell him. I think I've stalled long enough and my time is up.

Blowing out a deep breath, I pace in front of where X is sitting on the lounge and he watches me. He doesn't appear tense or frustrated which is a bonus, but concern swims in his eyes. I run my uninjured hand through my hair while I try to work out, how much to tell him.

"My mother is not what you'd call maternal. She never wanted me but dad did." I run a hand nervously through my hair again. "My father died four years ago and my mother took to the bottle and let's just say, it didn't take long to escalate into alcoholism. I visit every Saturday to check on her and clean up the mess in the house – empty bottles, overflowing ashtrays. This morning, I was washing up and grabbed a knife by the wrong end. I cut myself." I hold up my bandaged hand.

He nods and I don't miss the flash of anger in his eyes before I continue.

"My mother is convinced, because she's miserable, I should be too. She insists I have no right to be happy. This morning I let slip that I'd met someone. She said some terrible, nasty things which really hurt so, I got angry and said some bad things back to her. She shoved me against the wall and slapped me in the face."

I blow out a deep breath while tears trickle over my cheeks, resembling the rain running down the glass of the kitchen window. The quiet from behind me becomes too much to bear, the room seems to close in around me. The eerie silence settles deep in my gut and I turn away from the window to face him.

Xavier is barely holding onto his control. He's sitting forward with his elbows on his knees and his fingers so tightly interlocked, his knuckles are white. I think one wrong word would shatter the fragile hold he has on himself.

"Why doesn't your *mother*..." The word mother is spoken with contempt as if it leaves a bad taste in his mouth. He lifts his eyes to mine and I see the current of anger running within. "...believe you should be happy?"

Tension zaps between us in the small space. I really didn't want to give him any more information, I'm scared to death he will feel the same as my mother. But, if whatever this is we have stands a chance, he needs to know the whole story.

"S..she..." I will the dryness from my mouth so I can speak, take a deep breath and release it slowly. I wipe the tears from my face, gaze into his ocean blue eyes and tell him the truth.

"It's my fault my father died." I swallow past the lump in my throat as my voice cracks on the last word.

Xavier watches me for a few moments but I can't tell what he's thinking. Chills cause me to shake and I wrap my arms tightly around me. I wait for him to leave and flinch when he jumps up from the lounge. Fuck, the man can move fast, he wraps me in his arms. He sits back on the lounge, drawing me onto his lap. I melt into his chest.

"How is it your fault, Sweetness?" His deep whisper washes over me as he kisses my temple.

The chill this time touches me bone deep.

"When I was eighteen, I met a boy. He seemed nice enough but after a few months, I found out he was anything but." I push from Xavier's hold after taking in his scent and letting it cocoon me. Reluctantly, he lets me go. I can see by the look in his eyes, he's not happy but I can't be touched right now. With my back turned to him, I take in a few deep breaths. Turning back, I continue.

"Luke, my ex and I met just over four years ago. I was working part-time in a Newsagency in Maitland down the road from where I lived with my parents. I was living there to save money while I studied to become a Librarian. He used to come in every morning, he was a handyman in the area. I didn't pay him much attention at first, guys weren't on my radar at the time. I just wanted to work and get my Master's degree. He'd flirt and I found myself flirting back." I pause for a breath.

"So, one afternoon after my shift was done, I stopped at the local shops for a few things and ran into him. One thing led to another and a week later I agreed to go on a date with him. It was good and we started seeing each other whenever we were free. He knew I was busy and didn't push or demand my time. Then, one night he seemed weird from the time he picked me up. I thought he must have had a bad day at work, he was more agitated than I'd ever seen him. He accused me of cheating on him."

Time for another deep breath.

"I honestly didn't recognise him, his eyes were dark and wild. Looking back, I knew something was off but instead of listening to my gut, I tried to calm him down. After I reassured him I hadn't cheated on him, he seemed to settle. We were at his place and had just finished dinner when a friend, Steven, from my class started messaging me about an assignment which was due in that week. It set Luke off again. He dragged me by the hair to his bedroom."

I hiccup and try to calm my racing heart, I've been pacing back and forth while I was speaking. When I stop, Xavier is on the edge of his seat, fingers white from gripping the edge of the cushion. He nods for me to keep going.

"He threw me onto the bed. He'd always been a little on the rough side but I hadn't minded it. This time it was different. The walls seemed to close in on me, I was terrified. I begged him not to do what I knew he was about to, but my pleas fell on deaf ears. A split second later, my clothes were gone and he was inside me." I close my eyes and visions of his wild eyes looking back at me fill my mind. It's as if it's happening all over again. "I gave up," I whisper. "I stopped fighting him and that angered him more. He said he knew I liked it rough and that he was just getting started. I didn't know what he meant until I felt a burning pain slide down my leg and I screamed out in pain."

I scrub the tears from my face and turn away from X. I can't look at his gorgeous face while I speak such ugly words.

"When I looked down I saw he had slashed my thigh with the pocket knife he always carried. My cries of pain seemed to urge him on, it was like he couldn't get enough of my agony. He would stick his fingers in the wound until I screamed and then run his bloodied fingers over my body. After he'd finished with me and he passed out, I called my dad to come and get me the hell out of there. I'll never forget the look on dad's face when he saw me. It took everything I had to stop him from killing Luke and when he regained control, he took me to the hospital. I had never seen him cry before, but something broke in him that night and it also broke me."

My chest heaves on a sob as I replay the horror in my head.

"My father stayed with me while I was being checked at the hospital and speaking with the police. He held onto me and listened to every detail about what had happened. Luke was charged and I thought that was the end of it. Two months later I was proven wrong. What he'd done to me that night was nothing compared to what happened next. He showed up at my parent's home. When I opened the door, I saw the glint of madness in his eyes. Seconds later, pain exploded in my stomach and when I looked down, a knife protruded from me. I remember stumbling backwards, tripping on the hallway rug and hitting the ground hard. I heard my father yelling then, nothing. I woke up in hospital a week later, the room was empty. Later, a doctor said I'd had a close call and it would take months for me to heal properly. When I asked about my dad, the expression on his face changed to one of sadness. He explained, my dad hadn't made it."

I feel like I've just run a marathon and sit on the lounge to get my emotions back in check. I wait for the questions X is bound to have, but again the room is silent except for his heavy breathing. Oddly enough, his breathing has a calming effect on me as my fingers twist in a hole in my pajamas.

Energy from X fills the room and has my stomach twisting in knots. I feel the fear, like lead, sit heavy in my belly at the thought he will stand and walk out of the apartment. I wouldn't blame him, I'm a lot to take on. I feel like a hot mess most of the time and I'm just fighting to get through day by day. But, something about this man has me hoping he could be my compass and lead me from the nightmares that haunt me.

I study X closely and swear every word I have just spoken, shows on his features. From the way his eyes track every move I make to the way his muscles flex and relax as he fights for control. I know he's angry, it surges off him in waves. I don't think it's me he's pissed with, but the events of my past. I want to crawl into his lap and never leave, the feelings he evokes consume every cell in me. I'm broken from my thoughts when his voice washes over me.

"Never again. You're mine now."

A gasp slips from my lips when I hear the truth in his voice.

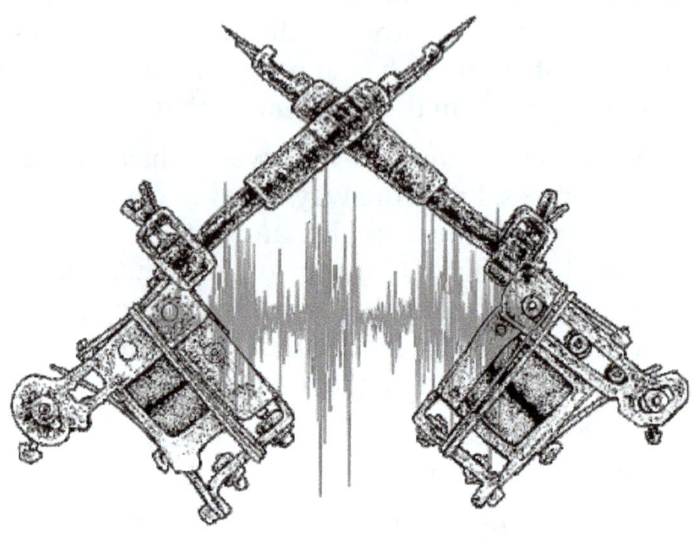

CHAPTER TWELVE

Xavier

"Didn't....."

I hold up my hand to prevent her from continuing and she wisely closes her mouth. It guts me to see so much fucking sadness in those beautiful eyes of hers and I wish she didn't feel this way. I know if she says one more word about not wanting to be with me because of this bullshit. I'll lose what little control I have right now. I need a fucking minute to soak in everything she's just told me, to try and calm my ass down before my anger takes control and makes this situation a lot worse than it already is. Exhaling a deep breath, I run my hand across the back of my neck to relieve the anger and tension knotting the muscles there.

"Never in a million years did I think I would find somebody and have the chance to settle down. Then, I found you." I pause and look into her wide eyes. "I knew there was something about you, something drawing me to you, but in my eyes, you seemed

92

untouchable. You'd put a shield in place which I thought I didn't have a chance in hell of penetrating. This past week has opened my eyes to so much more than I ever thought possible. Now, when I look at you I see a future. It plays out in my head as clear as crystal. I understand that shit may scare you because fuck, it did a number on me to begin with. But, I know what I want and what I want is you." My words finish on a growl.

"I'm scared." Her murmur is barely above a whisper but I heard it.

I get why she's scared but I need her to realise, she has nothing to be scared of when it comes to me.

"I know."

"What if I let you in and shit goes south?" There is more strength in her words now.

"Sweetness, life's about chances. I can't do this on my own, I need you to be on board."

"X, he had sugary sweet words on his lips but the devil was in his eyes."

I suck in a deep breath at her words. I'm barely holding it together. How could she even think I could be capable of anything like that piece of shit?

"What do you see when you look into my eyes?" I speak between clenched teeth.

She studies me for a moment and I can practically hear her mind ticking over. Then, her face softens as if she understands. Closing her eyes, she speaks words which ingrain themselves deep inside every cell and muscle in my body. I know if I touched her right now I would be lost in her forever.

"When I look into your eyes they have a calming, soothing effect like the ocean. They consume me like the waves crashing over the rocks. Center me like the white wash which crawls over my feet as I stand in the sinking sand. When the grey clouds roll in and a humid sticky feeling coats your skin before a storm comes - your eyes, like the storm, have an energy so consuming it surrounds me. I want to hold on to that feeling and never let it go. I want it to soak into every cell of my body and live right there, in that moment. Forever."

She breathes out slowly, trapped in the moment. She remains motionless as if she is feeling everything she has just described. Goosebumps break out across my skin at the sight. I don't remember ever having goosebumps from only words.

She shakes her head and seems to snap out of her trance-like state. When she looks around and her eyes meet mine, she ducks her head. A pink tinge colors her cheeks.

"I'm sorry," she whispers.

Her words knock the wind from me and before she can blink, I drop to my knees before her. I run my hands up her thighs and grip her waist. She tenses and I flex my fingers but then, she dissolves into my touch. Raising one hand, I lift her chin until her eyes meet mine. Freckles are scattered across her nose like confetti and I resist the urge to kiss every one. Forcing my eyes to meet hers, I open my mouth to speak but have no words.

Keeping my eyes on hers, I lean forward and brush my lips over her soft pink blush lips, resisting the urge to push inside for a taste. Knowing, the sweet taste of her ecstasy will pull me in. I wouldn't be able to stop and I want to give her what she just gave me.

"Your eyes remind of a sunrise on a Spring morning, when the sun's golden rays bounce off the dew-covered leaves."

She sucks in a breath as my mouth hovers over hers and I whisper the words across her lips. But, I don't stop - I need her to understand how fucked up she has me. "Did you know, when the sun hits your eyes, not only do you have a gold band which wraps around the pupils and shines but when you turn your head this way or that way....." I guide her face from side to side.

"....they catch the light? They become luminous and I could spend hours staring into them, wanting to learn every emotion flickering through them. There is so much passion lying in those green depths and I'm a greedy bastard - I want all of it."

I blow out a deep breath as her eyes begin to glass over and a tear sticks in her long lashes. When she softly blinks, it falls and races down her check. Reaching up, I run my thumb over the wetness and rub it into her soft, milky skin.

"Fuck, I sound like a fucking pussy right now but I'll be damned if I'll let you think that my actions are just a way to make you let down your guard. Never in my fucking life did I ever think someone so sweet could be interested in a brute like me. Fuck. I'm not backing off, babe. You have become my reason to get up in the morning and to sleep at night. You center me and I am not giving you up without a fight." I feel my muscles tense at the thought of her walking away from me and I close my eyes against the feeling.

"Okay." She rests her uninjured hand against mine on her cheek as she whispers.

My eyes snap wide and lock with hers.

"Yeah, Babe?" I wonder if I heard her right.

Nodding, she leans forward, brushes her lips across mine and whispers *yes* into my mouth. It's the softest touch, like a feather brushed across my skin. I growl and can't hold back this time. I thread my fingers through her silky hair and take her lips in a deep kiss. A kiss I have been craving since the moment I saw her. It's everything and much, much more than I ever expected.

Pulling her tight into my hold, I moan into her mouth when her body melts into mine. Her uninjured hand runs up the side of my face before gripping my hair. She twists her fingers through the strands, her nails scrape against my scalp. Turning her head to a better position, I run my tongue along hers -

devour and consume every whimper and moan escaping her throat.

After a moment, I pull back, needing to stop before I take her on the lounge. I lean my forehead against hers as we both catch our breath. I feel the warmth of her breath wash over my face and it grounds me knowing this woman is mine. Pulling back a little, I grunt at the satisfaction which runs through me at seeing how swollen her lips look, branding her as mine.

"You're mine," I breath out.

"I'm yours." A shy smile curves her lips as she speaks.

"Fuck, your gorgeous, babe." Leaning forward, I plant a chaste kiss on her lips before pushing to my feet and reaching down for her. Taking her uninjured hand, I pull her to her feet. I gasp when her chest pushes against mine. Fuck. Fuck. Fuck. I need to get my shit together. I glance at the clock on the wall to see it's almost 8:30pm.

"You have had a big day, babe. You must be tired, how about you lie down?"

Right on cue, she yawns and I chuckle.

"Yeah, I'm pretty beat." She snickers but I don't find her words one bit funny at all.

"Sorry, too early for jokes." She turns and heads towards what I assume is her room and I follow.

I'm pissed as fuck with her words, but she has dealt with enough today, she doesn't need me losing my shit too. It's taking every ounce of control I have to not demand to know where her bitch of a mother lives. I know it wouldn't help the situation though and right now I want to be here for my woman.

When I step into her room, I notice there isn't much in here, like the rest of her place. A queen bed is flanked by a bedside table on each side. A small built in wardrobe with two mirrored doors is on one side of the room and on the other, a television sits on a small plywood stand. The wall in front of her bed has an old-style picture window which looks out over the street. Turning back to Ally, I notice her fidgeting with the hem of her singlet shirt, her eyes downcast and looking at the floor.

"Let's get into bed." I wave my hand towards the bed and bite back a chuckle when her eyes widen and she looks back and forth between me and the bed.

"Just to sleep, babe." I reassure her and she nods before climbing onto the bed.

I have to readjust myself at the sight of her ass in the air and struggle against wanting to rip her clothes off and take what I want. *She has been through enough for one day,* I keep reminding myself as I slip off my shirt, remove my belt but leave the jeans on – needing a barrier between us for her sake.

I hear her gasp and our eyes lock before I make my way to the other side of the bed. I bite my lip to prevent a groan at the sight of her licking her lips as her eyes take in my bare chest.

"Do you wanna watch some TV?" I lie down and notice she is way over the other side of the bed. Not liking the distance between us, I pull her into my arms and as she rests her head on my chest, I breathe in her sweet scent.

"If you want," she whispers.

I tense when her warm breath flutters over me and her fingers trace the tattoos covering most of my chest.

"Why don't you have any tattoos here?" She lays her hand across my heart.

"I didn't know what to put there." I both love and hate the way she is exploring my body. My dick is as hard as steel and straining against my boxer briefs. I definitely think I made the right decision leaving my jeans on. It's painful as fuck but worth it to prove I'm not just here for a good time.

Reaching over me, Ally grabs the remote control off the bedside table and flicks through the channels before settling on a movie - *Road house with Patrick Swayze.*

"Good choice, babe." I kiss the crown of her head and feel her smile against my chest.

"I loved this movie growing up. My dad gave up watching it with me when I learned every single word and couldn't help but say them out loud." She giggles at the memory and I chuckle.

Her giggle has to be the best sound in the world, nothing will ever compare to the sound of her laugh.

"Try and get some sleep, babe." Wrapping my arms around her, I pull her closer and let the feel of her warm breath wash over my bare skin. It settles the anger sitting like a weight inside me, I'm content to lie here with my girl in my arms.

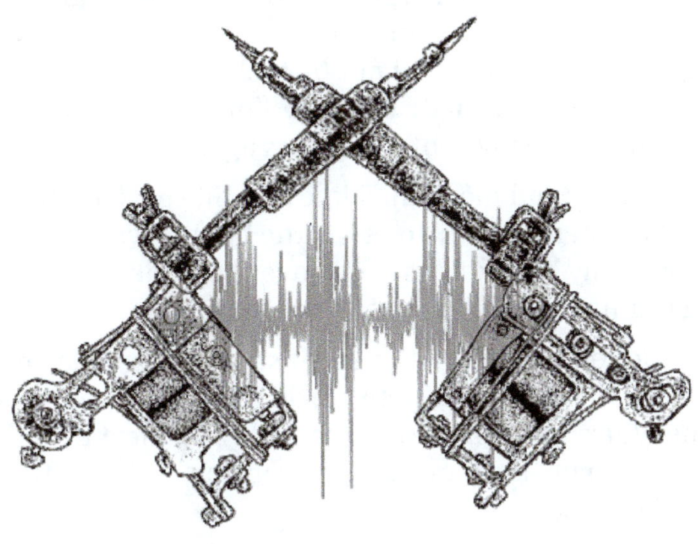

CHAPTER THIRTEEN

Ally

Feeling warmth surround me, I snuggle deeper into the blankets, not ready to wake just yet. As I wriggle down, I realise I'm not alone. I'm snuggling into something hard and not the softness of my pillow. I blink my eyes open and stare straight at the defined, tattooed chest of Xavier. Everything which happened yesterday floods my mind. I tense but the sound of X's light snores along with the rise and fall of his chest has me relaxing again, not wanting to wake him.

I replay the words which were spoken last night, I can't believe he stayed and admitted I affect him the way I do.

I know he's angry about everything I told him and I saw he is keeping some part of him from me. Do I come off as being so vulnerable that he needs to hide from me? I sure as shit don't want him hiding a part of himself from me. If I'm really his, then

99

it means he's mine and I deserve to see every side of him. Something at the back of my mind is scared shitless about knowing but I cannot and will not be fooled by a wolf in sheep's clothing. I've been through enough. I'm stronger now and I won't repeat the mistakes of four years ago.

With my mind made up, I know I will speak to him when he wakes but I'm not ready to break the bubble we have created just yet. I rest my head on his chest, over his heart and allow the soothing thumping to lull me back to sleep.

I'm jolted awake by the shrill sound of my alarm going off. Groaning, I reach blindly towards my nightstand to locate my phone. Vibration from a deep chuckle and the feel of fingers caressing my hair, stop me and I drop my hand to the hard planes of X's chest.

"I've got it, Sweetness."

His deep, sleepy voice fills my ears and I hum as tingles break out over my body.

"You're not much of a morning person, are you?"

He runs his hand down my back and my body reacts by arching like a cat into his side.

"Coffee," I mumble. My single word answer causes him to chuckle more.

I raise my hand and rub the side of my mouth, making sure I haven't drooled on him. I wince and a whimper escapes when I move and realise I've had my weight on the injured hand. Moving faster than I thought possible, X shoots up in the bed, taking me with him.

"What's wrong?" Concern furrows his brows.

"I slept on my hand." I cradle it too my chest and feel a light pounding as the blood rushes back into it.

"Let me take a look."

He reaches out to take my hand but I shake my head. There's nothing he could do and I don't want to talk about it anymore. I want to enjoy today with him before we have to go back to work. I run my fingertips down the side of his face which is full of tension.

"It's fine, X, I promise."

He nods and I change the subject.

"What do you want to do today?" I smile as the tension disperses and his eyes soften.

"How about I make us breakfast and then, if you feel up to it, we can meet up with Beau and Justin at the beach this afternoon."

"The beach sounds good but I can make breakfast."

When I attempt to get out of bed, I groan loudly. An ache seems to radiate through my neck and the arm of my injured hand. Damn, it friggin' hurts. When I get to my feet, I rub at the ache and the pain causes me to wince.

"Babe, go and have a shower, you'll feel better. I can make breakfast."

Before I can protest, he's walking from the room.

"You can't tell me what to do," I mutter a little louder than I thought because he calls back.

"Watch me. When it comes to your health, you'll soon realise, I'm in control."

"Stubborn ass," I growl and hear him laugh.

I smile as I make my way to the bathroom.

Feeling a little better after my shower, I throw on my favorite beach cover-up over my swimmers. It's white with crochet trimming around the edges. There aren't arm holes, you pop it over your head and let it hang from your body. I wrap my wet hair up in a towel the best I can with my sore hand and head to the kitchen.

When I reach the kitchen door, I pause and take in the sight before me. X is standing at the stove making pancakes, but what has me transfixed, is his naked back and the way his muscles flex and ripple. I study the tattoos which cover every inch of his skin. The focal piece of art is a scene of the ocean and it's breathtaking. I swallow a moan when the thought crosses my mind, this man is mine.

"Babe?"

Xavier's voice breaks into my thoughts and I quickly lower my eyes as heat creeps up my neck. Xavier chuckles, I guess I wasn't quick enough and he saw me ogling him.

"Damn, babe, you look as hot as fuck."

His deep growl makes my skin prickle. I'm not sure what too say so I head for the fridge and grab the orange juice. Before I reach the table, I feel the heat of his body as he wraps his hands around my waist. Turning my head to the side, I feel his hot breath wash over me and squeeze my thighs together to stave off the ache. My breath hitches as he plants kisses up my neck before his teeth make contact with the lobe of my ear.

"Sweetness, nobody sees what is mine so, let's keep the cover-up on. It shows enough and it's taking everything in me not to rip the flimsy piece of material off you."

He draws the material to one side and it slips from my shoulder. I'm about to protest until he runs his tongue over my shoulder blade and applies a little pressure to my collarbone. I grip the handle of the fridge to keep me from falling to the ground when my knees weaken and shake. He takes a step back and I yelp when he slaps my ass.

"Plus, you can't swim for another week."

"Fine, you win this one but only because I don't want to ruin my tattoo." I grumble while I concentrate on stopping my head from swimming and turning to a pile of goo on the kitchen floor.

"I always win, Sweetness." He sounds so damn sure of himself.

"Cocky Bastard," I mumble before taking a seat at the table.

He chuckles harder and I suck my bottom lip between my teeth to stop the smile which wants to spread across my face.

I close the glass door to my building and when I turn, X reaches for my hand, we make our way to the beach. I decide now is as good a time as any to bring up the discussion from last night, but I'm struggling to figure out how to convince him to open up to me. To let me see every part of him and not keep anything hidden.

"Sweetness, whatever it is, spit it out."

"What do you mean?" I ask dumbly, I didn't think I looked so transparent.

"Whatever is bothering you has been running through your head all morning. I know you want to say something so, just say it."

Well shit, I really am that transparent. I lick my suddenly dry lips and fix the sunglasses which have slipped a little down my nose before taking his advice and just saying it.

"Why are you hiding a part of yourself from me?"

Xavier pulls me to an abrupt stop and I'm swung around to come face to chest with him. When I look up, I take in his dark messy hair and the five o'clock shadow which seems to be permanently on his handsome face.

"Explain."

"Last night....." He holds up his hand but I push on, I'm not going to let him stop me this time. "Last Night I told you some pretty messed up shit and I could see you were angry, but then you spoke sweet words to cover up the anger. You acted like you were fine and I think you're hiding something." I blow out a breath. "I'm strong enough to deal with whatever it is X, you don't have to hide that part of you from me."

I finish on a whisper, looking into his eyes. I can't see what's in his eyes because he has sunglasses on, but I feel the tension which has suddenly surrounded us. The background noise of cars passing fades out and it's just him and me standing on the side of road. I hear the echo of my heart beat thumping in my ears while I wait for him to speak.

"Of course, I'm pissed, Ally," he growls.

I open my mouth to speak but he cuts me off by grabbing my hips in a possessive hold. It has my blood pumping faster and not in a bad way.

"How the hell would letting my anger out help? Besides scaring the fuck out of you and having you running away faster than you were already trying to do before I turned up."

I hear the anguish in his voice and it makes me feel sick to my stomach. He turns away from me for a moment and composes himself before speaking again.

"Sweetness, I would like nothing more than to find your bitch of a mother and teach her a fucking lesson, but that's just not me. I don't raise a hand to women or harm them with talk. I don't think she deserves any more of our time. As for your ex, he's a fucking cock sucking coward and yes, if he was standing in front of us right now I probably would kill him. I'd make him pay for everything he did to you and your dad, but babe I'll say again, seeing me lose control would only scare you off. So, you tell me, what good would you seeing me angry do? What would come of it because the only thing I see is at how fast you would run and I can't live with that." He blows out a deep breath.

I don't know what to say so instead I rise up on my tiptoes and brush my lips over his.

"I want to know you. I want to know how you feel and when I say that, I mean I want to know *every* side of you." I close my eyes and pray to my father above, hoping I'm making the right decision when the next words slip through my lips. "I promise, I won't run."

The words are no sooner spoken than I feel myself being lifted into the air and X's mouth lands hard on mine. I'm already so addicted to his taste, I open to him and run my tongue along his, moaning at the taste of coffee and mint which I seem to be craving more and more lately.

I pull back, slightly breathless. "Damn, I forget how tall you are until you lift me and we're chest to chest." I laugh and X chuckles.

"You're so tiny, I could put you in my pocket, Sweetness."

He runs a hand over my ass and gives it a squeeze before lowering me back onto my feet. Locking his fingers with mine, we continue towards the beach. The air around us feels lighter and the background noise begins to seep back through. I feel hopeful that I've made the right decision then, it hits me like a truck - despite everything we have spoken about, we haven't talked about his dinner with his parents.

"How were your mum and dad the other night?"

His hand tenses for a few seconds in mine, but he doesn't say anything. I'm guessing he doesn't want to talk about it, but after a few moments of silence he begins to talk and my heart hurts for him when I hear the sadness which coats his words.

"Mum seems to be getting worse every time I visit and I can tell what a toll its taking on my dad." He pauses for a minute before going on. "Dad pulled me aside before I left to tell me her doctor thinks it's time for her to be placed in a care facility where she'll have around the clock care. My dad argued that he'd hired a nurse and their house is familiar to her. He doesn't want to take that away from her too. So, everything is up in the air right now and I guess I'm still trying to process it all."

He sighs and I feel a sadness on hearing what he says. I don't know what to do to help him so, I pull my hand from his, wrap it around his waist and try to get as close to him as possible without tripping over. Leaning down, he presses a kiss to the crown of my head and wraps his arm tightly around my waist.

"It's hard you know, the woman who raised and loved me seems to be vanishing right in front of my eyes. No matter what I do, I can't stop it. I can't imagine how lost and confused she must feel. I can't imagine the pain at feeling so lonely and trapped inside my body. Not knowing, or only remembering part of who I am, or the people around me. I don't know how my father does it."

"He loves her," I murmur into his chest.

"With every fiber of his body, but this disease is slowly killing him too. She's a shell of the woman he loves and knew, I know it's tearing him to pieces. I guess I just want to know how to help, but dad has always been so strong and he thinks he needs to do it all by himself."

Xavier takes a sharp breath and I watch him rub at his eyes. My heart breaks a little more for him and it has me wishing I knew how to help. I stay quiet, listening to him breathing as we approach the beach. Once we're at the wooden fencing which leads to the concrete steps, he stops and wraps both his arms around me.

"When I told you last night that you were the reason I can sleep at night, those weren't just empty words babe. I need you in my life. You have become so deeply ingrained in me that you have become a part of my routine."

"X we only met a week ago, how does that even make sense?"

Pointing towards one of the old wooden benches, he takes my hand and continues. "I sat here every lunch break for over two months just so I'd get the slightest glimpse of you." Dropping his hand, he wraps his arms around me and I place mine against his chest. I close my eyes when I feel his lips on my forehead. "You became a part of me the moment I first saw you and it took for you to walk into my studio to seal the deal. I'm playing for keeps, Sweetness so, you'd better jump on board and hold on tight. I can't promise we won't fight and disagree on things, but I can promise you, I would never intentionally hurt you."

Leaning down, he takes my lips in a deep kiss as if he's sealing the deal by kissing me. I'm kind of glad because I have no words to reply. Pulling back when we hear voices calling out, I duck my head, burying into X's chest as a shyness takes over.

"Get a room you pair," Beau laughs.

"Let the girl breath," Justin calls out.

"Leave them alone you candy asses," a girl shouts at them from where she sits on a towel on the beach.

The men laugh and when I lift my head, I recognise her from the tattoo shop. She's the girl who threatened to stab Beau in the nuts with a pen.

"Come on babe, I want to introduce you to the guys."

Taking my hand, X leads me down the steps. I slip my thongs off and sigh when the cool sand hits my bare feet, making him laugh at me.

"Fuck you're cute, babe." He leans down and brushes his lips over mine.

"Call me cute again and see what happens." I growl, causing him to laugh harder along with the two men who have joined us.

"Fuck, I like this girl already." The woman laughs as she climbs to her feet, dusts off the sand and heads towards us.

"Erica, this is my girlfriend Ally. Ally, this is Erica, she works at the shop."

I can hear the pride in his voice when he calls me his girlfriend, sending butterflies swimming in my belly. Smiling I turn to Erica and I hold my uninjured hand out to her.

"Hi," I manage to say before I'm engulfed in a hug.

"Hey, nice to meet you, I could do with a bit more estrogen around here, I was feeling outnumbered." She laughs and I laugh with her.

"Can you give me tips on how to handle this big lug?" I laugh as I point to X and it earns me a slap on the ass.

"Behave, woman. Erica, if you like working for me, watch it," X growls but I can tell he is joking.

"You go and swim with the boys, leave us girls alone." Erica waves her hand in the air, shooing them away.

"At least put on some decent music," Beau grumbles.

When I glance down at the towel where Erica had been sitting, I notice the set-up she has going. There's a portable CD player, a small cooler which I guess has drinks in it, crackers, cheese and cabanossi which is cut up and ready to eat. There is also a bag of chicken flavoured potato chips.

"Shut it, Beau before I get the urge to drown you."

Beau wiggles his eyebrows. "Promises, promises, Peaches."

"Beau, I swear you'll be lucky to live another day if you keep it up," she snaps out. "I thought this song was kind of like our theme song," she laughs.

"Come on baby keep talking dirty to me, you know how much it turns me on. I'll take any theme song you want, Peaches." He chuckles and winks before turning away and jogging to catch up to the other two men who are at the water's edge. Looking back at Erica, I notice the smile on her face before a cheeky grin breaks out. She bends down and turns up the music so lyrics to 'Back to You by Louis Tomlinson ft. Bebe Rexha' ring out loud and clear. X and Justin laugh while Beau shakes his head and mutters something to the other two. Being so far away and with the music blaring I don't hear it.

I study the men as they stand side by side and notice how similar they look. They are all covered in tattoos and are around the same build and height. Damn, they're all sexy as hell but my man in the middle oozes *sin* and sex. I can't wait to be alone with him tonight. Licking my lips at the thought, I sense Erica come up beside me.

"Inked perfection," she says, barely above a whisper.

I don't know how to respond to her words but notice she is staring straight at Beau. There is sadness in her eyes but I don't ask her about it. I get the feeling she doesn't want to discuss what has put the look there and since she hasn't asked about why I'm so beaten up, I'll respect her privacy.

CHAPTER FOURTEEN

Xavier

"Where you going brother?" Beau calls out but I ignore his ass as I make my way out of the waves and onto the sand. I make a beeline for my woman who is currently laughing at something Erica has said. I like the feeling that settles in my gut knowing her and Erica are getting on so well.

Ally notices me heading towards her and I watch as her pink tongue darts out and swipes along her lush bottom lip. When her eyes rake over my body, my cock jerks in response.

Fuck, what I wouldn't give to be alone with her right now and the nasty things I want her to do with that tongue of hers.

I hear someone call Ally's name and she turns her head towards the steps which lead down to the beach. It's her friend, Cynthia and I assume the boy she has with her is her son. I don't miss the wince of pain which crosses Ally's face when she pushes to her feet and the muscles of my stomach tighten. I hate that she's in pain with her hand.

She jogs to her friend and they hug before Cynthia draws back and rests her hands on Ally's shoulders. I note the look of concern on her friend's face and when she turns to me and scowls, I almost recoil with the pain of her thinking I was the one to hurt Ally.

Cynthia's focus turns back to Ally's when she speaks and I watch as her shoulders relax and she nods. Ally bends and gives the boys hair a ruffle before she hugs him, I love the smile on her face. Damn, what I wouldn't do to keep that smile on her face all the time.

I feel the other men come up behind me.

"Is this going to be an issue, Justin?" I snarl, not wanting another episode like last week.

"Nope, I'm gonna marry that girl one day so, it's best she came to me before I tracked her ass down."

His words shock the shit out of me and I spin around to see if he's serious. The expression on his face as he watches Cynthia tells me, he's dead fucking serious. I nod at him. I understand because it's the same look I've had every day since I first saw Ally. Regardless, I still need to warn him.

"Don't fuck this shit up because I wouldn't want to beat your ass." I don't give him a chance to reply, I make my way over to the girls when they reach Erica.

"Erica, this Cynthia and her son, JT."

Cynthia smiles and says, "hello."

"Nice to meet you." The kid holds out his hand to shake with Erica.

The boy has manners, I like that.

"Lovely to meet you too, JT." Erica shakes his hand and smiles.

I watch as Cynthia's attention is drawn to something over my shoulder and her whole body tenses. It doesn't last long before she relaxes again and starts pulling things out of her bag.

"Mummy, I want to hit the waves." JT jumps from one foot to the other as he practically begs. I chuckle at his impatience.

"In a minute, baby, let's get some sunscreen on you first."

The little boy grumbles but listens to his mother.

I crouch down and hold out my hand for him to shake. "Hey, little man, my name is Xavier but you can call me X."

"That's a cool name, my name is Just...."

"JT!" His mother cuts him off, her eyes dart around us and she blows out a relieved breath. Glancing over my shoulder, in the direction Cynthia had looked, I notice the other two dipshits slowly making their way up to us. They would have been too far away too have heard what was being said.

Cynthia goes back to putting sunscreen on JT and I look to Ally but she just shakes her head and I nod in response.

"Okay, little man, lets go for a swim." Cynthia pulls off her dress and my eyes catch the numerous tattoos covering her body.

"Shit girl, I didn't realise you had all that ink under your clothes."

Erica laughs, taking it all in, but my eyes have zeroed in on one piece of ink which has alarms going off in my mind. I begin to put two and two together. On her left collar bone are the words - *His Queen*, it's identical to ink Justin has but his says -*Her King*.

Well, I'll be fucked. If the kid's name is Justin as he started to say then, it's not too fucking far fetched to believe it's his kid. Anger bubbles in my belly at the thought he left her with the kid and didn't own up to that shit. I thought he was a better man than that. Just as the thought crosses my mind, the man himself walks up beside me, his eyes wide as he looks at Cynthia.

"What the fuck?" he spits out.

I squeeze my hands into fists when I hear the anger in his voice and I'm about done for the day.

"Cover yourself up, woman, no man should see what's mine," Justin growls.

Cynthia looks up and there is so much anger in her eyes, I'm amazed Justin isn't dead.

"Don't fucking look at me like that, cover your ass up."

I feel the tension and anger roll off him in waves and I'm about to say something but Cynthia beats me to it. I'm pleased to see Ally and Erica take JT down to the water and away from what is sure to be a confrontation.

"You lost the right to tell me what to do years ago, Justin so, pull your fucking head in. I'm only here because I haven't seen Ally for a couple of days so, if you will excuse me." She straightens her shoulders and starts to walk past us, but Justin reaches out and grabs her arm.

"We need to talk." His voice is more controlled now.

She stares down at the sand and takes a few deep breaths before her spine straightens once again. "No, we don't."

She pulls away from his hold and heads to where the girls are.

"Justin," I caution.

"X-man, fuck this shit. I need to get my head on straight."

"Yeah, you fucking do. You don't deserve her time if you left her years ago with your kid." Anger is clear in my words.

"What the fuck you talking about?" He gives me a pissed off look before staring at the girls and JT. I can almost see when it all makes sense to him.

"Son of bitch!" he spits out while running a hand through his hair. "I need to fix this." Frustration laces his voice and the anger in me settles a little when I realise, he probably didn't know.

"Today probably isn't the right time, mate. It might be best to give her some time."

"What the fuck would you do if Ally had your kid and didn't tell you?"

I open my mouth then close it again, not sure what to say. If Ally had my kid, I know without a doubt, I would be a part of his or her life. Nothing, fucking nothing, would stop me.

I squeeze Justin's shoulder. "A word of advice - if he is your kid and you plan to marry that woman, take your time. Give her the space she needs and prove to her you're willing to wait for her for as long as it takes."

With that said, I turn away, allowing my words to sink in as I head to the girls.

Beau runs out of the waves, grabs Erica around the waist and throws her over his shoulder. We all laugh while she screams, threatening death to him while hitting his back with her hands. I hear the smile in her voice until a wave comes up and he drops them both into it.

On the way back to Ally's apartment, we grab fish and chips so we don't have to cook. It's just after six when we finally get home. After we eat, I reach forward and start to wrap up all the rubbish scattered over the coffee table. Ally giggles and stares at me like she is trying to work something out. I smile back at her.

"What's so funny, babe, what's running through that head of yours?"

"It's nothing." She waves me off and tries to stop herself from laughing.

"Spit it out woman" I grunt taking a seat next to her again. After a few moments she speaks.

"I was just trying to work out what kind of music I would put on a CD for a playlist."

I must have given her a strange look, because she quickly explains what the hell she is on about.

"At the beach today, Erica told me how much Beau hates most of the music she listens to. So, she put together a CD, one she always plays whenever Beau is around. On the CD its written - *How to annoy Beau.*

I bark out a laugh. "That shit with those two wouldn't surprise me, babe." As I push to my feet, in I hear her whisper. Her tone is serious now. "She's sad."

"What do you mean?"

"I can see it in her eyes, X and every time she looked at Beau today, it seemed more apparent."

"Babe, I'm sure things will work out. Beau doesn't give up. When he wants something, he will work his ass off to make it his. Erica was doomed from the minute she started working for me and Beau met her for the first time."

"What do you mean?"

"She captivated him from the minute she stepped foot in the shop. I always knew Beau as a ladies' man, he doesn't take a lot seriously, but with Erica he's different."

"Do you think he still sees other women?" Ally scrunches up her face in disgust at the thought.

"I don't think so. Well, I haven't seen him with anyone else."

"I hope they figure it out," she murmurs.

I notice how tired she looks and leaning forward, I run fingertips over her soft cheek. A faint smile graces her mouth as she hums. I chuckle, she is so damn cute.

"Why don't you go have a shower, Sweetness, while I clean all this up?"

"I can help," she protests in a sleepy voice. When she begins to stand, I notice her wince.

"Babe, I've got this. Go and have a shower then, we can relax for the night."

"Are you staying?"

"I'll stay for a bit, but I don't have any other clothes with me."

I hadn't planned on staying last night because I wasn't completely sure how things would go. I only had what I was wearing along with spare boardies and an extra singlet which I keep in the car. Most days when me and the boys finish for the day, we end up at the beach.

When she pouts, I growl and leaning over, I suck her bottom lip into my mouth. She moans as her eyes flutter shut.

"Go and have a shower."

"Want to join me?" she murmurs above my lips while sweetly staring up at me through her long lashes. She grips the front of my shirt while I rest my hands on her hips and give them a squeeze. She relaxes into me.

"Next time, babe. Let me clean this mess up and I'll race out and grab my clothes from yesterday out of my truck. I'll head home early in the morning and get changed before work."

Her eyes shine up at me when I say I'll stay, she leans up and brushes her lips over mine before turning and heading towards her bathroom, but not before I smack her ass for good measure, making her laugh. Fuck, I'm so hard. I want nothing more than to push inside her as soap runs down her curvy body, but she looks so tired and I know she's in pain. I don't want to hurt her and she needs a good rest.

Making quick work of cleaning up, I calm my ass down as I head out to my truck and grab the clothes. Thankfully, I thought to grab her keys on my way out, otherwise, I'd be fucked and have to disturb her in the shower to get back in.

When I get back inside, I don't hear water running so I head to the bedroom. She's curled into a ball, asleep and I choke out a breath at the sight of her in a pair of purple boy-shorts and another one of those fucking singlet shirts that I can practically see through. Balling my hands into fists, I take a few deep breaths to stop myself from touching and disturbing her. Stripping off, I drop my clothes on the floor in the corner of her room and grab a clean pair of boxer briefs I found in the truck before heading to the shower and making quick work of cleaning the salt water off my skin.

Stepping out of the shower, I dry myself off, throw on my briefs and make my way to the bed. It's going to be hard as fuck sleeping with her tonight with so little between us. I thought it was hell last night and she had more clothes on. Fuck, seeing her like this, I know I'll be lucky to get ten minutes of sleep. Palming my hard cock, I give it a squeeze through my briefs and will my ass to calm down.

Blowing out a deep breath, I lay down and pull her into my arms so her head rests on my chest. I soak in her sweet smell and let it surround me. She shifts and her leg wraps around my waist. I close my eyes and grit my teeth when she brushes my hard cock. I attempt to think of something else except the way she is draped around me, but my cock hardens even more. Planting a kiss to the crown of her head, I bury my nose in her hair and try to sleep.

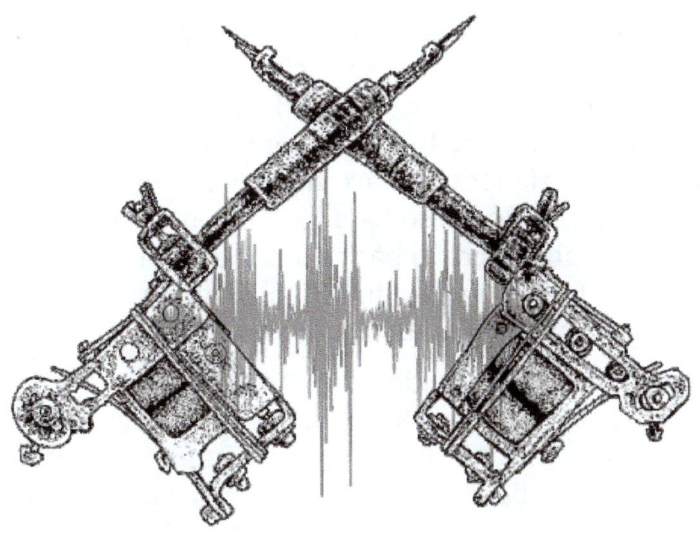

CHAPTER FIFTEEN

Ally

I stir awake when I feel X's warm breath wash over me and I hum deep in my chest. Blinking my eyes open, I notice it's still dark out, the glow of the moon filtering through my curtains. I look over to the bedside table and note the time is just after one in the morning. I can't believe how tired I felt earlier. I remember going to the bathroom for a shower and getting changed, thinking if I wore next to nothing, it might seduce X, but I must have fallen asleep. Looking down, I see how much of my body is wrapped around him. When I push up a little, the pain in my hand rockets through me and it starts to throb. I ignore it and try to escape X's hold which seems to tighten with my movement. Leaning over, I kiss his cheek and whisper that I'm just going to grab a glass of water. He grunts and loosens his hold enough for me to slip out of bed.

Heading to the kitchen, I grab the water and flick the lights off which had been left on last night. I leave the light in the small hallway and make my way back to the bedroom. I stifle a laugh at the sight of X in my queen bed which he looks too damn big for and bite down my lip to prevent a moan from escaping when I take in the sight of his bare chest with the sheet wrapped around his waist. He looks so bloody delicious. Placing my glass on the bedside table, I crawl back onto the bed trying not to jar it too much so I don't wake him. Right now, I want to explore every dip, curve and valley on display.

As I run my fingertips slowly down his chest, I feel goosebumps break out over his skin and his muscles tense. I lift my wayward fingers slightly when he shifts and wraps one arm under the pillow. I lick my lips at the sight wishing it was my tongue instead of my fingers exploring him. Slowly, I ease the sheet back from his waist my breath hitches at the sight of him in tight black boxer briefs.

Slipping from the bed, I make my way to the bottom end and crawl up slowly, pushing his legs apart so there is enough room for me to kneel between his thighs. I release a breath when I manage to do it without one of his legs falling over the edge of the bed. Running my nails lightly over his inked chest, I reach the waistband of his briefs and rest my hands on his hips. I lean forward and ghost my lips across his chest before moving to one hipbone and dragging my tongue above the elastic of his briefs to the other hipbone. I can taste faint traces of salt from the beach mixed with my green apple body wash, my mouth waters.

I snap my eyes to X's face when a deep groan leaves his throat and pause to make sure he doesn't wake. I'm feeling naughty at my exploration and needing more. I feel myself getting wet at the thought of what I'm about to do. Squeezing my thighs together to control the pulsing need in my pussy, I grip the band of his briefs and slowly drag them down until his cock bounces free. Leaving them at the top of his thighs, my eyes drink in his already hard cock and I caress the head with the tips of my fingers.

Something hard grazes my fingers and when I look closer I see the metal ring through the head of his cock. A shudder of excitement runs through me. *Shit that's sexy as fuck.* Running my fingers down the shaft, I watch as he gets harder and X groans again. He shifts a little and I pause my exploration, waiting until he settles again. After licking my palm, I wrap it around him and slowly stroke up and down. He grows harder in my hand and I come to realise how thick he really is, there's a good inch between my thumb and middle finger. Suppressing a moan, I grip him harder, lean over and swipe my tongue across the tip, collecting the pearl of pre-cum that's gathered there. I hum with delight as the salty taste coats my tongue. Not being able to stop myself, I give the metal hoop a little tug and feel X's legs tense around me.

Needing more, I grip his hip with my injured hand - ignoring the pain and squeeze him tighter with my other hand as I suck the head of him into my mouth. Wrapping my tongue around the piercing, I can't stop playing with it. I love the feel of it in my mouth.

My eyes snap up to lock with X's when he hisses and his fingers wrap in my hair.

"Fuck," he grunts as his hips lift from the bed, pushing more of him into my mouth.

I take his reaction as a good thing and increase my efforts. Releasing the hand I have wrapped around him, I grip his other hip. Breathing in and out through my nose and closing my eyes, I take more of him into my mouth and swallow around the head of his cock. Tingles fire through me as the hoop scrapes the back of my throat. I ignore the gag reflex as his deep groans fill the otherwise silent room, pushing me to keep going. After a few moments I slowly pull back, running my tongue along the underside of his shaft as I go and feeling him shudder.

Humming around the head, I feel his fingers flex in my hair and wait for the bite of pain to start tingling down my spine. Expecting it, wanting it, but it doesn't come. I raise my eyes to his and see the storm brewing behind his orbs and tingles race through me. His eyes seem darker in the glow of the hallway light which shines into the room, creating a shadow over his face. He's holding back, I can feel it in the way his body tenses as if he's worried he'll hurt me. Concentrating on the tip with my tongue, I reach one hand up until I close over X's hand in my hair and give it a squeeze, silently telling him what to do. After the third squeeze, I press my nails into the back of his hand and watch as with the simple move, his control melts away. Primal need replaces it.

"Fuck, babe." His voice is gravelly with need and I feel wetness coat my inner thighs at the erotic tone.

I reach between my legs and run a finger over my pulsing clit, my body shudders at the simple touch. Gripping my hair tighter, he pulls and I moan as I take him deep into my throat. The vibrations in my throat against his cock, causes his growls to fill the room. Sucking my cheeks in, I keep eye contact as he lifts his hand and rubs my cheek with the pad of his thumb. His body tenses and shudders. His eyes follow the movement of my hand as I lower it to between my legs and massage my clit.

The motion pushes him over the edge. He grits out curse words, his eyes roll back and returning my hands back to his hips, I swallow around him as best I can before his salty hot cum begins to slide down my throat. I keep sucking, making sure to get every drop until there is nothing left. Pulling my mouth away, I lap at the tip and watch as his cock jerks at the action. I can't prevent the giggle which escapes.

"Come here," he growls, his voice heavy.

He grips under my arms and slides me up his body. Before I can say a word, his mouth slams against mine in a deep kiss filled with raw intensity.

"I bet you taste better." He gives one last suck on my tongue before I find myself on my back.

He crawls between my legs and grips the sides of my undies. I start to lift my ass so he can remove them, but he places a strong hand against my belly and pushes me back into the mattress. His other hand fists and he rips them from my body. I gasp as a stinging sensation shoots straight to my clit.

"Damn!" I shout, making X chuckle.

"Not yet babe, but soon."

He slides up until he's at eye level with my pussy. Reflex has me trying to close my legs but X grips my thighs, keeping them apart. My body jolts as he nips the inside of one thigh, adding a new sensation to my already pulsing clit. It's completely consuming and overtakes my body. I feel like a puddle of goo. I wait for the first swipe of his tongue, but it doesn't come. Opening my eyes, I look down, wondering what the hell he could be doing.

"X?"

"Shhh," he whispers.

I'm not sure of what the hell I should do, I feel like I'm on display in a bloody gallery. The pulse in my clit seems to echo through me and I'm not sure how much more of this I can take.

"It's starting to hurt," I whisper on a moan as his thumb finds my clit and starts moving in a circular motion.

"Patience, Baby." He slides a finger inside me and my muscles clench around the digit, pulling a groan from him.

My breathing ticks up, mouth goes dry and I have to keep licking my lips to get moisture back on my tongue. Moving up, his massive size envelops me as he inserts another finger. My ass lifts from the bed when he curls his fingers inside, hitting the spot that makes my toes curl into the mattress. He continues the motion of his thumb on my clit while his gaze takes in every emotion he is creating as they play over my face. I bite down on my lower lip to stop my moans, but he isn't having any of that. As he pushes deeper inside me, I open my mouth on a moan and he swoops down to take my mouth in a bruising kiss. It sucks every one of my moans into his body. My legs shake and my belly flips. A sheen of sweat coats my skin and goosebumps break out. I sway on the edge, but before I can cum, he stops moving his fingers inside me and pulls back from the kiss, resting his forehead against mine and breathing heavy while we try to catch our breath.

"You cum on my cock only," he growls out on a deep breath.

He goes all caveman on me, the cocky bastard. I start to protest but he cuts me off with another deep kiss, intoxicating my mind. Every thought disappears as my mind turns to mush. I feel him harden against my belly and he flexes his cock. I shudder in response, but instead of sliding down and pushing inside me, he moves back down my body. Before I realise what is happening, his warm tongue lashes over my clit and I almost buck from the bed. Removing his fingers from inside me, he pins my hips to the bed. I whimper at the loss, but it soon turns into a moan when he lowers his head and starts sucking my pussy juices into his mouth before moving back to my clit and nibbling on the tight bud. He sets a maddening rhythm and my body becomes confused with the duel sensations. Sweat from my forehead rolls down the side of my face and pieces of hair stick to my cheeks. Not being able to control what he is doing to me, I bring my hands up my body taking my singlet as I go and ripping it over my head. Gripping one breast in my hand, I squeeze, knead and pinch my nipple until I need more and my back arches. With my other hand, I grip the hair on top of my head as tight as I can, forgetting about the pain in my hand, and lock my eyes with X. Fire smolders in his eyes as he watches what I'm doing and he growls into my sensitive flesh. I don't want him to know how close I am to coming, but he feels it when my legs start to shake and lock up. My body is so tightly wound it won't take much to shatter so, I pull away.

"X, please," I beg.

Sliding up my body, planting kisses as he goes, I feel X's lips hit the scar on my belly and tense.

"Shhh, Baby." His deep voice washes over me and his fingers run up my sides until he reaches the underside of my breasts. Feather-light touches back and forth cause me to tremble. After lavishing my scar with sweet kisses, he makes his way over the rest of me with his mouth. He nips, sucks and tongues until he nudges my hand away from my breast and takes the nipple into his mouth. He sucks hard before releasing it with a soft pop before giving the same attention to the other nipple. I whimper on panting breaths, not sure how much more of his teasing I can take. He plants his elbows on each side of my shoulders and runs his tongue along my collarbone, to the hollow in my neck I push my head deep into the pillow, giving him the space he needs. Turning my head slightly, he works his way along my jawline and up my neck. Raising his hand, he places it around my neck and turns my face back to his, taking my mouth in a deep kiss. Moaning around my flavor on his tongue, I run my nails up his sweat slicked back and feel his muscles flex and ripple. He hisses and arches into my touch. I've never liked the feeling of sweat before, but right now, it's my new favorite look on my brute of a man. I draw back from the kiss to catch my breath and lock eyes with him. His fingers flex at my throat and I don't want to admit that I like it so, I tell him what I want instead.

"Fuck me."

He sucks in a breath.

"Such a dirty, pretty mouth you have, Sweetness." He runs his thumb over my bottom lip before leaning forward and sucking my bottom lip into his mouth, giving it a nip before releasing it with a soft pop.

"I love your teeth on me, X."

I moan and arch like a cat into him, my nipples rub against his bare chest and I flex my nails into his shoulders. Lowering towards me, he places his mouth over the area between my neck and shoulder and applies slight pressure with his teeth. Not enough to pierce the skin, but enough to have me moaning for more. I don't give a shit how desperate I sound, I need him inside me. Now!

"Please... please...please," I beg while panting in an attempt to catch my breath.

Every sensation he's creating inside me seems amplified with his teeth on me. I writhe beneath him. My hands slide down to reach his ass but he's so big, I can't reach. I settle for wrapping my legs around him and plant my hands on his lower back. I can feel the indents there. I pull him down to me and push up at the same time, wanting to scream until I get what I want. Damn this man and his teasing. I feel him flex his muscles but he doesn't move an inch. Not giving up, I beg over and over again, hoping my words will spur him into action. I release his back and raise my hands above my head, gripping the wooden panels of the headboard. Locking my legs tighter around his waist, I push with everything I have and raise my lower body, pushing against his heavy cock. I whimper at the contact.

"Fuck me... Fuck me... I want to feel you stretching me." I'm gasping, desperate for everything this man can give me. The smell of sweat and sex surrounds us and my head is cloudy and dizzy with the combination.

"Fuck," he curses.

I feel him flex into my lower half as he leans up on his knees, one hand is still around my throat. He runs his fingers over every sweat coated curve before grabbing the base of his thick cock and swiping the hard head over my aching clit. I feel the cool metal of the cock ring graze me.

"I wanted to savor this moment, but fuck babe, even a fucking saint wouldn't be able to hold back. Don't move."

He snaps out the last two words with so much dominance lacing his voice I feel it to my very soul. We're breathing fast, our heartbeats echoing around us and my body locks up when he swipes the head of his cock back and forth over my aching clit. I whimper when the ring catches my clit and a low growl rises up my throat at the teasing. It's followed by a moan as he pushes the head into my pussy, my inner walls clench, wanting more. The hand on my throat flexes and his other hand grips my waist tighter. I groan at the thought of him leaving his mark on me.

"More," I choke out.

Shit, I can feel the ring sliding over my inner walls creating an unknown awareness which runs through my body.

Breathing heavy, he nods and eases inside a bit more. I wriggle my hips as I adjust to his size, it causes a groan to erupt from deep in his throat. I grip the panels of the headboard tighter, dig my heels into his ass and push forward, needing all of him inside me now.

"Fuck, Ally, I wanted to take this slow but if you keep doing that, my plan will go to shit."

His teeth are clenched and it's obvious he's struggling to control himself. I suck in a breath when I feel more of him enter me.

I moan and move my hips up and down, loving the fullness and not wanting him to hold back.

"Ah, fuck it." He slams into me, all control now gone.

My body jolts with the force of his entry and our deep groans fill the room. He doesn't move.

"X," I moan.

"Fuck, you know how to test a man's patience, Babe."

"Is that a bad thing?" I giggle before he pulls out and pushes back in, cutting my giggle off.

"Nope." He lifts the hand from around my throat and rests it on top of my head, tangling his fingers through my hair. Leaning forward, he brushes his lips over mine.

"I wanted to be slow and sweet with you, Babe, you deserved that. But, feeling your warm pussy wrapped tight around me, I don't think I could give you that right now." He pecks at my lips again.

"I don't want soft and sweet, X, I just want you. Hard and fast. Taking what you keep calling yours."

As he looks into my eyes, I see a fierceness cross his face. My body becomes hyper-aware of every single breath, touch and smell in our bubble.

"You're mine and by the time I have finished with you, you're going to know how *mine* you are."

He repeats the words from last week to me, making me shiver. Before I can reply, he starts a slow pace - moving in and out of me. My chest rubs against his, like the finest of silk, our bodies slide against each other as my pussy clenches around his hard cock.

He pulls my head back by my hair and little prickles of pain slide down my back as he buries his face in my neck and snaps his hips back and forth. Heavy breaths, the echo of skin slapping is almost enough to have me coming undone. I can feel liquid heat racing through every vein, searching for an escape. I allow my body to take over as my head begins to spin from the build-up. I meet X at every thrust. My arms strain above my head, but I soak in the pain from gripping the panels for too long.

X's dirty words in my ear send me into a state of euphoria like I have never known before.

"Fuck, so wet. I can feel your pussy juices running over my balls." He sucks the lobe of my ear into his mouth -such sweet torture. I don't know when it's going to end and I'm not sure I want it to.

"Harder," I moan as X's groans vibrate in my ear when I squeeze my inner walls around him.

"Greedy fucking pussy." He latches onto my neck with his teeth before leaning back and gripping my hip with one hand while the other returns to my neck, squeezing every so often as his thrusts pick up speed.

"Come on, Babe," he grits out before moving his hand from my hip and rubbing my clit.

One more hard thrust, swipe of the finger over my pulsing clit and he has me screaming out his name as a kaleidoscope of colours flash before my eyes. A loud grunt fills the room a moment later and X tenses. The warmth of his cum floods my pussy setting off small tremors through my body.

"Fuck, Babe," X says on a hard breath.

I place my hands over my chest and hum as I try to suck in as much oxygen as I can. Cracking an eye open, I look to the bedside table and after my heart settles a little more, I prop myself up on one elbow and reach for my glass of water. Taking a generous mouthful, I pass the glass to a chuckling X and watch as he drains the rest of the water. Licking my lips, I watch as his adam's apple bobs up and down and his muscles flex in his arm. Damn my man is too friggin sexy for words.

"Babe?"

My eyes snap back to his and he chuckles at my reaction to him, but I feel my spine stiffen when a serious look crosses his face.

"What's wrong?" I whisper, all my insecurities racing back over me.

I reach for the sheet to wrap around my naked body.

"Hey…" He reaches out to stop me, ripping the sheet from my hands, then grips my chin so I'm looking at him again.

"Don't hide from me babe" he runs his fingers softly down the side of my face.

"I just wanted to tell you, we forgot the condom." His voice is tense.

Oh shit, I have never forgotten about making sure the man is using one before.

"I'm on the pill and I haven't been with anyone since…" he cuts me off before I can say Luke's name and I'm kind of thankful for that, not wanting to bring him up while I'm naked.

"Me too. I never forget to wear one. You send my head spinning, Babe and I can't think straight when I'm around you." He crawls up to lay beside me and wraps his arms around me, shifting I place one leg over his lap and rest my head against his chest

"I know the feeling," I murmur as he runs his fingers up and down my naked back.

Looking towards the clock without moving my head I notice it's just after 4am. Holy shit where the hell did the time go? Shifting a little, I notice the dull ache between my legs which tells me exactly where the time went. And, for the first time in a long time I feel whole and a feeling of lightness rushes over me as I feel X's lips at the crown of my head.

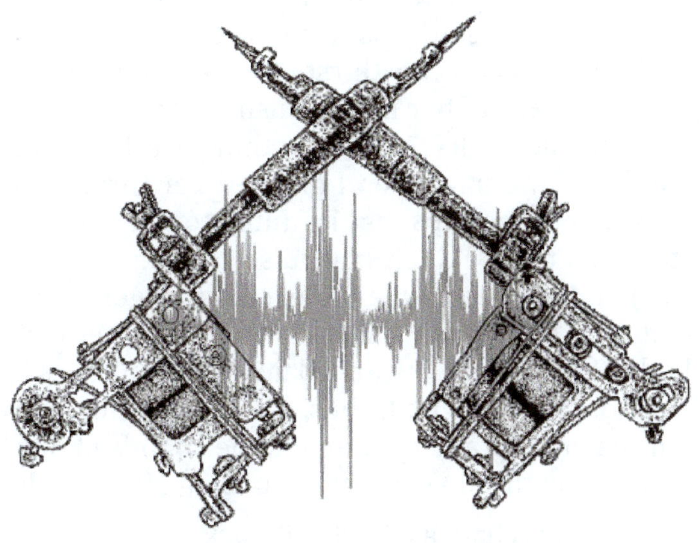

CHAPTER SIXTEEN

Xavier

It's been three days since Ally gave herself to me and fuck what a night it was. After our first time, I couldn't wait for another taste.

Rolling her over I'd begun devouring her body all over again until those dirty words I loved were flying out of her mouth. Sin dripped from her luscious pink lips and I'd wanted more. Flipping her to her stomach, I'd kneeled behind her and lifted her so her back was flush with my chest as I fed my impatient cock into her greedy pussy. Fucking heaven was what it felt like being inside her and I didn't want it to end. I was worried my dominance and possessiveness would scare the shit out of her, but she soaked up everything I gave her and by the end, I wanted everything she had to give.

I'd felt her body begin to shake as I bit down on her shoulder, tasting the saltiness from the sweat coating her smooth milky skin, making me thirsty for more. Raising my hand and gripping the back of her neck, causing her body to bow for me was a fucking heady feeling, but nothing was better than the way her body went crazy when I gripped her throat. So much passion spilled from her lips that I wanted to soak in it. Turning her face towards mine, I'd felt her pulse race under my fingers and the hitch in her breath when I flexed my fingers, caused me to growl into her mouth as I sucked every one of her whimpers into my body. Pulling back, I watched her sex drunk eyes looking up at me through her thick lashes. She begged for more as I slammed into her over and over again, the sounds of our heavy breathing mixed with skin slapping bouncing off the walls.

I shift in my chair as my hard cock pushes against the zipper of my jeans and wonder how much longer it is until I can see her again. We haven't had sex since Monday morning, when we finally pulled apart from each other.

Monday was a long ass day and by the time I got back to Ally's later in the night, we were both exhausted and crashed out watching a movie.

Yesterday I had dinner with my parents. I'd tried to talk her into coming with me, but she didn't want to meet them while she looked all banged up. My parents wouldn't have cared, but I let her off the hook because she had dark circles under her eyes and seemed to be coming down with a bug of some kind. Next week is a totally different story though, there's no way she's getting out of it.

Glancing up at the clock, I note it's only 10am. Pushing to my feet, I grab my now empty coffee cup and head towards the kitchen for a refill. A loud crashing sound grabs my attention followed by my name being shouted out. *What the fuck is going on?*

I race out front and find Cynthia standing in the doorway with her hand on her heart, trying to catch her breath. Her eyes are wild and searching the room until they land on mine. The look of terror in her orbs has pure panic pumping through my veins.

"What the fuck is wrong?" I check behind her for Ally but Cynthia is alone.

"X," she gasps as tears form in her eyes.

My heart is pumping out of my chest. Rushing to her, I try to persuade her to tell me what the fuck is going on. Resting my hands on her shoulders, I give her a little shake and she seems to snap out of the shock she is in.

"Ally." She hiccups and tears begin to roll down her cheeks. "She passed out at work and wouldn't wake up."

"Where is she now?" I feel my body lock, needing to get to my girl.

"I called an ambulance and they took her to the John."

"Fuck, I need to get to her."

Pulling my phone from a pocket, I dial Beau's number, I don't have time to race around looking for him. Fortunately, he's in the stock room at the back. I explain I need to leave as I make my way out the door with Cynthia close on my heels.

"What the fucking hell is going on?" Justin asks as I brush past him.

"It's Ally, she's in hospital." Cynthia manages to tell him between sobs.

"Oh fuck, let me drive brother." He holds his hand out for my keys.

I know I'm not in the right headspace to be driving so I chuck him the keys, hurry out to the car, pull open the front passenger door and climb in. Cynthia climbs in the back.

For the next twenty minutes or so everything passes in a blur - the traffic, the noise and even the sounds of Cynthia's quiet sobs in the back seemed to all fade to black. I only have one thing running through my head right now and that is, I need to get to my woman and make sure she's okay.

I'm unable to find the words to speak when we race into the emergency department, but Cynthia speaks with a lady behind the desk who's stopping us from getting to my woman.

"Sir, are you family?"

I snap my eyes to hers as she takes me in from head to toe assessing me and I know if I don't say yes then she won't let me back there.

"He's her husband," Cynthia says coolly.

I snap my eyes to Cynthia, but she isn't looking at me, she's staring straight at the nurse daring her to say I'm not.

"It's not listed here that she has a husband." The nurse checks on a computer.

"They just got married on the weekend," Cynthia insists.

"And you are?" The nurse asks Cynthia.

I'm about done with this conversation, it's keeping me from Ally's side.

"She's Ally's sister," I grit out as Justin races in after parking the car.

"And, that's her husband." I point to Justin and hear a long drawn in breath from beside me, but I ignore Cynthia's reaction.

"Are we about done with the chit chat?" I growl.

I try to control the rage in my voice, but when the nurse's head snaps back, I figure I haven't succeeded.

"Sir, there is no reason…"

"Look, he's worried about his wife. So, if you would kindly push the button to let us in, we'll get out of your hair." I can hear the tears in Cynthia's voice.

The nurse looks at her and I see sadness swimming in her eyes. She nods, reaches over and pushes the button which releases the double doors so we can enter.

"Thank you," Cynthia says from behind me as I push through the doors. We head down a small corridor and when we reach the end, I note the nurses station in the middle. To my left is the Paediatric area, to the right are larger beds so I start off in that direction. Blood is pounding in my veins and my heartbeat thumps in my ears. I swallow in an attempt to bring moisture back into my mouth. Before we can go much further, the nurse from our previous encounter appears out of nowhere, stands in front of me and holds her hands up.

"I'm sorry, Sir, but you can't go any further. I need you to come with me."

"Like fuck!"

She looks as pissed as I feel now. "Sir, I will call security if you don't calm down. I need to escort you to the waiting area we have just over there." She points to a small room off to one side. "A doctor will be with you shortly to explain what is happening with your wife."

The word 'wife' settles deep in my belly, it sounds so right. As I open my mouth to protest, I hear raised voices coming from a room ahead and look over the nurse's head to see a flurry of activity. Without hesitation, I move past the nurse and cross the couple of meters separating me from the room where instructions are being barked out. When I reach the open doorway, nothing could have prepared me for what I see. My Sweetness, as white as the sheet she is lying on. She's not moving, her eyes are closed and a tube is down her throat. Wires are coming off her everywhere and what I assume is a heart monitor is beeping – but it's not strong or steady. I suck in a deep breath and stumble back into the wall behind me, my woman is helpless and so fragile looking.

"Sir," a deep voice from my left says with authority lacing his tone.

I glance over and notice a man dressed in a security officer's uniform. I don't give a shit what he says, I'm not leaving. I need to be right fucking here for when she wakes up, because she *will* wake up.

"I'm not fucking leaving," I snarl between clenched teeth.

He steps forward and lifts his hand to my shoulder. He stops in mid-air when I speak.

"Touch me and see what happens. I'll make sure you'll be using your feet to eat for the next month."

"X-man." Justin attempts to calm me down but fuck that.

"Sir I will call the police and have you removed from this hospital for good"

"X." Cynthia's soft tear-filled voice draws my attention to her and she grabs my arm. "Please, let's go to the waiting area and wait for the doctor."

She looks to the security guard, he has a pissed off look on his face, but he nods.

Fuck him. I take a few deep breaths, not wanting to move, but I either go with Cynthia or my ass gets kicked out or thrown in jail. Neither will do Ally or me any good. Steading myself, I push off the wall and make my way towards the waiting area. It's not much to look at - there are two small couches pushed up against different walls in an L-shaped configuration and a small coffee table is in front. On the far wall is a small kitchenette with tea and coffee supplies for those who are waiting.

Taking a seat, I rest my elbows on my knees and bow my head into the palms of my hands, trying to get my breathing under control. Dampness coats my hands and when I wipe a hand over my face, I realise they're tears. Fuck, I need to get my shit together. I look up when the door opens. I expected it to be the doctor but it's the asshole security guard from before. He shoots me a warning look before leaning against the wall near the door and folding his arms over his chest.

Cynthia places a cup of coffee on the small table in front of me. I have no desire to drink it, but I need to settle my churning head. Taking a sip, I let the flavor coat my tongue and wince at the bitter taste.

"Tell me what happened, Cynthia." I run a hand down the side of my face, blow out a deep breath and steady myself to hear what happened to my girl.

"She didn't look well when she came into work this morning. She was pale with dark circles rimming her eyes, like she hadn't slept all night. She said she thought she was coming down with something because her muscles felt achy. I tried to tell her she should be at home in bed, but she just waved me off and took off to get the book trolley. All of a sudden she seemed unsteady on her feet and in a blink of an eye she was on the floor." She blows out a deep breath, sniffs back her tears and continues. "I didn't know what had happened or what to do. I fell to the floor beside her and tried to wake her, but she didn't respond so, I ran to get my phone and called the ambulance. Everything after that is like a blur. I was on my knees beside Ally and the lady on the phone kept trying to talk to me, to keep my focus until the ambulance turned up."

Tears fall from her eyes and it guts me to see. Reaching over, I grab her hand and give it a squeeze. Justin wraps his arm around her back. I feel her tense at his touch, she doesn't pull away, but she doesn't lean into his touch either.

I'm not sure how long we sit there or, how many of these god-awful coffees we drink between us, but finally the door opens and a middle-aged man steps into the room with a grave look on his face. He's holding a grey flip folder in his hands. My ass is off the couch and in front him before he can open his mouth. I sense the security guard step to my side, but I ignore his ass.

"How is she?" I demand to know

"My name is Doctor Tannersen, I'm Miss Malone's doctor and you are?"

"Xavier - Ally's husband." Heat travels through me when I say the word 'husband' and I realise, I really want it to be true. "This is Cynthia - Ally's sister and her husband, Justin." I wave my hand behind me.

Nodding, he indicates the lounge and when I sit down, he sits beside me and flips open the folder.

"When your wife was brought in, she was unconscious. The paramedics inserted an IV to get a vein open and they started saline solution. Although she was given oxygen via a tube, she struggled to breath and her heart rate was increasingly rapid. Her BP was dangerously low so, they had no choice but to intubate. By the time the ambulance turned up and she was wheeled in, we had a team ready to assess what was happening. A thorough examination was conducted to check for external wounds. The bandage on her hand was removed and a swollen, red and oozing cut was revealed. We administered a large dose of Amoxicillin immediately to counteract the infection and blood was drawn to further analyze and isolate the type of infection."

My head is spinning and I'm fucking glad I'm sitting down. "What does this mean in plain talk, Doc?"

"I put a rush on the blood work and we just received the results back. They show what we initially suspected. The cut in your wife's hand is Septic – it's Septicemia. Your wife is extremely ill."

"Septicemia?" I repeat slowly. I'm trying to remember what it is, I know I've heard the term before but my brain has turned to mush. Thankfully, the doctor explains further.

"Septicemia, or blood poisoning, develops when our bodies are overwhelmed by infection. Our immune systems successfully fight off most of the bacteria which attacks our bodies. Usually if bacteria do gain access, we might feel achy and feverish for a day or so, but our bodies usually overcome them, often without antibiotics. Most of the time we have no idea we've even had bacteria invade because our immune system fights it off so quickly. However, sepsis is a different story. It infiltrates a wound and spreads into the bloodstream, the chemicals released by the immune system to fight the infection end up causing the body to become inflamed throughout. As in Miss Malone's case, when Septicemia is present, the heart rate soars, blood pressure crashes and the patient struggles to draw oxygen into their lungs which causes them to become unconscious. This can deteriorate into Septic Shock and death if precautions are not immediately forthcoming. Thankfully, when Miss Malone did collapse, someone was there to call for an ambulance." The doctor turned to Cynthia. "You, young lady, probably saved your sister's life."

Cynthia crumbles into Justin's hold and starts to sob. Adrenaline is rushing through me, I need this man to tell me, Ally is going to be okay.

"She'll live though now, won't she?" I refuse to think about the alternative.

"At the moment, Miss Malone is stable and for the next 48 hours we'll be monitoring her closely and pumping her full of antibiotics to keep her that way."

"Can I see her?" I need to touch her, smell her sweet scent, I crave so much. Let her know I'm right here for her.

"We're just getting her moved upstairs to ICU. I'll send a nurse in soon to bring you up to sit with her." He turns to leave the room but stops before exiting. "Sir, your wife is unconscious, extremely pale and has a lot of machines hooked up to her. You might want to prepare yourself."

Nodding I understand, I blow out a deep breath and relax in the knowledge, she is still with me.

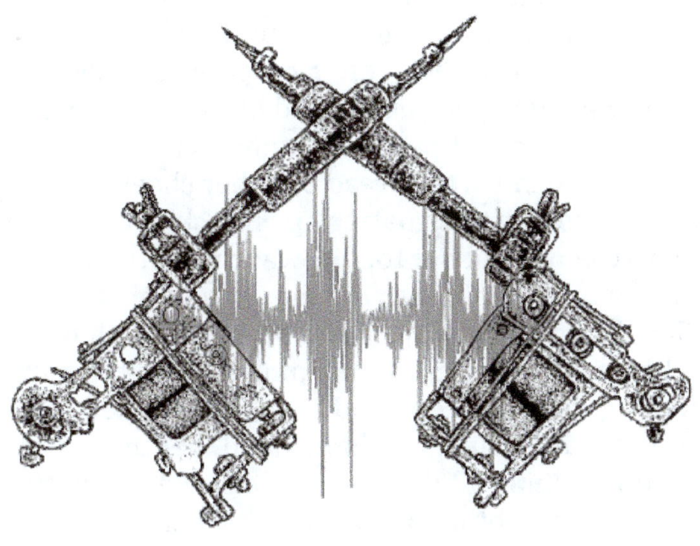

CHAPTER SEVENTEEN

Xavier

Nothing, and I mean nothing, could have prepared me for seeing my woman the way she was. Nausea swirled unrestrained in the pit of my empty stomach on seeing her hooked up to machines left, right and centre. My heart felt as if blood in my body had become tar and was no longer flowing freely. I struggled to stay calm as I was confronted with how pale her normally milky white skin had become. It seemed transparent, paper thin and I was worried even holding her hand would cause her pain. As gently as I could, I laced my fingers with hers and watched as a machine by her bed pumped up and down, breathing for her. For the first time I can remember, I prayed. I prayed out loud to anyone who would listen and begged for her to come back to me. She's already been through so much in this life and I haven't had the chance to show her how true happiness could be.

Lifting her hand slowly, I gently laid my other hand over the top, willing the heat from my body to travel into hers. I study every intricate detail of her soft face, from the shape of her brows to the way her eyelashes rested like crescent half-moons against her soft cheeks. I pause for a moment, waiting for the pink flush I love so much to spread over her cheeks, but it never comes. My eyes follow the smattering of freckles down her nose to the dip between it and her top lip. wanting nothing more than to suck the sensitive spot into my mouth and tease it with my tongue. Shaking my head, my eyes take in her plush bottom lip. Even her lips don't have their usual pink flush to them. I place a kiss to her fingers, one by one and keep them locked with mine. I rest my forehead against our hands and feel the tears, which have been threatening all day, begin to fall. Having nothing left inside me to keep fighting, I close my eyes and allow them to trickle over my cheeks.

"Xavier."

A deep voice much like my own calls out my name and through the heavy fog of sleep, the voice seems to get louder. Feeling stiffness in my back when I attempt to move, I groan and stop short when everything hits me at once, piercing my heart. Snapping my head up, I ignore the sharpness in my muscles as my eyes swing towards Ally. The afternoon sun streams over her from the window in her private room. She continues to lie still, so still. The beeping, whooshing sounds of the machines around the bed fill my ears and grief slams hard into my chest.

"Son."

My father's voice has me turning to where he stands on the other side of the bed.

"Dad." My voice sounds husky, sadness and sleep coating my words.

"It's okay, son."

Nodding, I don't say anything more, but turn back to Ally again. I refuse to look away, needing to soak everything in from the rise and fall of her chest to her thick lashes fanning over her soft colourless cheeks. I hope her eyes will flicker with awareness, but still they stay closed.

My bottom lip trembles at the thought of her not coming back to me. Emotions from earlier swirl around me and I bite down on my lip to still it, to stop me from breaking down. My father steps up behind me and without saying a word, he places his strong hand on my shoulder and squeezes. My shoulders heave with the emotion I was trying to stop, floods to the surface. My hands shake and tears sting my eyes. Releasing Ally's hand, I squeeze my hands into fists and a lone tear slips down my cheek. Closing my eyes, I will myself not to break, but it's no use. More heavy tears fall, deep sobs tear from my throat and I break. Not a word is spoken, only the sounds of the machines and my heavy sobs echo in the room.

After what feels like an eternity but was probably only minutes I wipe my face and blow out a deep breath. Dad releases my shoulder and takes a step back when I stand to stretch my legs. I head to the window and watch the sun setting. The trees sway in the light breeze and the faint sound of cars below floats up towards me. Everything appears normal as life goes on around me, but my chest tightens at the sight of a couple embracing down on the sidewalk.

Glancing over my shoulder, I notice my father has left the room. He probably thinks I need a moment to get my shit together, but fuck, it's gonna take a lot more than a moment. Sitting down again, I bring her hand to the side of my face, wanting nothing more than to feel the heat of her skin to soothe me. Like the colour in her cheeks, the heat is non-existent. Palming her hand, I place it against the stubble on my cheek for a moment before turning my face into it and letting my lips linger on a kiss. I breath in her sweet apple scent but even that seems to be fading as well.

"Son."

Turning my face away, I lower her hand gently to the bed and reach out for the coffee my father has brought.

"Thanks dad, but I think I've had enough of this hospital piss to last me a lifetime."

Chuckling softly, he takes the seat on the other side of the bed.

"I thought as much so, I went down to the cafe."

I take a mouthful and find it's not as bad as what I have been drinking.

"Thanks." I take another mouthful, letting the taste linger on my tongue for a bit longer than necessary. We stay quiet while we drink our coffees and then dad speaks.

"You love her."

As the words leave my dad's mouth, my body feels like it ignites and my heart stutters in my chest. My breath comes in pants, but all of a sudden, a calmness washes through me.

"Yes." It's all I say as I reach forward and place my hand gently on Ally's and entwine my fingers with hers.

"I didn't know what this feeling swirling in my gut was, but it's enough to drive me to my knees and anything this strong must be love." I rest the hand holding my coffee cup on my knee, not wanting to let go of Ally's hand.

Dad whistles low and when I turn to him, he's smiling.

"What?" I scrunch up my eyebrows, wondering what he is smiling about.

"Son, you just described how I felt when I first saw your mother."

I see the sadness in his eyes at the mention of mum and my stomach knots.

"How is she?"

Waving his hand around, he sits up a little straighter.

"She's fine but today isn't about your mum, it's about your girl. One worry at a time, son."

He nods towards Ally and I nod back, knowing he's right. Then it hits me, how the hell did he know where I was? I haven't left Ally and I haven't thought of anything except her since this morning. I don't know where the hell my phone even is.

"How did you know where I was?"

"I stopped into the shop and Beau told me your girl had been rushed here. I knew you wouldn't be anywhere else. Shit that reminds me...." He digs into the pocket of his jeans and pulls out my phone. "I ran into Justin in the carpark when he was leaving with Ally's friend, Cynthia to grab some of Ally's stuff. He said you left it in the truck. He thought you may need it since he needed to take your truck.

"Thanks, it must have fallen out of my pocket earlier." I take it from his outstretched hand.

"Oh, Erica said she'll stop by in the morning."

"Okay."

After a few moments of silence, dad speaks again.

"Beau told me a little about what happened with Ally and that she passed out at work, but he didn't really know the details. Why don't you fill me in?"

"On the weekend she cut her hand..." I tell dad some of what happened. How her and her mum argued and she picked up the wrong end of the knife when she was doing the dishes and it sliced her hand. I then fill him in on what happened today and what the doctor had said, it brings a lump to my throat talking about it. I watch as the colour drains from his face and I swear the old man's eyes glass over, but I can't be sure. "Now, I guess we play the waiting game."

I look down at Ally and place a kiss on her fingers.

"She's strong, dad. She's been through so much shit in her life and still came out swinging. I bet there were days she didn't want to even get out of bed, but she did. I know in my heart she's a fighter and I need her to kick this disease's ass and come back to me. I need to show her what kind of life she is meant to have, the kind of life she deserves.". I close my eyes and pray for a fucking miracle for probably the hundredth time today.

"Why don't you try and get some sleep, it's almost nine o'clock and you've had a long day."

Shaking my head, I glance to the window and realise how dark it is, the time has flown by.

"I'm good, dad. I need to be here for her when she wakes." I will *not* let her wake up in a cold, sterile fucking hospital room by herself. Not happening. I'm amazed the nurses haven't come in and kicked us out, but I suspect my dad probably had something to do with that, he can be pretty convincing when he wants to be.

"Well, at least rest your eyes and I'll stay right here with you both."

Looking at my dad, I nod. I have no intention of sleeping and I'm so fucking thankful he's here.

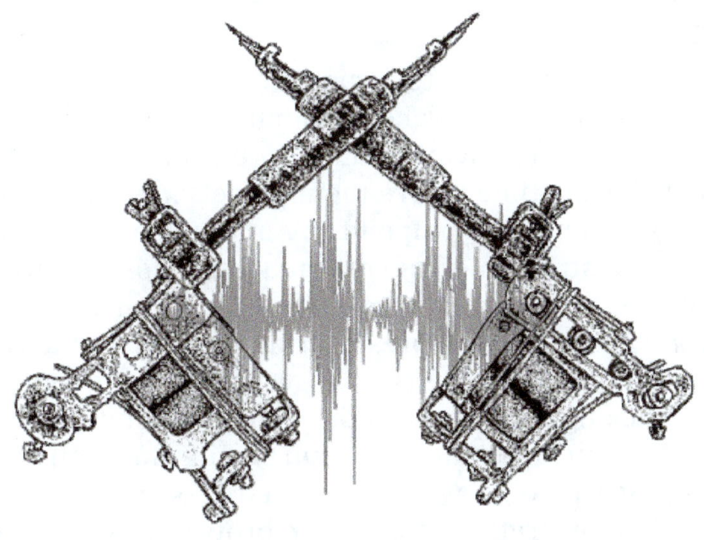

CHAPTER EIGHTEEN

Ally

My heartbeat vibrates through me, steady and strong. Without opening my eyes, I take stock of my body as a stiffness in my joints makes itself known. Blowing out a breath, I note the rise and fall of my chest is smooth. Lifting my hands, I rub my face they feel unused and weak.

What is wrong with me? Where am I?

Blinking my eyes open, blurriness fading away, my surroundings become crisper and stark whiteness flashes before my eyes. *Damn why is it so bright?* Closing my eyes again, I sit up. This time, I open my eyes slowly and attempt to take in my surroundings. All I see is a white haze, like someone has turned on a fog machine and forgotten to turn it back off. Thick fog surrounds me and I wait for the cold to creep in, but instead, a calmness washes over me – a calmness I haven't felt for a very long time.

I blink and attempt to focus on where I am. Everywhere is white. I thought I was awake, but I mustn't be. I look down to find I'm wearing my white summer pajamas and I try to remember the last time I wore them, it feels like it's important to remember, but I can't pinpoint it. An aroma of salt air floats in the air and distracts me from my thoughts. I close my eyes and breath in deep, intoxicating my senses. Cool water washes over my feet and I jump back before lowering my eyes. I watch as the white fog dissipates and, in its wake, whitewash and sand come into view. Flexing my toes, I feel the cool grains squish between my toes. I look up to feel the warm sun beating down on my face. The crashing sound of waves against rocks has me looking around, taking everything in. My eyebrows draw together in confusion when I wonder how I came to be on the beach. Off in the distance, a man with dark hair stands tall. His strong back is to me as he looks out over the water. He turns slightly and I notice strong tattooed arms folded across a broad chest. Without a conscious thought, or a choice, I begin to make my way towards him. Moving faster, my heart picks up speed and my breaths come in pants as a familiar feeling runs through me - home he feels like my home. I move faster but the man seems to be moving further away.

"Don't leave me!" I call out, but no matter how fast I move, I can't reach him.

Splashes of warm water hit my cheeks, then my chest and I raise my hands to my face to stop the tears from falling.

"Please, stop," I croak out on a broken sob, but again he doesn't hear me.

The calmness I felt from earlier is gone leaving a chill in its place and I wrap my arms tight around myself in an attempt to ward off the cold. Slowing my footsteps, I watch as the man seems to disappear and the foggy white haze from only moments before seeps back in, taking over the beach. I'm left with nothing but white surrounding me once more as an echo of a whisper bounces around in the wind.

"Come back to me, baby."

Falling to my knees, white fog billows up and around me, cocooning me and leaving me cold and alone. Sitting on my butt, I pull my knees in tight to my chest, bowing my head as gut-wrenching sobs rake through my body until I'm gasping for breath and my head begins to swirl.

I startle on feeling a warm hand rest on my shoulder, but I don't lift my head - afraid if I do, they'll disappear too. After a few moments of silence, a deep voice – one I know so well and miss so much more, reaches my ears and cuts off the sobs still escaping my mouth. I freeze in place as my head spins with his words.

"Shhh, Buttons, I've got you."

Not wanting to believe what I'm hearing, I take in a few deep breaths. I'm worried my head is playing tricks on me and when I do look up, he'll be gone again.

"When you're ready, I'm here," he whispers near my ear.

I swear the breath from his words glides down the side of my face as he wraps a strong arm around my shoulders drawing me into his side. I breathe in his familiar scent as I feel the warmth of his body seep into mine and the beat of his heart begins to vibrate the side of my face as I lay my head on his chest.

"Dad," I whisper.

He places a kiss to the crown of my head and rests his chin there. After a few beats, I let myself relax into his hold and finally build up the courage to look into eyes. Eyes so much like mine. I let the tears fall, not wanting to wipe them away.

"Where am I?" I suck in a small breath and grip my father's shirt until my knuckles turn white, attempting to stop my hands from shaking and cementing me to the spot.

Without a word, he turns his head away from me and I follow his line of sight. The white fog slowly evaporates again, revealing a lush green field which we are sitting in. We're surrounded by trees and off in the distance in a clearing is a child's playground. It reminds me of the one my father used to take me to when I was little. Birds chirp around us, but otherwise the area is deserted. The whole scene sets off an ominous eerie feeling in my bones and I can't stop the tremble as it rapidly races through me.

"I've got you Buttons, just watch."

My dad's deep voice washes over me again and I take a few deep breaths to bring myself under control. Looking around, it seems like everything is moving in slow motion until it all comes to a stop. Everything becomes still.

No movement.

No breeze.

Nothing, until a small child's joyous laugh floats through the air and then, a cool breeze picks up, fluttering my hair around me.

"What are we waiting for?"

"Just wait," my father says calmly, squeezing my shoulder.

After a few beats, the joyous laugh sweeps around me and sets off a current of heat running through my veins. Not knowing what to do and not wanting to let my father go, I squint through the clearing and notice a young girl smiling, laughing as she runs towards the swings tugging on her father's hand. I'm confused but something about it feels so familiar.

"Some of our best memories were when I took you to the park," my father says wistfully.

Snapping my eyes towards my dad, I realise we're heading towards the park.

"What's going on?" Confusion laces my words and I watch the little girl being pushed on the swing. Squinting, I take a closer look at the man. He looks like my dad, only younger. I blink rapidly, convinced I'm seeing things, but then, it's like a total time shift happens right in front of my eyes. The park disappears and in its place the beach materializes. I see myself on the shore, a young teen, laughing as I fall off the surfboard which lies still on the sand. My father is trying to teach me how to stand properly. My lips curve into a smile at the memory.

"Why are we here?" I whisper while watching a younger version of my father.

His head is thrown back on a deep laugh, he can't understand how I could fall off a board while it's stationary on the wet sand.

"I wanted you to see how happy you were."

I nod and try to soak it all in before it disappears again.

"I'm so sorry, dad." Guilt prickles and claws at me.

"Why are you sorry, Buttons?"

Gripping me by the chin, he turns my face to look into his. A lone tear escapes down the curve of my cheek before he thumbs it away.

"You know why?" I choke out as my bottom lip starts to tremble.

Turning my face away once more, I try not to blink as the beach disappears and flashes of me riding a bike for the first time, my first school dance and graduating high school play like a movie around us and then everything stops. No motion what so ever. Everything goes dark, but not for long. Image after image pin to invisible curved walls, creating a circle surrounding me. My eyes dart around as I try to take it all in, but what I fixate on, is my father's proud smiling face in each image.

"It didn't matter what I did, you were always proud of me." I turn in a circle with my arms out at my sides. "You always showed me you loved me."

I come to a stop in front of him, a smile tugs at my lips as I look into eyes which never failed to lift me up when I fell.

"Ally, my beautiful girl." He rests his hands on my shoulders and I soak in his comforting touch, never wanting him to let me go. "You hold so much guilt, but you have nothing to feel guilty about. None of what happened was your fault." I open my mouth to protest but he places a finger over my lips.

"You deserve to be happy, you deserve a life with someone who will always show you they love you."

"But..."

"No buts, Buttons, it's time to fight for what you want in this life, push through the hard shit so you can finally have the good you deserve."

"You were killed because of me, dad." I sob as pain lances through my chest and my heart squeezes so tight, I gasp for breath.

"I died protecting my daughter."

I connect with his eyes again, my vision blurry and attempt to soak in his words. It doesn't prevent the hurt flowing through me. Sobs cause my chest to heave as his whispered words seem to get further and further away.

"Let him in, let him be the person you fall into. trust he will catch you. You fight for your life; don't you dare give up."

"Don't leave me," I whisper. "Not again. Please. Please. Please," I beg on broken sobs, but he doesn't respond and before I open my eyes, I know he isn't here anymore. The feeling of safety and warmth floats away with him and I'm left feeling cold and alone.

Opening my eyes, I look frantically around, but as I suspected, dad is no longer here. The only things which remain are the numerous images floating around me. A chill slices through me when the fog begins to seep back in, but this time it's gray and an ominous, eerie feeling returns with it. The photos shatter like glass around me and a blood curdling scream rings out. Dropping to my knees, I feel around for anything to get me out of here, but the fog is never ending.

Gasping for breath, I attempt to fight the invisible mask pushed against my face which is stopping me from breathing. I watch in pure shock as my white pajamas turn crimson red and grip my stomach. I put pressure on my wound, but the blood is coming too fast. Ripping my shirt off, I search frantically for where the blood is coming from, but it's no use. Laying on my back, I push the shirt onto my stomach and coolness overtakes me, starting to turn everything numb.

"I got you baby, stay with me." Xavier's deep gravelly voice surrounds me and I can only hope he's telling the truth.

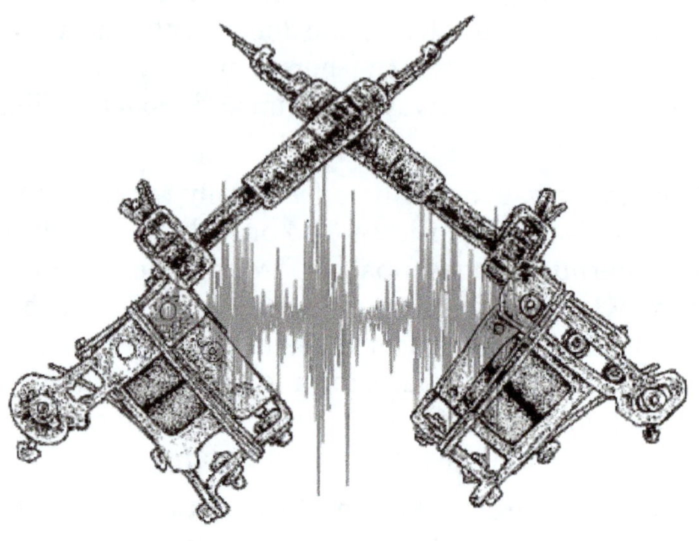

CHAPTER NINETEEN

Xavier

I stretch my neck from side to side and fist my hands, feeling the stiffness in my muscles from sitting in an uncomfortable plastic chair all night. My father finally convinced me to go for a walk and grab some coffee. I didn't want to leave Ally's side, but he promised he would stay with her until I got back. So here I am, waiting for our coffees and when I glance at my watch, I note it's almost 9 am.

After Ally's vitals where checked earlier this morning, the doctor came in and removed the breathing tube from her throat. Relief washed through me when she began to breath on her own. After he left, the nurse explained, the doctor would check back around nine when he did his rounds. I don't want to miss the update.

I look around, trying to focus on everything around me. Anything to take my mind off the mental ticking of a clock hammering inside my head like a jack hammer. It doesn't work. Everyone is going about their business as usual, but instead of faces and clear crisp sound, everything is just a blur of static noise.

I will my mind to stop counting down and try to concentrate on the artwork hanging from the cream washed walls. They seem to me to be dull, lifeless. Realistically, they are probably beautiful pieces of art designed to calm and welcome you, but they are making me more anxious as my brain keeps wondering about the what ifs....

What if I had taken the time to check her wound when I arrived at her place on Saturday afternoon?

I knew she wasn't looking well, she was pale, tired.

What if I'd persisted on the other numerous occasions when I saw her wince in pain and asked if she wanted me to check her hand?

What if I hadn't let her brush me off?

I didn't see the signs that were right in front of my fucking eyes.

I rub my eyes and scrub at my tired face, feeling the roughness of my beard. I haven't shaved yet and you know what? I don't give two shits about it right now.

The anger I feel with myself ripples through my veins like a wildfire licking at the doors of Hell. My mind is my enemy right now, insisting I failed to keep her safe. Running a hand through my hair, I grip the base of my skull and feel the tension and anger swirling through my muscles, cording up tight and ready to snap at any minute.

Why the fuck is this task of getting coffee sending me into an anger filled argument with myself? Fuck, I need to be upstairs with my girl, not down here standing in line waiting for my order like I haven't got a care in the fucking world. I never claimed to be a saint, but fuck if she recovers...

No! Fuck that...

When she recovers, I will spend the rest of my life worshipping the very ground she fucking walks on. I just need her to open her beautiful eyes and let me show her how happy we could be together. Blowing out a deep breath I shake my head to clear the dark thoughts from invading my mind further. Cracking my neck from side to side, I try to work the stiffness out and calm the anger - anger won't help the situation right now. I look to the line of people waiting to order then, to the barista behind the counter - I will him to hurry the fuck up and find it hard to prevent annoyance rushing through me. I know it's not his fault, they're swamped with orders and are moving as quick as they can, but an ominous feeling settles deep in the pit of my stomach. I'm about to say "fuck the coffees" and get back to my girl, when my number is called. I sigh with relief and head to the pick-up counter. I ignore the girl blatantly checking me out and fluttering her eyelashes and grab the cardboard takeaway tray. I grunt out a thank you before making the trek back upstairs to Ally.

Moving quicker than probably necessary, I head upstairs, not bothering to wait for an elevator. I take the steps two at a time until I reach a long corridor. I round the corner at the end and almost collide with an orderly pushing a patient's bed.

"Shit, sorry," I mumble, the orderly nods and keeps on going. He's probably used to it happening.

"Shit, get your head on straight or you'll be no good to anyone." I chastise myself quietly and say a silent vow not to leave Ally's side again until we can walk out of here together because even the simplest task of getting coffee seems to be to fucking hard for me right now. Passing the nurses station, I quickly ask if the doc has been by yet.

"You just made it." The far too cheery nurse looks at the watch attached to her scrubs. "He'll be about ten minutes, Sir, he's just finishing up with a patient in room four."

"Thank you." I feel a little less anxious now.

"You're welcome." She smiles brightly before returning her attention to the papers in front of her and I head in the direction of my woman's room. I step through the door, expecting to see my father sitting in the chair reading the newspaper a nurse dropped off earlier this morning. But, that's not what I see. I freeze, my muscles tense and lock and then, I catapult forward. The coffees go flying and I ignore the hot liquid which splashes my jeans and coats the floor. Machines are beeping loudly around me.

"Get the fuck off her!" I reach for the woman holding a pillow over Ally's face and reef her back hard. She stumbles backwards and lands on her ass.

Anxiety, adrenaline and pure rage race through every cell in my body, my fists shake as I snatch the pillow up and throw it to the floor. I keep my back to the woman and try to take calming breaths so I'm not tempted to kill her. I spin around, my jaw is clamped tight, teeth grinding together and anger is rolling off me in waves.

I glare at the woman who is now standing and straightening her all too tight clothes for someone of her age. I take a step forward, ready to rip her fucking head off. She watches me advance and I see the fear flash through her glassy eyes, but it's gone as quick as it comes. She straightens her spine and pushes her shoulders back.

"What the fuck!" I bellow between gritted teeth.

"Who *are* you?" she sneers.

"Better question is, who the fuck are *you* and what the fuck do you think you were doing?" It's taking every ounce of control I have to stand here and speak instead of dragging her by the hair and throwing her out of the room.

"I don't know what you're insinuating." She feigns ignorance and waves her hand towards the bed. "I was fixing her pillow."

"You had the fucking pillow over her mouth," I shout.

"You can't prove that. She's my daughter and I can do whatever the hell I want!"

I instantly hated this woman. Her chin juts out at me and I want to slap her.

"Now, tell me who the fuck you are because I know you're no-one important?" She slams her hands on her hips and taps a foot as she eyes me up and down.

The wind is knocked from my lungs at her statement and I stumble back a step, bumping the bed in the process. Through the red haze of anger, I really take her in. From her blonde/grey hair which doesn't look like it's been brushed in weeks. Rough tanned skin that reminds me of leather and then I notice her blood shot eyes, before I can say anything else, a voice cuts in from the door.

"What is going on in here?" A nurse demands to know, arms crossed over her chest. The smile from when I spoke to her a few moments ago, gone. In it's place, a pissed off expression. She moves to check Ally and reset the screeching machines, the beeping returns to normal.

"I'll tell you what's going on." I fight to hold back my rage from bubbling over. "You need to call security because I walked in and found this woman...." I wave my hand towards the woman dismissively. I don't say Ally's mother because this piece of shit doesn't deserve the title. "....was smothering my woman with a pillow." I flex my fists at my sides and breath deep to try and control myself, I smell the stench of alcohol lingering in the air.

"She's been drinking," I spit out in disgust before fixing my cool gaze on the woman. Her face morphs into an expression of intolerant disgust.

"You have no right and no proof!" Pure hatred and false shock laces her voice and I notice the way she stands a little straighter to try and prove me wrong.

I see her wobble as she goes to take a step towards Ally, there is no way in hell I'm letting her anywhere near her.

Pushing my shoulders back, I fold my arms across my broad chest, stand close to Ally and dare the bitch to come closer.

"What the fuck!"

A loud shout erupts from near the door and I turn in time to see Erica explode through the door, almost knocking the nurse over in an effort to get to Ally's *mother.* Beau is hot on her heels and grabs her around the waist, lifting her up so her feet come off the ground. Erica kicks her legs out, trying to connect with her target. It would actually be quite comical if the situation wasn't so serious.

"Who the fuck, do you think you are coming here?" Erica screams.

She's still kicking out so, Beau takes a step back so she doesn't connect.

"I'm Ally's mother," she says with an arrogant curl to her lips.

"You ain't no mother!" Erica shouts. "Beau, put me the fuck down."

"Fuck that, Peaches, if I let you go you'll rip her head off." He grunts as Erica's elbow connects with his ribs but he doesn't let go. "Not that she doesn't fucking deserve it." He turns a disgusted look on the fucking bitch who keeps saying she's Ally's mother.

The word 'mother' has never tasted so foul on my lips, I can't even bring myself to say it. I look back to the nurse, but she's nowhere to be found. I'm hoping she has gone to get the security guards and to call the police.

"You have no right to be in this room."

The bitch directs her statement at me and all the anger I've been trying to control and the band holding it all together, is blasted to smithereens. Before I know what I'm doing, I'm in the bitches face, my heart beats faster and my breathing comes hard and fast.

"Xavier!" My father's voice rings out loud and clear, but I hear the anger and worry lacing his tone.

"She's not worth it, X." Beau says while still trying to hold Erica back. She claws at his hands, making him hiss.

From the corner of my eye, I see him whisper something in her ear. She settles a little, but I see the hatred in her eyes as she stares at this piece of shit. I'm so amped up I don't notice my father move until I feel the weight of his hand on my shoulder.

"Touch me and I'll have you arrested." She sneers, looks up into my eyes and puffs out her chest.

I would *never* in my life hit a woman, but right now, in this moment the bitch deserves everything coming to her. I flex my hands into fists at my sides and feel my knuckles pop under the strain.

"Son," my dad says calmly while squeezing my shoulder firmly.

"You bitch, are the one who'll be led away in handcuffs and I will personally make sure you never see the light of day again. I hope you drank enough this morning to get you through." Malice laces my tone and I feel the hatred for this woman deep in the marrow of my bones. I guess she hears the conviction in my words and she visibly pales.

"Son," my father repeats.

"What?" I ground out, not taking my eyes off the piece of shit in front of me.

"How's your girl?" he asks.

Snapping my eyes to my dad and then to Ally still lying motionless on the bed, worry swims through my veins.

"Dad."

"I've got this, look after your girl." He nods his head towards the bed.

Giving one last look at the drunk bitch, I turn and cross to Ally's side. Gently gathering her hand, I hold it to my cheek before leaning down and letting my lips linger on her forehead for a moment. I whisper in her ear to stay with me and tell her, I have her now.

"I want to speak to a doctor." The bitches demand is a little weaker now.

"Not going to happen," my father says. "Let's step outside and wait for the police to get here. As you can see, my son is the one who belongs here."

I turn in time to see him grab her upper arm, he doesn't hold her tight enough to hurt her, but enough to keep control of the situation. He begins urging her from the room, but she doesn't leave without a fight - throwing insult after insult at him and struggling to pull her arm free, before swinging her free arm out to slap him in the face. My dad reacts fast and catches it before she can connect.

"Get your hands off me," she yells as he drags her through the door.

"I'll go and grab someone to help clean this mess up." Beau releases Erica and nods to the spilled coffee on the floor.

I nod as I soak in Ally's touch and catch my breath.

Erica grabs Ally's other hand gently so as to not bump the needle in the top of her hand and in a voice the softest I have ever heard she asks me, "Is she going to be okay?"

I notice how glassy her eyes are before she turns her head towards the window and blinks a few times.

"I don't know, Erica." I answer honestly, pain lacing my words.

"I'm gonna go and see if we can get a doctor in here to make sure that bitch didn't do any more damage."

Erica gently places Ally's hand back on the bed before turning and heading out the door.

Dread crawls through my body just thinking the woman might have caused my girl more harm. Again, I wasn't around to protect her. Instead, I was downstairs in a line of fucking people waiting on shit ass coffee that I didn't fucking want to begin with. Fisting my free hand into the sheets at the side of the bed, I bow my head against the edge feeling soul crushing emotion shatter straight through me. Squeezing my eyes tight, I try to fight off the regret, I need to keep my shit together for Ally.

Lifting my face, I release the bed sheets and run the tips of my fingers over her soft cheek, pushing her hair behind her ear. My breath catches in my throat when I notice slight imprints from the pressure of the pillow being pushed down on her face. Leaning closer, I notice what looks like the beginning of bruises forming on her neck. Being so pale, they stand out like a flashlight in the night. Fuck. Standing, I lean over and notice the same on the other side. Running my hands through my hair, I begin to pace as it slams into me - her own fucking mother tried to kill her.

"What's wrong?" Beau asks as he reaches me and places his hands on my shoulders, stopping me from pacing.

I open my mouth to answer, but nothing comes out. Bending down, I grip my knees and take a few deep breaths. It feels like I have been run over by a semi.

"Fuck, Beau. Ally has bruises forming on her throat. Her fucking mother tried to kill her."

"What the fuck?" He drops his hands from my shoulders and moves closer to the bed to take a look. "Sonofabitch!".

"Do you think she tried to strangle her own fucking daughter, but then decided the fucking pillow was a better option?" He kicks out at the offending pillow, sending it sailing across the room.

My head begins to spin and I have to sit down. Resting my elbows on my knees, I drop my head into my hands and suck in deep breaths to ease the tightness in my chest. How the fuck could a mother do this to their own child?

"X-man, fuck mate, breathe. You need to be thanking some fucking miracle that you were here in time."

"I nearly wasn't," I whisper.

Lifting my head, I lock eyes with Beaus' and he must see the guilt written all over my face.

"But, you were!!" His voice is fierce.

"I was in fucking line waiting for fucking coffee while my girl was up here struggling to fucking fight for her life. I should never have left this room. She's mine to protect, Beau and so far, by my count I've fucked up and failed her twice already. There will *not* be a third time. Trust me, brother, that bitch is lucky I didn't rip her fucking heart out." I point wildly towards the door.

"X-man, you can't think like that, it will fuck with your head." He blows out a deep breath and runs a hand through his hair. "You need to push that guilt shit away before it eats you alive and concentrate on being here for Ally. Between all of us, we'll make sure that drunk bitch doesn't get anywhere near your girl again."

I know what he's saying is true, but I know these feelings won't go away until she opens her eyes and smiles at me. In response, I nod and turn back to my girl.

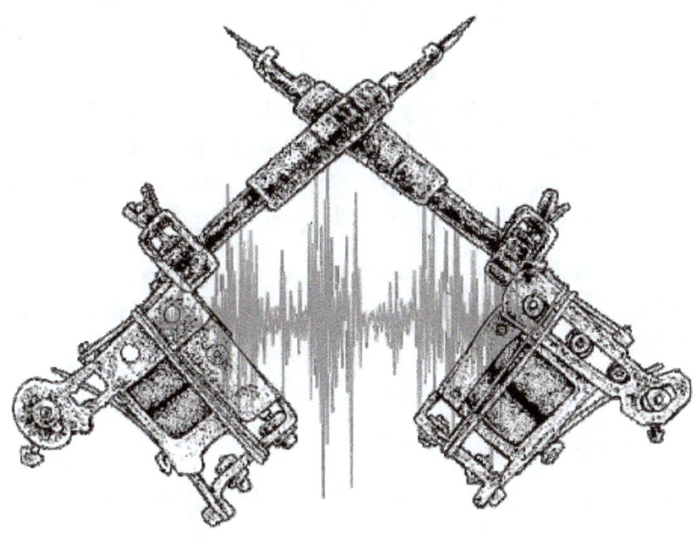

CHAPTER TWENTY

Ally

Screams bounce off invisible walls around me, I'm scared to open my eyes and watch as crimson blood drains from my body. I tremble as chills spread deep within me. I feel frozen in place. Then, like the flip of a switch, tingling starts at my toes, shoots up my legs and settles in my chest. Warming me before I experience severe stinging as I seesaw between feeling blistering cold bordering on frostbite, to intense heat which feels like I'm trapped in a sauna.

My eyes look wildly around, my mouth opens on a silent scream. I'm gasping for breath and sweat pours from my face. I try to swipe away the wetness, call for help, but it's no use. Closing my eyes, I curl into a ball, rest my head against my knees and fight against the overwhelming feelings.

After what seems like an eternity, my heart steadies and I'm overcome with a feeling of weightlessness. I open my eyes to find I'm standing, floating. The gray haze from earlier surrounds me once more. My surroundings blur at the edges as if the world that I know is being erased around me. Invisible chains seem to drag me down into nothingness. I don't know if I have the strength to fight what is happening.

The fight leaves me and I close my eyes as tears run unchecked down my face. Everything in my life was becoming better – I'd made new friends.

I had a great guy.

Is this my reality check?

Am I being reminded that I should never be happy?

Is this my life now?

Refusing to believe this is it, the end, I use what little strength I have left to push to the surface, away from the dark abyss. I look above and white light breaks through the gray haze.

My father's voice comes from the right of me. "It's time to fight."

Xavier's deep voice, from my left. "Keep fighting, Baby."

They give me the extra push I needed.

With their whispered words echoing around me, I float towards the blinding light. As I get closer, the gray haze morphs into white smoke which swirls around me.

The light is huge now and I push closer, away from the darkness for the first time in what seems like forever. As I near, I feel as if I'm being put back together – pieces are no longer missing, everything is where it should be.

I breathe out a deep breath as relief washes over me. Glancing around, there is stillness. Nothings moves. Even the swirling smoke is now motionless. I step forward and listen – quiet. Not a sound.

Feeling lost and not sure what to do, I keep moving forward, away from the darkness.

After taking a few steps, shadows form into figures ahead. Feeling a surge of energy, I move faster, hoping they won't disappear as I get closer.

Then – chaos.

Has someone turned on a radio? I listen carefully.

Machines are beeping, pinging. Muffled voices can be heard and as I step closer, they become clearer, less like static.

The smoky haze clears and I take stock of where I am. The smell of antiseptic wafts past my nose. Pristine white, sterile walls appear around me. Realisation hits me – a hospital. I'm in a hospital room. The shadows become larger and morph into people.

No....not just people. My friends. Xavier is leaning over a bed holding someone's hand.

Beau is seated by an open window, a pained expression on his face. An ominous feeling of dread sends chills through me. Confusion clouds my mind.

"What's going on?" I whisper, afraid of the answer. *Is it X's mum?*

"Beau what if..." I hear the pain in Xavier's deep voice and it's enough to bring me to my knees.

"Don't," Beau says, cutting him off "Just don't. She *will* be fucking fine. There is no other option." I watch as he drags a hand through his hair.

"What's going on?" I speak a bit louder this time, worried they didn't hear me. But, I still don't get an answer. Why won't they answer me?

"What happened?" Erica's worried voice comes from the doorway and I turn to find an extremely disheveled Erica standing beside an even more worried Cynthia. They hurry into the room and straight past me as if I'm not even here.

Feeling frustrated, I move towards the bed and place my hand on X's shoulder. I expect him to melt into my touch, but when he doesn't, I turn my focus to the bed. I freeze and feel the blood cool in my body. My eyes fill with tears at what I see.

It's me......

Wires are coming out of me everywhere. I'm attached to a bank of machines – the beeping I heard.

I slap my hands over my mouth. "Oh, God, what is wrong with me?"

I'm pale - deathly pale and I have purple bruises on my neck.

Oh, God, this can't be happening.

This can't be real.

This is another dream or, nightmare. Yes, that's it. It's a nightmare. I try to think but my head starts to spin and my stomach roils.

"Come on Baby, fight!" Xavier's voice breaks and he bows his head to the bed. Gripping my hand for dear life.

"I'm here, Babe. I'm fighting." It's no use they can't hear me.

"I thought you were tougher than this. Fight, damn you." Erica sounds angry and as she wipes the tears from her eyes, Beau pulls her into his side and kisses her head.

Cynthia moves to the other side of the bed and grips my free hand. When she speaks, I'm lucky to catch the words as they're torn from her throat on broken sobs.

"I-I need you, Ally. Y-you're my be-best friend," she hiccups, tearing my heart out.

I jump when I feel a hand on my shoulder and looking to my side, I see a sad smile on my father's face.

"Dad."

"You need to fight, Buttons. They need you as much as you need them."

"I don't know what I'm fighting."

"You need to fight to live and be happy." A watery smile graces his face.

"Every time I try, something knocks me back down."

"Fight, honey. If not for yourself, for each and every life you have touched since you opened yourself back up to the world."

"I...." I pause and look around the room.

In only a few short weeks, these people have become my family. They have come to mean everything to me. I focus back on Xavier and know I would do anything to feel his touch again.

"I will. I promise," I whisper, not taking my eyes off X's back. Worried that in a flash, he'll disappear again.

"Live and be happy, Button's."

Dad's whispered words catch on the wind coming through the open window. I don't need to look to know he is no longer standing beside me. Moving closer to the bed, I crawl up and lie over my still form. Blowing out a deep breath and closing my eyes, I allow the love in this room to soak deep into my bones.

I get ready to fight.

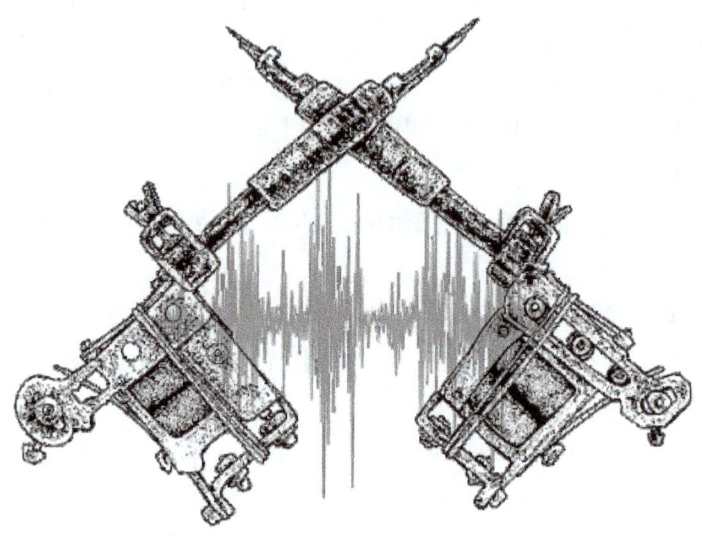

CHAPTER TWENTY-ONE

Xavier

I feel absolutely, fucking defeated. Scrubbing my hands down my tired face, I feel like I've aged fifty years in the last hour. All I want to do is crawl into bed and wrap my arms around my girl, keep her safe. Glancing around the room, I take in everybody's grave faces. They look as bad as I feel.

"Where's Justin?" I ask, trying to take my mind off all this shit running through my head.

"He's finishing up at the shop," Beau answers.

"Fuck." I remember I was booked solid today.

"It's all good, mate. We contacted everyone and told them you had a family emergency. Everyone rescheduled except one person we couldn't get hold of. Justin stayed for the appointment then, he'll close up shop and head here."

Nodding, I look at my friends. "You guys don't need to be here."

"Like you could stop us and as if we would be anywhere else right now." Erica crosses the room to close the window, there's a cool breeze blowing in.

"Leave it open, please." My voice takes on an edge even though I try to stop it.

"There's a chill in the air, X," Cynthia argues.

"Well get a fucking jumper!" I regret the words immediately. "Shit, sorry." I drag a hand over my head and try to explain my reaction. "Ally loves being outside."

Cynthia places a hand on my arm. "I understand, but she may get too cold and she's sick enough." Swinging my head towards the window, I watch as dark gray clouds begin to splash across the sky, overtaking the crisp blue of the morning. Without saying another word, I nod my head, indicating it's okay to shut out the cold. I fix my gaze back on my girl.

"Xavier." My father speaks from behind me and I turn in time to see a doctor move past him.

It's not the same doctor who was in the emergency department yesterday.

"Doctor." Relief sounds in my words.

"I've heard there's been some drama going on with this young lady this morning." He gives us a disapproving look.

I explain what I'd walked in on and without a word, he makes his way to Ally's side. He begins checking her and I move out of his way to give him all the room he needs. After a few minutes, the doc examines the fresh bruising around her neck which seems to be getting darker by the second. He checks readings on the machines and writes stuff down in her patient folder. The continuing silence begins to sit like lead in the pit of my stomach and I'm about ready to rip my hair out when he finally speaks.

"We won't know the extent of the damage caused until your wife wakes up. Sir, you need to prepare yourself for any complications."

"When will that be?" I manage to get past the lump in my throat which rose the minute he said the word 'complications'.

"At the moment everything is looking the way it should, *but* I won't know for sure until we wake her up. The damage to her throat is considerable and I won't know what it's done to the vocal center until she wakes. I'll come back this afternoon and start to bring her out of the coma."

I nod and turn to the window. The clear blue sky has vanished completely, overtaken by dark clouds and adding to my already shitty mood. I clench and unclench my fists to try and stop the rage swirling heavy inside me.

"I'll pop downstairs and grab some coffee." I barely hear Cynthia's voice over the pounding in my head.

I take the few steps to the window and lean against the ledge, watching as the sky above opens up and the rain begins to fall hard.

"X-man, would you like a coffee?" Beau asks.

I shake my head and watch as a crack of lightning flashes across the sky.

"Son." My father's voice penetrates the sound of the rain and anger at him takes hold.

He was supposed to be here. He promised he wouldn't leave Ally alone while I was gone. I feel my back muscles tense when he places a hand on my shoulder and grind my teeth together in an attempt to control my anger. I know there has to be an explanation. Not trusting myself to speak, I wait for him to talk.

"I'm sorry I wasn't here, son. There was a call from your mother's nurse, your mother had a fall and hit her head."

The guilt riding his voice tears at my heart while anger simmers in my veins. Then, it hits me - fuck I'm a selfish prick. My dad is here with me, holding me together when he should be with my mother. I grip the window ledge a bit harder and bow my head. I feel ashamed of my attitude.

"I'm sorry, dad. Fuck...." Pushing myself to stand straight, I pace the floor, running my hands through my hair in dismay.

"You have nothing to be sorry about, no-one could have predicted what the fuck happened today with your mother or with your girl." He blows out a frustrated, tired breath and I study him while he peers at the ground. His shoulders are hunched and he looks completely fucking defeated. I know there's something he isn't telling me and I steel myself for what he has to say.

"What is it?"

Locking his eyes with mine, I notice the worry lying there and the hesitation before he opens his mouth to speak.

"Ally's mum got loose, she took off and no-one can find her."

"What the fuck?" I head for the door, ready to go and find the bitch.

"Shit! Xavier, stop!" Dad races up behind me and grips me firmly on the shoulder to stop me leaving.

"You need to stay and look after your girl, let the police do their job," he grunts out.

I swing around to face him.

"How the fuck am I supposed to let them do their job when they lost her to begin with?"

"It wasn't their fault, son. The security guard allowed her to use the bathroom and she climbed out a window.

"Fuck, dad." I'm at a loss as to what to say, climbing through a window to escape is the oldest trick in the book.

"Listen to me. You stay the fuck here. I'm going to go and check on your mother and when I get back we'll take it from there.

"Fine." I'm torn between finding the bitch and making sure my woman is fine.

Dad reaches over and squeezes my shoulder before leaving. I sit my ass down and gather Ally's hand in mine. When I glance around the room I find everyone is gone, probably to get coffee.

"I'm right here, Baby." I kiss each of her delicate fingers.

The dark clouds from outside linger over my head, I know in my heart, the clear crisp blue sky won't return to my life until my girl is awake again.

I'm not sure what time it is, everything seems to be passing in a blur. I was aware of the doctor coming in with a nurse and as the she checked Ally's vitals, the doctor injected some medicine into the cannula on the back of her hand. It's supposed to bring her out of the coma they put her in, but the doc said it could take a few hours and when her body is ready for her to wake, she will.

I place Ally's hand on the bed, lean back in my chair and stretch my back. The guys are back and Cynthia is on the other side of the bed reading a book out loud. I must have really zoned out not to notice, or even hear, her reading. I raise my eyebrows at the next sentence out of her mouth.

"What the fuck are you reading to my woman?" Confusion laces my voice, but I can't help the chuckle which leaves my lips. It feels good to laugh.

Stifling a laugh herself, Cynthia manages to answer me. "It's called Broken Bastard by A.L Simpson, I found it on Ally's bookshelf. It's book one in the Broken Series I brought book two with me also. The blurbs on the backs of the books sounded really good so, I thought I'd give them a try."

She shrugs, reaches down for the bag she's packed for Ally and pulls out another book. She holds it up so I can see the cover. When I look at the guys who are leaning against the window, they shrug their shoulders and continue to stuff their faces with food. Catching Erica's eye, I see she is smiling around a mouthful of food before she covers her mouth to speak.

"It's a great story so far. Don't stop, Cynthia, keep going." She laughs and the guys groan.

I think I'm a little intrigued about this story if it makes the guys groan like that.

"I got you a sandwich from the cafe downstairs." Erica reaches down and grabs a sandwich in a sealed packet from her bag.

"I'm good." I shake my head, not interested and not sure if I could stomach anything right now.

"X, you need to eat something," she insists, but I shake my head again and wave her off.

"You're going to need your strength for when Ally wakes up." Stubbornness coats Erica's words, it becomes obvious she won't be taking no for an answer. She stands, rounds the bed and thrusts the sandwich towards me. I still don't take it.

"Just eat the fucking sandwich, brother," Beau growls.

I'm about to snap, but then I see the worried look on all their faces. I try to think of the last time I ate but nothing is coming to me. Reluctantly I take the package and open it to find a simple ham, cheese and tomato sandwich. Lifting it to my mouth, I take a bite. Seemingly satisfied, Erica sits back down and the boys go back to stuffing their faces. The sandwich is bland, tasteless and every bite seems to lodge in my throat before sitting like lead in my stomach. I eat a couple more mouthfuls, wrap the other half up and place it on the small bedside table for later.

Erica mumbles something to the boys, but I don't give a shit. I know my appetite won't be back until my girl is awake and eating herself.

Picking Ally's hand back up, I entwine her fingers with mine and try to relax. Resting my head against the side of the bed, I watch my girl. I'm hoping any moment now to see the slightest movement telling me she is coming back to me. The moment Cynthia starts to read again, a phone ringing cuts through the otherwise silent room. Bending over and rummaging through her bag, Cynthia finds her phone, places it against her ear and answers the call.

"Hey, Jace, is everything okay?"

She listens to the guy on the other end of the phone and from the corner of my eye, I notice Justin has stopped eating and is standing straighter with a possessive look on his face.

"Thank you so much for this I owe you big time." She rubs her forehead as a small smile graces her lips. "Hey little man, are you behaving yourself for Jace?"

She listens intently and I'm guessing she's talking to her son.

"Oh wow, you're one very lucky boy." She pauses. "Okay, well put him back on the phone and I'll either see you tonight or in the morning ... I love you too, buddy."

She's quiet for a moment and it seems everyone in the room has stopped what they are doing to listen in.

"Jace, I can never thank you enough for doing this. If you take him on the back of your bike again, please drive carefully," she stresses before laughing at something he says in answer. "Okay, bye." She ends the call before placing her phone back in her bag. The tension, which has been building in the room since she first answered the call, is finally broken with a pissed off sounding Justin.

"Who the fuck was that?"

"It was..." Cynthia starts to speak but Justin is on a roll and cuts her off.

"Whoever the fuck it was better back the fuck off!"

I watch as Cynthia's shoulders stiffen. "No matter what *you* think, Justin, it is none of your friggin business." Her voice is colder than ice.

"Like fuck it isn't," he spits out.

"My life does not fucking concern you anymore, you made that quite clear years ago so, don't start to pretend to give a fuck now." She speaks angrily before picking the book up from her lap and turning to where she left off.

Looking over at Justin, I see the pain etched into his face at her words. He opens his mouth to speak but I shake my head.

"Now isn't the time for this shit, save it for later."

Justin throws his hands in the air and blows out a hard breath before apologizing. Cynthia nods and mutters a quiet 'sorry' before she clears her throat and begins reading again. After a few moments, the air around us settles and I concentrate on listening to her soft voice. The words about the guy in the book waiting for the love of his life to come back to him, ricochet around my head. I swallow as the pain in my chest seems to intensify with each word is spoken. I draw my chair up closer to

Ally's face, bend down and whisper in her ear to keep fighting. I beg her not to give up on me now and promise that I will prove to her every day that this is where she belongs -next to me. I vow, no matter what, I will always be here. Right next to her fighting when she can't.

CHAPTER TWENTY-TWO

Ally

In the back of my mind, my father's whispered words float around - telling me to wake up, demanding I don't give up. He orders me to simply open my eyes. "It's not that hard, Buttons, just remember life is worth fighting for." His voice slowly fades away. A slight hum slides up my throat and passes my lips in response to the feeling of warmth which surrounds me. I take comfort in the feeling, too scared to open my eyes in case I get thrown into another dream which turns into a nightmare. I try to take stock of my body as the same feeling of stiffness in my back makes itself known. At the same time, a beeping noise resonates through my foggy head.

Is this real or will I wake only for this moment to be stolen away from me again? I'm absolutely bloody terrified of the answer.

Breathing in short sharp breaths, attempting to gain my senses, I feel something laying under my nose. It's not enough to stop the familiar scent of mint and coffee which wafts around me, helping clear the fog from my head. It's a smell I know well and the way it lingers around me is like it's welcoming me home. I try to lift my right hand but something is weighing it down. I attempt to move my legs, but again, something heavy feels like it's keeping me pinned to the bed. I give up and try to wiggle my fingers instead, even this is a huge effort. Taking a deep breath through my nose, I will myself to open my eyes. Counting to three in my head, I slowly peel my eyes open only to find everything is a blur. I blink rapidly to clear my vision and find I'm in a dimly lit room with incessant beeping coming from machines beside my bed.

I look over to my right, trying to figure out what is weighing me down. Xavier's arm is draped over me and his handsome, rugged face is resting on the side of the bed. His fingers are laced with mine, his hold tight as if he's worried someone is going to tear me away from him. My heart fills with so much emotion at the sight. Staring at him, I take him in. His eyes are closed, dark lashes resting against his cheeks and his breathing is even. His dark hair is a disheveled mess and he looks like he hasn't shaved in days. Not wanting to wake him, I move only my eyes to look around the room. Chairs line the far wall where Beau and Justin are asleep. Erica is curled up asleep on Beau's lap. Cynthia is asleep in a chair on the left of my bed, a book upside down in her lap. Warmth washes over me at having them all care enough to be here with me. I look towards the window and notice it's dark out, I wonder how long I've been here. Focusing back on X, I note the lines of worry in his face. As much as I don't want to wake him, I need to know what the hell is going on and how I ended up in a hospital. Swallowing the saliva in my mouth, I try to find my voice. I wince as a slice of pain spears through me as I croak out his name.

"X."

He seems deep in sleep so, I try to flex my fingers in his before lifting my other hand to his face. I see the cannula attached to the back of my hand. Shaking my head, I slide my nails across X's strong jaw, ignoring the heavy and sluggish feeling of my arm. Sucking back the pain, I try again to speak.

"X, Babe." Using what little strength I have, I squeeze my fingers around his and I'm thankful it was enough.

When he jolts awake, two pained and tired blue eyes lock with mine.

"Ally," He whispers, his voice hoarse.

He clears his throat as a single tear ghosts down his cheek.

"Don't..." I want to tell him not to cry, but another pain grips my throat. I take my hand from X's face and wrap it around my neck.

"Don't speak, Babe, let me call the nurse." He leans over me to press a button before bending and kissing my forehead.

"Thank fuck, you came back to me," he whispers into my hair. I don't miss the catch in his voice.

"Am I dreaming?" I wheeze out.

"If so, let's never wake up," he replies into my lips before planting a soft kiss to my mouth.

Instinct has me running my tongue across the seam of his mouth and a low growl slips from his throat. I needed a taste to ground me and tell me this is all real.

"Babe," he chastises.

I can't stop the hint of a smile which curves my lips on hearing his deep delicious voice, I've missed it so much. Before he can say anything more, a nurse with blonde hair enters. A badge attached to her uniform tells me her name is Georgia.

"I'll page the doctor," she tells Xavier and I watch her press a button on a device attached to her waist.

She steps closer and begins taking my vitals.

"How are you feeling?" she asks, placing a hand over mine.

"My throat hurts a little," I whisper in answer.

"When the doctor comes in, he'll talk to you and your husband about everything."

At the word 'husband', I raise my brows in confusion, wondering what the hell she is talking about. I look down at my hand – nope, no ring. What the hell is she talking about? Have I lost my memory, is that why I'm here? No, that can't be true because I knew who Xavier and my friends were straight away. An alternate universe maybe?

I look towards X hoping he can shed some light on whatever the fuck is happening. I notice the pleading look in his eyes. Is he pleading with me to remember? How could I have forgotten we got married? Fuck, how long have I been here? I feel my eyes glass over before the tears begin to fall.

"Is it okay to give us a minute?" X asks the nurse as she adjusts my bed so I can sit up.

"The doctor should be in any minute, but I can step out until he gets here."

"Thank you."

X gathers my hand in his but doesn't say anything until the nurse leaves.

Sniffing I wipe my free hand under my nose while avoiding dislodging the cannula.

"I'm sorry," I mumble and sniff again.

I look around the room to find the others haven't moved, they're still sleeping. I fix my eyes on the window so I won't have to look into X's eye's, worried about what I will see there. X gently turns my face to his with the tips of his fingers. I close my eyes for a few beats before slowly opening them. Instead of the hurt I expected to see in his eyes, there's a softness I have never seen before.

"What are you sorry about, Sweetness?"

"I don't remember." Tears well again.

"Remember what?"

"I don't remember...." Blowing out a small breath I try again, "that we're married."

I sniffle again and try hard to hold back the tears.

Chuckling softly, he runs his fingers down the side of my face in a soothing motion, but I'm confused as to why he's laughing at me.

"How would you feel if you couldn't remember," I grit out.

He stops chuckling, sits on the side of my bed and traces circles over the top of my hand.

"Ally...."

"What?"

"Listen to me, Sweetness."

Nodding my head, I keep my eyes closed.

"Look at me, Babe," he says gently while squeezing my hand in his.

"I don't want to," I whisper, sounding like a sullen child.

"Babe, come on," he coaxes.

Giving in, I open my eyes. I'm pleased he's stopped laughing at me. Bringing my hand to his mouth he plants a soft kiss to my palm which makes me melt a little.

"That's better. Now you listen to me, Sweetness. You haven't forgotten anything. We're not married. *Yet.* I had to say that to be able to be in here with you."

I blow out a deep breath, relieved I'm not going crazy and forgetting big life events like my own wedding. I open my mouth to apologize again, but he cuts me off before I can say a word.

"Trust me, Babe, when we get married it will be a day that neither of us will ever forget."

"When we get married?"

"Fuck, yeah Babe, there is no getting rid of me now." He leans forward and plants another soft kiss to my lips.

Pulling back, I look back around the room and wonder if there is more I should know.

"And them?" I ask, nodding to our friends.

Chuckling again. "Cynthia is your sister and Justin is her husband. Erica is my sister and Beau is her husband." He finishes on a deep, quiet laugh and I can't help but laugh with him until the pain in my throat causes me to wince. I watch as a pained expression crosses X's face.

"I'm okay." I try to reassure him, but he shakes his head at me.

"No, you're not and I will not let you brush it away, Babe. I told you when we first got together - when it comes to your health, I'm in charge."

I smother a smile as he goes all caveman on me but can't stop the tingles that race through me at his stubbornness.

"Okay, Babe." I agree, so he'll calm down.

As I lean back on the bed, X fixes my pillows.

"I bet the girls were happy with the fact you named the guys as their husbands." I try to change the subject but he isn't having any of it.

"Why don't you just relax while we wait for the doctor," he says gently before pushing my hair back off my face.

Cynthia squeals and tears stream down her cheeks then, she jumps up and before I know it, I'm wrapped in a hug. "I could have slapped him across the face." "I'm so happy you're finally awake," she whispers into my ear.

I wonder how long I was asleep for.

"So am I."

I watch as the rest of our friends wake up, thanks to Cynthia's excitement. Erica has a bright smile on her face and the boys are stretching and running their hands down their tired faces.

"You guys didn't need to be here, you look like you need some rest." Secretly, I'm so bloody happy they're all here with me.

"Someone had to control your man while you were out, I swear he was ready to rip someone's head off." Erica laughs as she crosses the room to me.

Cynthia releases me and Erica leans over and gives me a tight hug.

"Welcome home," she whispers, bringing a lump to my throat.

"Thank you," I manage to say just before the doctor walks in with nurse Georgia at his side.

"Welcome back, Miss Malone, my name is Doctor Vargas. I've been taking care of you." He reaches into the front pocket of his white coat, pulls out a pen-light and proceeds to flash it into my eyes. "How are you feeling?"

"My throat's a little sore." I glance towards X and notice a sad look on his face. Before I can ask what's wrong, the doctor starts to check me over.

"Is your throat the only thing bothering you?"

I nod in answer while he checks one of the machines beside me.

"I'm going to order a few tests for first thing in the morning." He writes in what I assume is my patient folder.

"How long was I asleep?"

"Just over thirty-six hours," he says, checking his watch.

"Holy shit, nearly two days! What the hell happened to me?"

"You don't remember?" Concern flashes over Doctor Vargas' features.

Closing my eyes, I try to remember the last thing I did....

X wanted me to go to dinner with his family, but I wasn't feeling well and stayed home to read. The next morning, I still wasn't feeling well, but I managed to go into work. I remember Cynthia telling me I should have stayed home and I started to agree with her when I felt like I was going to pass out. Everything after that is a blur. After explaining all this to the doctor, he nods and jots down more notes in my file. He instructs Georgia to remove the IV and start me on oral medicine first thing the following morning before turning back to me and explaining what happened and why I am here.

"You're a very lucky young lady. If it hadn't been for the quick thinking of your friend in calling an ambulance immediately, we may not be having this conversation. When you were brought in, you were in a coma so we stabilised you with the help of a breathing machine and checked you further. We noticed the bandage on your hand and removed it. The cut was badly infected and after running a few tests, we discovered the wound was septic. In other words, you had a severe case of blood poisoning. We kept you in a coma to give the medication a chance to work and allow your body to recover. It was a close call."

My mind is racing a million miles an hour at what he has said.

"Your throat is sore because you were intubated and ....

He pauses for a moment, he seems to be weighing his next words and the silence turns heavy. X takes my hand and the same look of sadness washes over his face again.

"What is it?" I whisper, worried about the answer.

"Your mum," Xavier starts.

I suck in a deep breath and my body locks up.

"What happened?" My vision blurs and cool tears slide down my cheeks.

X sighs. "I left to go and grab a coffee." I hear the anger and guilt coating his words and it breaks my heart. His words take on a hard edge as he continues. "When I came back to the room, she was here. She had a pillow over your face, she'd also attempted to strangle you." He blows out a hard breath, rubbing a hand down his tired face while his other hand squeezes mine.

I wait for the pain to slice through me but nothing comes. Looking around the room, I note the mix of sadness and anger on everyone's faces. I have no words. What does one say on hearing something like that? Again, the silence in the room seems to sit heavy around us until doctor Vargas speaks.

"First thing in the morning, Georgia will take you for a head and neck scan to check everything is as it should be. We don't know how long she smothered you for and I need to ensure there is no damage due to a possible lack of oxygen. I'll also run some blood tests to check the infection. If the scan comes back clear and you respond to oral medications, you should be able to go home in forty-eight hours. You will need to rest and take it easy for at least two weeks and I'll want to see you again in a few days to check the wound on your hand."

"Two days," I murmur, still at a loss for words.

"Let's just concentrate on getting you well again."

I nod and feel X's lips on my forehead as everything I have been told begins to sink in. I knew my mother hated me, but to try and kill me is a whole new level I didn't think she would stoop to.

"Try and get some rest and I'll be back in the morning to check on you. We'll look at disconnecting you from a couple of the machines if all is well." Doctor Vargas hands my chart to the nurse and I slump back on the pillow. My head swirls with the overload of information. Closing my eyes, I attempt to relax.

"Rest baby, I've got you," X breaths into the top of my head and the truth in his words comforts me, settling some of the swirling emotion swimming in my head.

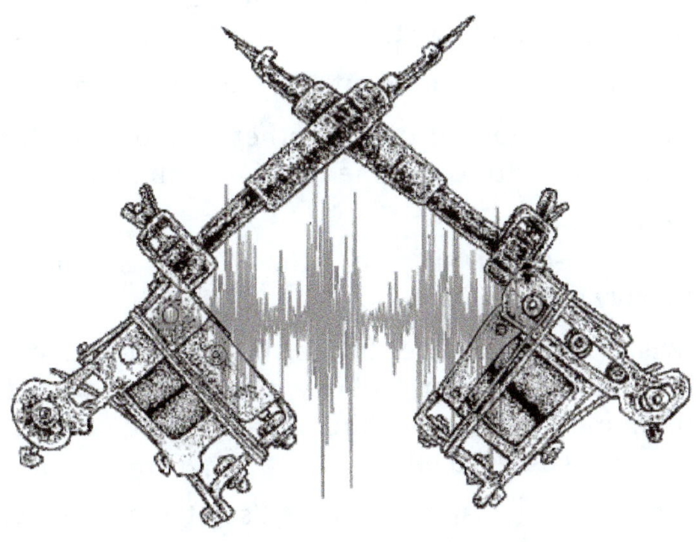

CHAPTER TWENTY-THREE

Xavier

"Rest baby, I've got you," I whisper into her silky soft hair. I'm hoping to catch the familiar scent of sweet apples, but it's no use -antiseptic and the smell of a sterile room overpower what might be there.

When I cast my gaze down, her eyes flutter closed and a tear squeezes through her thick lashes to roll over her cheek. I brush it away with the pad of my thumb before it drips from her chin.

My stomach churns with disgust knowing I had to tell her about her mother, but I sure as shit wasn't going to lie to her. As much as I hated having to tell her, she deserved to know.

Ally grips my shirt tight between her fingers and I watch as her knuckles turn white. A tremble races through her, she buries her head into my chest and sobs wrack her body. It breaks my heart to see her so upset. Sitting on the side of her bed, I hold her tight and kiss the top of her head.

"Can you give us a moment?" I croak out to Beau.

"Yeah, we'll go and grab another round of coffee." He heads to the door with everyone else following and we're left alone.

"H-how c-could she do t-that?" Ally stammers out between heavy sobs.

I wish I had an answer for her but I don't understand it either. Running my hand up and down her back in what I hope is a soothing motion, I try to think of something reassuring to tell her. Nothing comes to mind.

"I'm sorry," I whisper knowing it's not enough, but it's all I got. I'm sorry for all the years she's had to put up with the bitch.

When she leans back a little, Ally's glassy eyes lock with mine. Sniffing, she runs a shaking hand under her nose. Without a thought, I lean down and kiss her nose, chuckling lowly when I feel it scrunch up beneath my lips.

"That tickled," she breathes out when I pull back.

I close my eyes when I feel her nails trace over the two days growth on my face. I savor the feeling of her touch and the breath catches in my throat when I realise just how much I've missed her touch.

"Sorry, Sweetness." I slowly open my eyes and lock my gaze with hers, aware of our connection.

"Stop saying, sorry. You have nothing to be sorry about."

She drags her eyes away from mine, looks over my shoulder and blows out a deep breath before returning her gaze to me. So much sorrow swims within the deep depths of her eyes and I would give anything to be able to fix it. I'm snapped back to the moment when she speaks, her voice husky.

"I'm the one who should be sorry." Her words tremble with regret and sadness, each one causing my heart to twist and ache for her. Blowing out a deep breath, I try to free my heart from the crushing effect of her words.

"You didn't do anything wrong." I run my hand over her back.

She opens her mouth to speak but I shake my head, needing her to listen to what I have to say and she needs to rest her throat. I haven't missed the winces she tries to hide when she speaks. I place a finger to her lips.

"You didn't ask for any of this to happen and you didn't make your bitch of a mother the way she is, she did that all on her own." I pat my chest. "Lay your head here, close your eyes and try and get some rest."

I find myself needing to hold her, to feel her warm breath against my chest, to be soothed and reassured that she's alive. Laying her head against my chest, the vibration of her hum as she gets comfortable, settles me.

"X?" she whispers sleepily.

"Hmmm?"

"Thanks for being here, it means a lot to me."

"Always, Sweetness." I run my hand up and down her side before settling my hand on her hip when her breathing begins to even out.

After Ally fell asleep last night, I waited for the guys to come back with coffee to let them know they could leave. The girls moaned about wanting to stay, but finally agreed it was probably best to leave so Ally could rest. They left promising they'd be back today.

Rubbing my face, I lean back in the shitty plastic chair, stretch my arms over my head and roll my neck to stretch out the kinks which have settled there. A deep breath escapes my lungs. Nurse Georgia came in about an hour ago and took Ally to get some tests done. I wasn't allowed to go with her which irritated the fuck out of me. Georgia assured me she wouldn't leave Ally's side so, after an internal battle, I finally relented saying I would be right here when they came back.

"Why don't you go home and get cleaned up?" Ally had suggested, concern washing over her words.

"I'm fine, Sweetness. I'll wash up in the bathroom and wait for you to come back."

She shook her head in disapproval, but I didn't miss the smile which tugged at her lips before she sucked her bottom lip between her teeth.

I felt a growl rumble up my chest and squeezed my fists at my sides. I gritted my teeth and after taking several deep breaths, I managed to calm myself enough to place a kiss on her forehead. When she opened her mouth to argue with me again, Georgia reminded her, they needed to go.

So, now, after washing my face, I sit here staring through the window while I wait. Watching as the blue sky tries to fight through the heavy dark clouds which are liberally scattered about. I'm worried by the ominous feeling which has settled in the pit of my stomach.

"What did we miss? Where's Ally?"

I swing my head around to see a concerned Erica enter the room with the rest of the guys close behind.

"The nurse took her downstairs so they could run some tests." I get to my feet.

"How are you doing this morning?" she whispers in my ear as she gives me a hug.

"I'll be a lot better when I get to take my girl home."

When Erica releases me from the hug, Justin pats me on the back with his free hand and hands me a brown paper bag and a coffee from the other.

"We brought you a coffee and chocolate chip muffin, the girls are worried you aren't eating enough." He gives me a sheepish grin and shrugs.

"I stopped on the way and grabbed you a change of clothes, brother, while the girls gave your place a quick clean." Beau chuckles and hands me my gym bag.

I raise my eyebrows in confusion, wondering why the fuck they would bother, my place is usually pretty clean.

Cynthia steps up to give me a quick hug. "There were a few dirty dishes in the sink and clothes on the bathroom floor, it wasn't anything major. Erica washed the dishes while I threw a load of laundry on." She shrugs before going on. "I assume Ally will be going back to your place once she's released so, we thought we'd take care of it so you can just focus on Ally."

I'm blown away that they would do all this for me.

A grunting sound comes from behind me which I'm assuming is from Justin, but fuck if he has anything to worry about. The only woman I'll ever need or want is Ally. Fuck, she's the love of my life. Brushing away his jealousy, I turn and look at each of our friends while trying to work out what I can say that could convey how I feel and how much they mean to me.

"Thank you," I murmur, knowing it's not enough but I'm fucking speechless.

Turning, I take the few steps to the bedside table and put the coffee and muffin down before heading towards the attached private bathroom to change out of my dirty clothes, lifting my shirt to my nose as I go. I'm thankful for what they have done for both of us. Now, I need the test results to come back with the all clear so I can take my girl home and everything will be right in my world once again.

Making quick work of my dirty clothes, I throw on a pair of clean dark-wash jeans and the grey long sleeved Henley from the bag before looking in the small mirror above the sink. I run a hand over my unshaven jaw wondering if I should shave. The phone ringing from the floor distracts me. Reaching down, I pull it from the front pocket of my discarded jeans before throwing them back to the floor. I flip the phone over in my hand to see dad's name flash up on the screen.

"Hey dad, what's up?"

Heavy breaths come down the line but he doesn't say anything.

"Dad?" I become concerned he's rung me without realising.

"Son," he chokes out in a gravelly voice soaked in emotional pain which has the hair on the back of my neck standing on end.

I grip the sink in front of me, waiting for what he has to tell me.

"Your mother."

His voice breaks like glass and the shards shred my heart when he manages to get the next words past his lips.

"She didn't wake up this morning, I called the ambulance and we're on our way to the hospital."

His voice cracks on the last word and the frailty I hear in my father almost brings me to my knees.

"I, um-um." I squeeze my eyes closed as cool tears slide unchecked down my face. Taking a deep breath, I try to get words to pass my lips but it's a struggle. "Okay," I manage hoarsely. It's all I've got at this moment. My throat is dry, my chest tightens and muscles tense. I guess it must be enough when he repeats the word before ending the call.

I grip the porcelain bowl of the sink in both hands and bow my head as an onslaught of emotions slams into me. I have nothing left in me to keep me standing, I'm so fucking tired. Falling to my knees, the phone crashes to the floor. I rest my head against the sink and let the emotions consume me. The intensity all but chokes me, my shoulders heave, my breaths come in choppy pants and my sight is blurred with thick tears which refuse to stop.

"What happened, brother?" Beau's voice floats around me as if I'm in a tunnel.

Squeezing my hands hard on the sink, I hear the porcelain creak as it fights against the hold of the tiles on the wall. Sucking deep breaths in, I let them out slowly through my nose, trying to calm myself down, but it's fucking hopeless.

"X-man, talk to me, brother." Beau's voice doesn't seem so far away now.

I open my mouth and try to speak, but nothing wants to come out.

"Just breath, mate." A hand squeezes my shoulder and I try to follow his instructions. "Mate, ease up a little on the sink, you're gonna pull the fucker off the wall." A worried chuckle leaves his throat, he's becoming clearer now.

Loosening my hold just a little, I try again to speak.

"Mum," I get out before a sob tears through my throat.

"Fuck, what happened?"

"She wouldn't wake up this morning. I need to get down to ED. They're bringing her in by ambulance." Words tumble from my lips now as urgency overtakes me.

"Shit, okay we got this, mate. I'll get Erica and the others to stay here and wait for Ally while we go down there together." He squeezes my shoulder again.

Nodding is all I seem to be capable of right now as my gut twists for completely different reasons. I promised Ally I'd be here when she got back from her tests.

"Listen I'll let Erica know and give you a minute," Beau murmurs before leaving the bathroom letting the door close with a soft click that seems to echo around me.

Sucking back the gut-wrenching emotion, I grab the phone from the floor and pull myself to my feet. After a few deep breaths, I flip the tap on the sink and splash cold water on my face. I need to be strong right now. For my dad. For Ally. There will be plenty of time to break down later, right now I need to summon whatever strength I have left and push forward. My dad is going to need me.

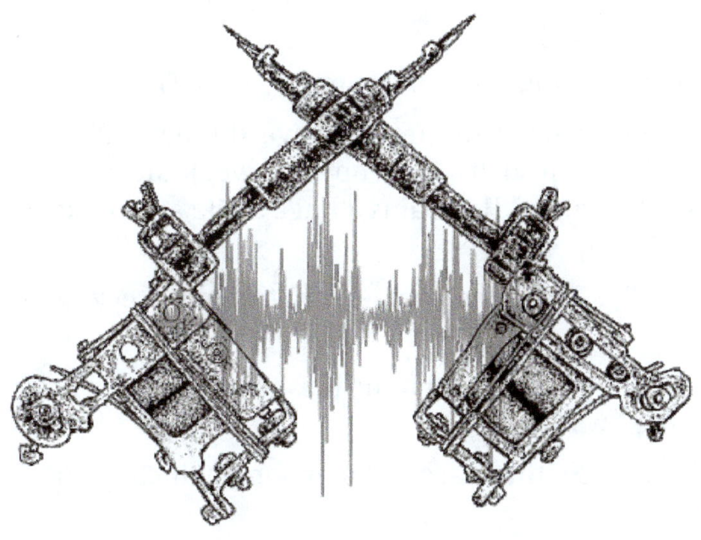

CHAPTER TWENTY-FOUR

Ally

"Are you nearly ready to go home?" Nurse Georgia approaches the side of my bed, she's way too bright for this time in the morning.

With effort, I plaster a smile on my face and answer. "Yeah."

"Well, don't sound so enthusiastic. Someone might think you actually don't want to leave us," she chuckles.

"I do, it's just been a long week."

I sigh as Cynthia walks through the door with JT by her side and glance at the clock on the wall to see it's 8am. "You guys are here early."

"We figured, the sooner we got here, the sooner we could take you home."

She smiles at me, comes to a stop beside the bed, bends and gives me a hug.

"How are you doing, little man?" I ask JT.

"Really good. Mum let me have the day off school. She said since I've been such a good boy this week, she's going to buy me a new PS4 game." He beams a huge smile and looks up at his mother with hopeful eyes.

"Really! That's awesome, what game are you going to get?"

Swinging his eyes to mine he shrugs. "Not sure yet, there are a couple I want."

"Of course, there are," I laugh, only wincing a little bit at the action.

The doctor told me yesterday that my throat may still hurt for another week or so, but my tests came back clear and I was allowed to go home as long as I promised to take it easy for the next couple of weeks.

"The doctor should be in shortly with your discharge papers then you're good to go," Nurse Georgia said.

"Thank you," I reply, eager to get out of here.

"Why did you call me to pick you up? Not that I mind, but where is X?" Cynthia asks.

A lump forms in my throat for my man.

"X's dad called late last night and asked if he could help him with the funeral arrangements for his mum this morning." My eyes glaze over and the words sound watery to my own ears. I bite my lip to stop the tears from falling, but it's no use, one escapes to trickle down my cheek. My heart feels heavy in my chest as guilt rides hard down my back knowing he was here with me and not with his mother.

"Fair enough." Cynthia stares through the window, sadness in her gaze, no doubt remembering how heartbroken X looked two days ago.

"When is the service?" she whispers.

I check on JT and make sure he's good before I speak. He's taken a seat against the far wall, pulled out his 3DS, popped his earbuds in and has immersed himself in his game. Satisfied he's occupied, I answer.

"Thursday at 10am."

Cynthia opens her mouth to say something before a voice comes from the door and Dr. Vargas walks in with what I assume are my discharge papers in his hand.

"Miss Malone, everything seems to be in order and you're ready to leave us. Remember, take it easy for a couple of weeks. You'll feel weak but your strength will slowly return over time. Apart from that, there shouldn't be any other issues."

"Thank you for everything, Doctor." I push the blankets off my legs and swing my feet over the edge. Trying to go slow as my sock covered feet touch the floor, I blow out a small breath and try to gear myself up to move off the bed. I hate how bloody sluggish my body feels. It will only be my second time out of this bed in a week. The first time, X was here to help me. When he took me for a short walk last night, his arm was wrapped around me for support and he watched every step I took.

"Let's get you changed." Cynthia grabs the bag she packed for me from the floor and pulls out some clothes before helping me to my feet. Once I'm steady, she helps me to the bathroom.

"Do you need me to help you change?"

I shake my head, feeling like shit that she thinks she needs to help me.

"I don't mind," she says softly, nothing but sincerity coating her words.

"I should be fine, but I'll call out if I need help."

"Okay." She opens the door and places my clothes on the closed lid of the toilet seat before walking out and closing the door behind her.

After stripping off the hospital gown, I grab my clothes off the toilet lid and throw them on, pulling my grey sweatshirt on over my bra. I stare at my black leggings, not sure if I have the strength to put them on standing up and I would probably fall on my ass if I lean against the wall. Blowing out a frustrated breath, I sit on the closed toilet lid and tug them on. Gripping the sink, I pull myself up and shimmy them the rest of the way over my ass. Still gripping the sink, I lean over, grab the hospital gown and pop it in the bin provided. Looking into the mirror, I run my hands through my unruly hair and despair that I now have permanent bed hair! Frustrated that it's not doing what I want, I pluck a hair tie from the shelf above the sink and throw it up in a messy bun on top of my head. It's just gonna have to do until I get home, have a shower and wash it.

Pushing the door open, I take a few slow unsteady steps into the room, pushing a wayward strand of hair behind my ear.

"Okay let's get..." I stop dead in my tracks and my heart flutters in my chest as Xavier strides into the room, as large as life.

He's wearing a pair of worn blue denim jeans and a black hoodie with Xtreme Ink written across the front in white. I take a deep swallow so I don't drool at the sight. He is sporting a short beard, he hasn't shaved for the past week and his dark hair is messy but sexy as fuck. His blue eyes drop to my feet and slowly track up every inch of my body. When they finally meet mine, a sexy smirk curls his lips and a look of primal hunger reflects in his eyes shooting want straight to my core.

"What are you doing here?" I wonder out loud, my voice shaky.

I struggle to get my body to behave.

"Babe, I'm here to take you home. Did you think I wouldn't be here?" His deep voice rumbles straight through me.

I clench my fists at my sides as he cocks a dark eyebrow, daring me to argue with him. I can't and don't want to stop the smile spreading over my face, but then it falls just as quick knowing he should be with his dad.

"I called Cynthia so you could help your dad and not have to worry about me."

"I will always worry about you, Sweetness, and no-one except me is taking you home. How many times am I going to have to keep telling you, when it comes to your health, I'm in charge? Now, let's get your stuff together and get the hell out of here."

While he speaks he closes the distance between us and wraps his arms around my waist. I lay my hands flat against his chest and gaze up into his calming blue eyes. I notice they're a little bloodshot thanks to so many sleepless nights. I melt into his warm touch, feeling centered for the first time since last night.

Bending down, he plants a light kiss to my forehead before his lips linger over my now sensitive skin. His warm breath washes over my face and the hint of coffee lingers around me.

"This helps." He whispers so only I can hear him. "Holding you grounds me and settles the raging emotions running rampant through me."

With my hands pressed to his hard chest, I push up on my toes and brush my lips over his, knowing exactly what he means.

"You help me breathe," I whisper across his lips and my voice catches on the last word.

Before I can suck down my next breath, his lips crash against mine, making my head spin. What I thought would be a hard and commanding kiss turns out to be the complete opposite. His lips seem to entice mine and conjure them to open as he runs his warm tongue across my bottom lip. I hum in the back of my throat when one of his hands twists into my messy bun and holds me in place, but not too hard that it frightens me. I know I could break free at any moment, but I don't think my body would let me even if I wanted to. Instead, a whimper slips free when his tongue glides across mine. My fingers gently twist into his messy hair and my nails scrap across his scalp. Time is lost as we soak each other in. Bursts of colour flash behind my closed lids and my body presses harder into his, wanting the safe warmth of his body to surround every inch of me. Pulling back after what feels like hours but was probably only a couple of minutes, we try to catch our breaths. Panting softly, my eyes flutter open, not wanting this all-consuming moment to end. I tuck my head under his chin.

"I've missed you," he breathes into my ear.

I burrow my head into his chest, letting the steady beat of his heart settle me.

"I've missed you, too," I murmur.

I'm worried he may not have heard me, but he squeezes me tighter, answering my unspoken question.

"Well, since you guys are good, I think I'll take little Mister here to get his game." Cynthia's voice breaks into our moment.

Looking over my shoulder, I feel the heat blaze in my cheeks. I was totally lost in the moment and had forgotten she was still in the room.

"Sorry," I mouth to her.

"It's fine. JT is too wrapped up in his game to have noticed, but I might need to get a cold drink on the way out," she laughs and waves a hand in front of her face, a smile a mile wide curves her lips.

X laughs, a deep belly laugh that vibrates through me. Releasing him, I pull Cynthia into a tight hug, promising to call her later and plan for a much-needed movie night.

"You'd better," she laughs before letting me go. Crouching down, she helps JT pack up his things.

"Will you come and play with me after I get my new game?" JT bounces on his toes in front of me, excitement spilling from him in waves.

"Try and stop me buddy." I give him a kiss on the cheek and a quick hug before they walk out the door.

Turning, I head to the bed to grab my bag but find X already has it in his hand.

"Come on, Babe, let me take you home." He holds out his free hand.

Taking X's strong, rough hand in mine, I revel in the feeling of it as it completely engulfs mine. Making our way out of the room X drops my hand and wraps his arm around my waist.

"I got you, Babe." He plants a kiss to the crown of my head.

Without doubt, I know he truly has got me. X has been by my side day in and day out, keeping me strong and pushing me forward. Now it's time for me to do the same for him as he works through the difficult days ahead.

Glancing over my shoulder, a secret smile on my face, I look through the window at the beautiful Autumn day. Noticing for the first time in days, the clear crisp blue sky with not a cloud in sight. A slight sway in the trees makes the golden, red and brown leaves dance gracefully. I'm reminded of the crisp chilly air we are about to face once we're outside and I snuggle deeper into X's side. A warmth runs through me knowing, no matter what, the man at my side will shield me from anything which lies ahead of us. Our strength together has me looking forward to the bright new days to come.

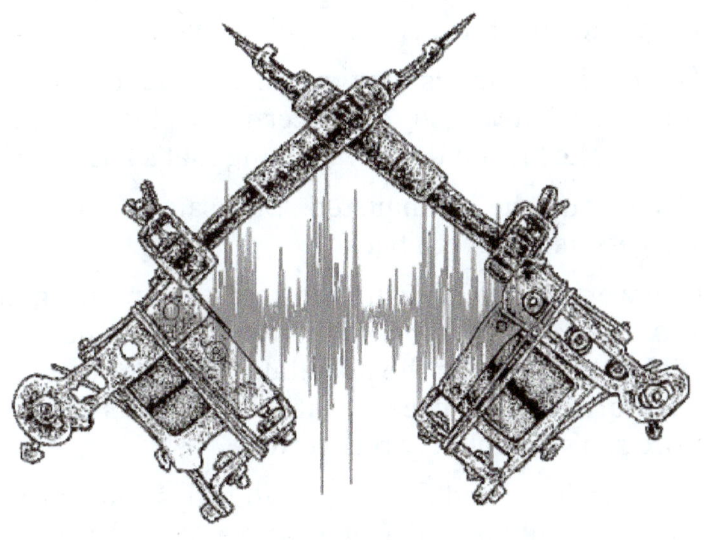

CHAPTER TWENTY-FIVE

Xavier

After settling Ally in my bed, I make my way towards the living room.

My apartment is fairly modern with an open floor plan. The kitchen, living room and dining room are all in the same large space and the far wall has sliding glass doors which open onto a huge balcony overlooking Newcastle Harbor in Honeysuckle. Summer time is absolutely breathtaking. There's nothing better than sitting outside, firing up the barbeque and throwing back a few beers on the outdoor lounge setting. Today, the doors are closed with the blinds rolled up to the ceiling, allowing the natural light to flood in. Shaking my head clear, I focus on my dad who is sitting on the black leather lounge, going through paperwork that's covering my glass coffee table. Heading towards the kitchen bench, I flick the kettle on and pull two coffee mugs from the cupboard.

"Coffee?" I ask while putting a teaspoon of coffee in each cup, already knowing the answer would be yes.

"Yeah." His voice is raw, gruff. He sounds absolutely, fucking defeated. "How's Ally?" Concern laces his voice, I know he's trying to take his mind off everything that's happened.

"Good, but she's exhausted. Doc said it'll be a while before she gets her strength back."

I answer while picking up the kettle and pouring the hot water into each cup. Ally looked better than she had in days when I picked her up from the hospital. The pink tinge I love so much has returned to her cheeks, but I can tell she still has a way to go before she's completely recovered.

"I'll head home today and give you guys some privacy." I look over my shoulder and watch as he leans back into the lounge and rubs his eyes, the paperwork pushed aside. Turning, I lean against the bench, crossing my arms over my chest. I take in his disheveled hair, his unkempt clothes and worry swims in the pit of my stomach. Looking towards the glass doors again, I blink a few times to clear my watery vision.

"Dad, you don't have to go anywhere," I assure him, huskiness taking over my voice. I know I would be worried as shit if he was at home by himself at this time. "Let's get through the next couple of days and see how you feel." I want him to know he's welcome here for as long as he needs to be.

"We'll see how things go," he murmurs before going back to the papers in front of him.

Turning back, I pick up the cups and make my way towards the lounge. Sitting, I move some of the papers out of the way and place our cups down. Grabbing the stack of papers I'd moved, I flick through them, noticing they're mums funeral arrangements.

"I pulled some steaks out this morning, how about we fire up the barbeque for dinner after the funeral director leaves? " I suggest.

"Sounds good." He picks up a photo of the three of us which was lying amongst the scattered papers, it's one mum always had with her.

Giving it a brief look, I try to swallow around the lump in my throat which seems to be permanently lodged there these days. Closing my eyes, I take a few deep breaths and bow my head when I feel my father's hand land against my back. No words are spoken, only the sound of our heavy breathing surrounds us as we both try to control our emotions.

"Thanks again, Donald." I shake the funeral director's hand before closing the front door behind him.

Placing both palms flat against the wooden door, I take in a few deep breaths, wishing this shit was just a fucking dream. Squeezing my eyes shut, I picture my mum's smile the last time I saw her and try to block out the memories of her lifeless body lying on a hospital bed with tubes coming out of her everywhere. I remember the chill to my lips when I kissed her forehead for the last time, a sensation I don't think I will ever forget.

Squeezing my hands into fists, my knuckles pop under the strain. Dropping my head against the door with a quiet thud, I let it rest against the wood and attempt to fight off the tears which threaten to fall. Moment by moment, the walls I'd put up a couple of days ago, the walls to keep me strong, begin to crumble around me. The tears I've fought to hold back begin to spill down my cheeks. Licking my bottom lip, I taste the saltiness. My body trembles uncontrollably, the chill from the memory of the kiss slides under my skin. Goosebumps appear, making everything fresh and raw once again. Pushing my fists harder against the door, the tremble escalates to shaking and the door vibrates under my hands.

Biting down on my tongue, I try to fight off the cyclone spiraling inward making my stomach twist in pain and my heart feel like lead. My eyes are burning and my breaths are coming in choppy pants. No matter how hard I squeeze my fists together, these overwhelming feelings won't go away.

My body tenses when small hands wrap around me from behind and her head rests against my back. Just like the night I went back to her after seeing my mother for the last time in the hospital, she holds me firm, comforting me, there is no need for words. I try to push down the brutal waves of pain, loss and despair which are trying to bring me to my knees. Blinking my eyes against the swirling and crushing rawness from only moments ago, I will it to fade to black. Not to fade completely, but enough for me to be able to think and to begin to build the walls back up again.

"You had me, now I have you." Her husky words hit my back and I don't need to look to know she is crying.

Leaving my head resting against the door, I lower my hands and cover hers where they rest against my stomach. I'm not ready to turn around and face her just yet. Taking another couple of deep breaths, I will my control, which I'm so well known for, to snap back into place before I face my father. After a few seconds, the rawness is buried deep enough for me to turn and wrap my arms around my girl. Resting my head against the crown of hers, I breathe in her sweetness, soaking it in enough to help calm my racing nerves.

"I need to be stronger," I whisper so my father doesn't hear me.

"For who?" Her glassy eyes capture mine, refusing to let them go.

So much passion lives behind her green orbs. My throat tightens and I'm afraid to speak in case it comes out on a broken sob.

"No one expects you to be strong at the moment, Babe. It's okay to break every now and then." Ally blows out a deep breath and grips the back of my shirt tighter. "This past week has been a whirlwind of emotions and broken moments. We'll get through this and be stronger.....*together.*"

This woman blows my fucking mind. After everything she's been through this past week, especially with her own mother, I didn't know what to expect but this was far from it.

"Fuck, Babe, after everything that's happened this week, I'm not sure how much more I can take. But, you standing here, your voice so fucking strong...." I shake my head. "I'm in awe of you, Baby."

When she raises up on the tips of her toes, I lift her at the waist and she places her lips over mine, breathing life back into my broken soul. Lowering her back to her feet, I wrap one arm around her and bring her into my chest. I cup her warm cheek in my other hand and turning her head, she places a soft kiss into my palm before leaning into my touch as her glassy eyes lock with mine.

"I love you." Truer words have never before passed my lips.

Her eyes widen before softening and I brush away a single glistening tear as it escapes down her cheek.

"I love you, too."

Hearing those words from her sweet lips are like a balm to my soul and I know we can get through this together.

"We got this," I grunt before bringing her lips back to mine.

"Together....." she whispers into my mouth as her lips touch mine.

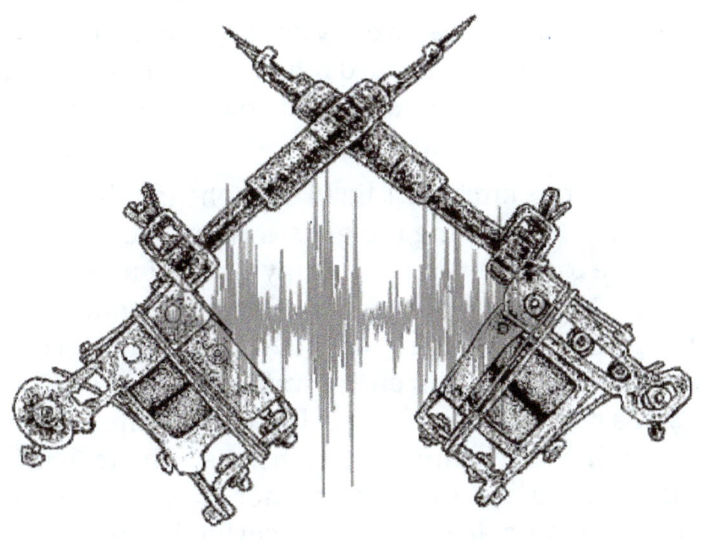

CHAPTER TWENTY-SIX

Ally

Running my hands down the front of my black shift dress to the hem which hits just above the knees, I smooth out a few wrinkles. I examine my black stockings, ensuring I don't have a run and let out a breath when I note I have managed to pull them on without tearing the flimsy material. I turn back to the mirror and fluff out my auburn hair which is simply styled with soft curls flowing down the sides of my face.

I hum along with the radio as I run the tip of my finger around the edge of my lips to make sure I have no smudges from the brown lipstick I just applied. I smack my lips together to make sure the colour spreads evenly and push my palms against my thighs when a slight tremble races through them. I will myself to find the control to get me through today.

It's Thursday, a day so much like any other but yet so different because it's the day we say goodbye to Xavier's mother. With a heavy heart I turn towards the bedroom door, deciding to leave the radio on to provide X some background noise while he gets ready.

Entering the kitchen, I head straight for the kettle and flick the switch on, knowing the guys will probably want coffee before we have to leave. Glancing at my watch, I note the time is only 7.30 am. We still have plenty of time but not enough to build ourselves up to do what we have to. Staring through the glass doors which take up an entire wall, I take in the clear, crisp day. The sun's rays bounce off the calm water in the harbour. It's as if the weather is conspiring against us – instead of being gloomy, depressing without X's mother here, it's sunny and bright and everything around us is cheerful. I bite down on my quivering lip and attempt to stem the onslaught of emotions slamming into me. I may not have had the privilege of meeting Emily, but through the stories shared over the week by X and his dad, I feel like I've lost someone before I even had a chance to savour and cherish her. Emily sounds like a woman you couldn't help but love. A tiny kernel of jealousy had swirled into my stomach and made my chest tighten as I listened to them tell story after story. I found myself wishing I had someone like that for a mother. I know it's irrational to feel that way, maybe it's the events from the past week with my own pathetic excuse for a mother being so vicious. I can't help how I feel, I would have given anything for a mother like Emily. She was obviously someone very special and I feel sad knowing I've missed out on knowing her.

"Are you okay, Sweetness?" X's deep voice sounds from behind me as he wraps his strong arms around my waist.

I hadn't realised I'd walked towards the glass doors and placed my palm against the cool glass, staring at nothing in particular, just letting my mind completely zone out. Shaking off the fog, I rest my hands over X's and lean my head back against his chest. I lift my chin and look up at him through my lashes.

"Yeah…just lost in thought, sad I didn't have the opportunity to know your mum."

X leans down and kisses my forehead, I close my eyes at the soft touch of his lips. I'm missing being intimate with him. Since we got here from the hospital on Monday, he's been so worried he would hurt me, he's refused to make love to me. I understand his reasons but I miss that piece of him. *Damn stubborn man.*

"How are you doing?" I whisper.

Looking up, I gaze straight into his soft calming eyes but it lasts for only a moment. I watch as they begin to churn and swirl with emotion, crushed by a tidal wave of raw hurt. They begin to glaze over and he doesn't say a word, he simply nods before taking a deep breath and blowing it out slowly. He struggles to hold back the tears and one lonely drop rolls down his cheek before he swipes it away. A sharp pain grips my chest every time a tear escapes his eyes, it's like his mountain of strength is cracking and breaking right before my eyes and all I want to do is patch him back up. I know it's killing him waiting on the autopsy report. Nothing is worse than not knowing what happened but waiting for the answer is a close bloody second. I wish I could take his pain away but all I can do is be here for him and try to take his mind off things even if it's only for a short period of time.

"I put the kettle on, let me fix you a coffee." I start to move free of his hold but he tightens his arms around me, holding me in a vice-like grip.

"In a minute. I just need to breathe for a minute."

I melt into his hold, loving that I do for him what he does for me.

"Okay," I murmur.

Turning in his arms so I can bury my face into his chest, I have to suppress a moan from escaping my throat when I notice the black as night suit he is wearing, because right now isn't the time to be drooling all over him. Squeezing my eyes shut, I try not to think about how his crisp white shirt is moulded perfectly to his hard chest, like a second skin.

"Are you okay, Babe?"

"Yep," I squeak out. Clearing my throat, I try again. "I sure am, why is that?" I'm hoping to the heavens above I sounded bloody normal and it wasn't the desperate whine my ears heard.

Chuckling softly, I feel his hot breath against the top of my head before he speaks. I squeeze my thighs together, trying to stop the sudden tingle in my clit caused by the vibration of his deep rumble in his chest.

"Babe, your squirming like a worm and your breath's kind of picked up speed."

Shit. Sometimes I wish he wasn't so observant.

"I'm good." I concentrate on trying to control my breathing.

"Come on, I want to show you something." X pulls away and grips my hand tightly in his.

"What?" My brows crease as I wonder what he needs to show me.

He doesn't say anything, just keeps walking in the direction of his bedroom with my hand in his. I have to quicken my steps to keep up with his long strides.

"I thought we were going to have coffee?" I question as he sets me down on the edge of his bed. Holding a finger in the air, indicating for me to wait a moment, he turns and heads towards the black tallboy which is against the wall. He picks up a small velvet pouch from the top before returning to sit next to me. Gripping the pouch in one hand as if his life depends on whatever is in it, he gathers up my hand in his free one and takes a few steadying breaths before facing me.

"What is it, what's wrong?" Worry laces my voice as I stare into his eyes.

Emotions flicker through them so fast, it's hard for me to figure out what's wrong.

Releasing my hand, he pulls the strings open on the pouch, and turns it upside down into the palm of his hand. The hint of gold catches my eye and I suck in a deep breath.

"We've got this, you and me?" He asks, releasing a breath.

"We have." I nod, feeling the words right to my core. "We can get through anything." I manage to say before his lips crash down on mine. I feel the cool of metal against my cheek as he palms the side of my face with one hand, the other holding the opposite side of my neck. Feeling cocooned in his warmth, I get lost in his kiss as his tongue slides against mine. Pulling back slightly on panting breaths, I suck my bottom lip into my mouth, savouring the tingling sensation his kisses always cause. Intense blue eyes meet mine, holding me captive and I struggle to draw oxygen into my lungs as pure primal need washes over them. His eyes dart to my neck and I follow his line of sight but don't know what he is looking at. When I raise my hand, it comes into contact with the cool metal of what I know must be a necklace. Getting to my feet, I cross to the free-standing mirror in the corner of the room. A gasp leaves my lips when I see the diamond encrusted star pendant hanging from a gold chain.

"Wow…." My voice is awash with shock as I finger the delicate jewel. "It's absolutely gorgeous." Words can't do the piece justice. The sun's rays streaming through the window bounce off each diamond casting a rainbow of colours around me.

Wrapping his strong arms around me from behind, he rests his chin on my shoulder and locks his gaze on mine in the mirror.

"On the darkest of days, you make everything brighter," he breathes out against my neck, sending a shudder ricocheting down my spine.

"Damn," I whisper, making him chuckle.

Love bursts through my veins as the lyrics to *Hungry Eyes* by *Eric Carmen* begins to waft in the air. Turning me in his arms, his lips land on mine before I can even catch my breath. Sliding his hands up my dress, he grabs my waist and lifts me off my feet. Pulling back from the kiss so, we are a whisper apart, he murmurs as he runs his tongue softly over my lips - "help me breathe."

"Always."

Wrapping my arms around his neck, I pull him back to my lips, needing to breathe him in as much as he needs to breathe me in. Feeling the soft bed beneath me, I expect him to rip my stockings and panties off, instead he pulls his lips from mine and a soft whimper of protest leaves my lips.

"I need this slow, Babe and you're still recovering so, I'm in control. I want you to lie there and take everything I have to give you."

"I'm okay."

Shaking his head, he cocks a dark brow. "Trust me babe, you're not ready for hard and fast."

"I do trust you."

Painstakingly slowly, he slides the stockings down my legs, once off he throws them to the floor. Lifting my left leg, he begins a torturous pace with his mouth, placing soft kisses along the inside of my leg. When he reaches my panty covered pussy, his warm breath washes over me, sending shivers racing through me. A soft moan leaves my lips, but he ignores it as his mouth slides back down my left leg. Pausing at my knee, he sucks the skin on the underside into his mouth. My leg tenses as heat rushes to my aching clit.

"X....." comes out on a whimper, but again he ignores my pleas for more.

Lifting my right leg, he repeats the action, setting my blood on fire. When he runs his nose over my covered clit, my head begins to spin. He pushes his hands up under my dress until they engulf my breasts. When he pinches my nipples with his fingers and continues his assault on my clit with his nose, my back bows off the bed. My mouth opens on a silent scream as my muscles tense, waiting for the fall to happen, but before I can get there he pulls away.

"Please," I whimper.

His fingers slide back down my body leaving goosebumps in their wake. When he reaches my panties, he grips the sides of the lace material and slowly pulls them down my legs. Sliding up my body once again, he pushes my dress to my waist as he goes. His mouth lands on my neck and I turn my head, giving him all the room he needs. I moan as his tongue slides down along my collarbone. My hips puch upward and I feel his hard cock rub against my aching clit. I gasp when the metal hoop from his piercing catches my clit sending a whole new sensation racing through me.

There's something sexy about us both being fully clothed as he enters me in one smooth, agonisingly slow thrust and I buck my hips, needing the friction against my clit. With one of his large hands wrapped through the strands of my hair and the other pinning my hip down to the bed, he's completely stopping my movements. A soft whine escapes my lips before his mouth covers mine in a quick kiss, effectively silencing me. I stop trying to move against him and lock my gaze with his.

"I need you," he grits out between clenched teeth, proving how much control he has and how close he is to shattering it.

"I need you too," I managed to respond as he flexes inside me and my body begins to hum.

Cupping my hands against his face, my nails rake through his now neatly trimmed beard and without breaking eye contact with him, I roll my hips the best I can while he's still pinning me to the bed. His head falls forward, his warm breath coats my face and his eyes stay locked with mine as a single tear rolls down his cheek. I lean forward and lap it up with my tongue before it has time to drop off his chin.

"Help me breathe," he whispers.

His words are so raw they cause tears to spring to my eyes. Slowly he begins to thrust, moulding our bodies together like a well-rehearsed slow dance. This isn't a race to the finish, this is us letting go of the hurt we've been through in the past week and melding our hearts back together, repairing the cracks which could have torn us apart but instead brought us closer together.

"Love me," I gasp out as my body arches on the cusp of what could only be described as pure ecstasy.

"For a lifetime," he chokes out on a deep growl, pushing as deep as he can go before letting go sending my body into a soul shattering climax.

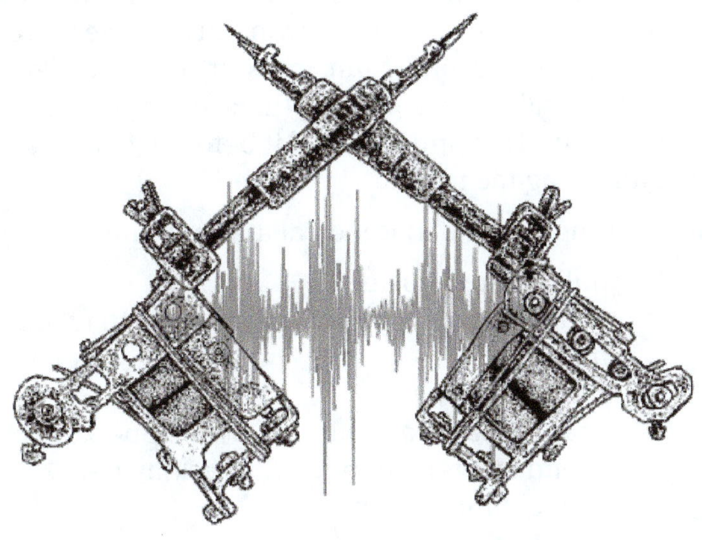

CHAPTER TWENTY-SEVEN

Xavier

The moment the town car pulls into the long driveway and slows to a stop in front of the open doors of the little chapel at Lake Macquarie Memorial Park, my heart squeezes as if caught in a vice. Sweat forms on my brow at the thought of getting out of the car. Stepping out makes it all too real, I can no longer pretend it's all a bad dream that I'll eventually wake up from. Fuck, how I wish this was just a bad, fucking dream. Blowing out a shaky breath, I squeeze my eyes shut as images of my mother's face slam into me, one after the other. My mouth dries, throat closes and I can't seem to swallow the dryness away. It's the same feeling I had when I woke up this morning. From the minute my feet touched the floor, I felt like I was stumbling and trying not to trip over invisible lines. I don't think I have ever felt so off center in my life. It was as if one more wrong move and my already flaky heart was gonna shred into tiny pieces. Every breath was like a shard of glass tearing through my throat, my eyes burned from forcing the tears back. It became worse the second I put my suit on. I felt like I was suffocating, the walls were closing in around me. I needed something to ground me and I needed it before I let the raw grief swamp me and drag me under.

Everything became methodical at that point:

- pull on boxer briefs.
- shirt on, takes forever to button with trembling fingers.
- roll on socks.
- drag on pants and fumble with zipper and button.
- spend an eternity tying the fucking tie.
- slip feet into shoes.
- shrug on jacket.

It had seemed to take hours as I'd struggled to ready myself and had turned into a battle I was sure I didn't want to fight. All I'd really wanted to do was crawl into bed and hold Ally in my arms until the pain went away.

Now, I'm here and I know I have to get out of the car. I'm not even sure my shaky legs have the strength to keep me upright. I fist my trembling hands on my thighs, needing a few moments to compose myself.

Warmth engulfs both of my hands, offering a promise of support, security. Peeling my eyes open, I look down to see Ally's small hands folded over mine. With that one simple touch, air gushes from me and I'm grounded in the moment. Knowing I have her by my side makes everything a little more bearable.

Stepping from the car, I button my jacket and pull the sunglasses down over my eyes. I suck in a deep breath, the surrounding chill a welcome respite from the stuffiness of the car. I glance around at all the people who are gathered, but don't take in their faces, it's all just a blur.

I reach out to help Ally from the car and fix her black shawl in place as it falls over her shoulders. Dad steps from the car on the other side and comes around to join us.

"Good to hear they're playing one of your mother's favorite songs," dad husks out while looking at the ground and before taking a few deep breaths.

Honestly, I didn't even notice. Turning slightly towards the door, I hear *A Thousand Years* by *Christina Perri* floating on the air. My mum loved the *Twilight* series and when this song was released, before she became sick, whenever it came on the radio, my father would dance with her around the kitchen. Mum loved to cook and ninety percent of the time, the kitchen was where you'd find her.

Ally grips my hand tight in hers and I realise my breaths are coming in heavy pants so, I concentrate on her touch and draw strength from it to calm my breathing. Flicking my eyes around, I notice the people gathered here have their heads lowered as if they're remembering a time with my mum and my heart does some funny shit in my chest.

The town car pulls away and a pristine white hearse pulls in at a slow crawl. The blue sky, the people, the music - all fade into a blur as the back door opens. I know it's my cue to step up but my feet feel like they're cemented to the ground. Releasing my hand, Ally presses a soft kiss to my cheek.

"You've got this, Baby," she whispers before stepping to my father's side and taking his hand in hers. Biting my quivering lip, I prepare to move when I feel hands hit my back. I'm so focused on mum's casket, I don't realise Beau and Justin have stepped up to my side. A few of my dad's fire buddies step up to the back of the car. With a little help from Beau, we take the steps separating us from the back of the car. Each man lines up and the pure white casket is slid from the hearse into our hands. I grip the gold handle and the smell of mum's favorite lavender flowers mixed with white roses hits my nose. My head spins with memories I thought were locked deep down for now. But the instant the smell hits my nostrils, my fragile mind is assaulted with sweet memory after sweet memory of a woman who made me into the man I am today - strong and loyal. Sucking in a lungful of air and with my boys by my side, I carry my mother – the woman who held me for so many years, on her final walk in this world as the final lyrics of *Let her Go by Passenger* floats from the chapel. One step at a time, one foot in front of the other are the words I repeat to myself as we carry her from the car to the chapel entrance. People whose lives she touched in some way are all here. Dad's firehouse crew stand a guard of honor as we breach the entrance. I look at the long walk way and pray my legs can carry us both up to the small table she will sit upon for the duration of the service.

I snatch a quick look back to see Ally behind us, her arm wrapped tightly around his waist. His body is hunched, pain and loss rolling off his tired frame in waves. Mum was his world. His life.

Donald, the Funeral Director, begins to speak but I tune out what he is saying. I'm not able to turn my mind completely off and hear soft cries as they echo off the high vaulted ceiling. They are like wrecking balls going off inside my head, pounding away. My eyes sting from staring at the wall ahead, willing the tears not to fall.

"Emily left a message for her loved ones," Donald murmurs into the microphone, his words capture my attention.

"As you know Emily suffered from Alzheimer's and before she lost herself completely, she wanted to leave something behind for the one's she loved most of all."

Shuffling papers around, he blows out a steady breath while a white screen descends from the ceiling behind the coffin. On pressing a button on the remote control in his hand, my mother's sweet voice flows through the speakers scattered above us. A photo appears on the screen, it's of the three of us smiling at the camera. I remember the photo – mum's brother had taken it when we were visiting him in Queensland one summer before he passed away. I would have been about seventeen years old at the time.

"If tomorrow you wake without me, know that no matter what, I will always be shining down on you. I'd like for your memories of me to be happy ones. Smile when the sorrow hits. Lift your face towards the sun and feel the warmth. If it's raining, lose yourself to the simple drops. Be thankful to everyone you encounter and love those closest to you for you never know when your time will be done. Cherish the simple things and guard those which are sacred to your heart. Find that one love, your true soul mate who both pushes and savors you and hold on with both hands."

Photo after photo fade in and out. Family. Friends. Vacations. Christmas mornings. Birthdays.

"To my son - I watched you grow and wished every day you would slow down so I could hold on just little bit longer. Just as the seasons changed far too quickly, before I knew it, right before my eyes my little boy had grown into a strong loyal man. I'm so very proud of you. Always remember, no matter where your path leads you in life, you are stronger than you believe. Mother's hold their children's hands for a short time but we hold them in our hearts forever. My son, I am so thankful that my heart held you in it for a lifetime."

I swallow down a deep breath as tears stream unchecked over my cheeks., Ally's warm hand keeps me grounded in the moment as the video continues to play. Photos from our life together fade in and out as my mum's voice sounds out clear.

"My husband. My best friend. My soulmate. From teenagers to adults, our love withstood the test of time. I knew, no matter what, I would always love you. I cherished every moment I had with you. In the dark it was your smile, our dreams, our life together which pulled me back to you. I realised

I was falling and I knew I had to do this one thing for you to hold onto forever. I know, even at my worst, your love, strength and desire will never waiver."

There was a short pause before she continued.

"Before I slide away completely, I want you to know, I saw in your eyes how much you missed the old me. I heard your words when you sat with me and told me stories of our love. Our son. You always had me wanting more – wanting to remember. I would smell your scent before you even entered the room and smile because I knew you would hold me. Read to me. Show me how very much you loved me. So today, I leave you, my husband, with these words....."

Tears streamed from my eyes and when I glanced around, there wasn't a dry eye to be seen.

"I want, no *need* you to know, I have always loved you with all my heart and I will miss you every day until you're back in my arms again. When you feel sad, cry – for the tears which creep down your cheeks will become mine and I will rid you of the sadness. When you're happy, the warm feeling you have will be me holding you close. When you're alone in the dark of night and a warm breeze kisses your cheeks, it will be me hugging you. Our story will live on in you until the time comes for you to join me. Until then, my love will be with you, guiding you from above. Your Emily. Your forever. Your Wife."

A picture fades in of my parents on their wedding day. It's a shot which was taken from off to one side, without them knowing. It's natural, beautiful. My dad's arms are wrapped around mum's waist and he's staring down at her with so much love and adoration in his eyes. Mum is facing the setting sun, a peaceful look on her face and a smile curving her lips. The sunset of oranges, reds and purples blankets around them.

After a moment when only soft crying can be heard, Donald speaks again.

"Xavier, Emily's son would like to share with you now."

Squeezing Ally's hand one more time, I gather the strength to stand.

On shaky legs, I make my way to the dais.

Blowing out a deep breath, I pull a sheet of paper from my suit jacket and with trembling hands, place it on the stand in front of me.

"My mother's soul was beautiful and wherever a beautiful soul has been there is a trail of the most beautiful memories. Those memories are all my father and I have left to cling to. Losing a mother, a wife, is well it's permanent and inexpressible. It's a wound that will never quite heal. Time will allow it to fade. Days will carry on. The nights will fall and the stars will dance in the sky. Me? I'll continue to be here in the fog of loss, like a cold blanket wrapped around me. Forever longing to look into her crystal blue eyes, to hear her telling me everything will be okay. Never will I watch a smile break out like pure sunshine across her face, filling me with comfort. I will never again hold her hand, feel the warmth of her touch or have her hug me. Hear her sweet voice which danced over me like the sun on the crystal calm of a blue lake. You will leave here today and your life will carry on. She touched all of you in some way or you wouldn't be here but she loved my dad and I more than breathing. Now we have to learn to breathe without her, to wake in the morning and find ways to move through the empty day which was always filled with her being a mother and a wife. She was always there - in the dark when, as a 4-year-old boy, a nightmare took up space inside my dreams. When, as a 10-year-old boy, I grazed my knees learning how to skateboard. Then, as an 18-year-old young man who had his first taste of love and heartbreak. She was always there to hold me. Kiss me. Take away the fears, the pain, the tears. A lifetime she was my strength, my light and my life. A lifetime which was far too short. I regret that it took me so long to find what her and my father have, a deep love where just looking at that person takes your breath away. I hate that a disease took her memory before I could introduce her to the woman I have fallen in love with. The woman who loves me unconditionally. I will take my mother and all our memories with me as I travel throughout the rest of my days. I will strive to show those I encounter, some of the love she showed me. The world will be dimmer, maybe a little bitter and colder than when my mother was in it. My mother – my first love."

Biting my lip, I pause for a moment and lock eyes with Ally as she rubs dad's back. Silent tears stream down her cheeks, but with a small nod of encouragement from her to keep going, I blow out another breath. Gripping the stand in front of me, I steady myself.

"Today, I'll hold my head high knowing she taught me how to be the man I have become. She showed me right from wrong, held my hand and picked me back up when I fell. Today is a day I fall but tomorrow I will get back up even stronger, knowing she taught me how. Even on her weakest days she held her head high, pushed harder and continued to smile. I remember her telling me, the best thing in life was finding that one love who could help me overcome any obstacle. To always live for today and reach for my dreams. I have always lived by her words so, today I stand before you a better man because I had her love and guidance. I have said goodbye a thousand different times and ways in my life, but this is by far the hardest goodbye I have ever had to say. So, today I won't say goodbye. I refuse to utter the word and I will end this by saying – Mum, you were one in a million and will forever live on in my heart. Until I see you again, know that even in death, you will never be forgotten. I love you, Mum."

Folding the paper in my hand, I take the two steps separating me from the coffin.

Thick tears fall free as I place my hand against the cool wood - *Close your Eyes* by *Michael Bublé* floats around me.

I stood watching as people who cared about my mother approached her coffin and placed flowers on the wooden top. Pulling dad and I into their arms, kissing our cheeks and saying, "I'm so sorry for your loss" and "She was beautiful, so beautiful."

I feel numb, she was my mother and now I have to live without her. I'm battling to go through the motions of being polite before they file from the chapel. Sun's rays filter through the pretty stained-glass windows to illuminate the coffin and it seems so appropriate. I run my fingers over the small buds of flowers which cascade over the side of the coffin in a rainbow of colours

My memory drifts to a time when, as a child I was in the garden with my mother helping her to cut flowers which she'd arrange in vases throughout our home. Her fingers would entwine with mine as we walked back to the house, the sun shining down on her, lighting her up like the angel she was.

I'm startled when my father places his hand on my back.

"Sorry son, it's time."

My father's voice breaks as he tells me we now have to carry her from this room, filled with so much light from the heavens above and take her to a much smaller one. The time has come to truly say goodbye.

Sucking in a lungful of air, I hold it until the burn hits my lungs and my body screams at my brain to breathe. I welcome the pain, it reminds me I'm fucking human and life hurts.

My boys flank me, our hands find the gold handles of her coffin and we lift her up. Leaning down slightly, we lift her high onto our shoulders, our arms linking over each other's. I grip Beau's shoulder tight as my arm begins to shake and he squeezes mine in return. Bracing the coffin on our shoulders, our free hands hold her in place, her final ride high on the men who loved her almost as much as we did.

The doors to the small cremation room open, this room is filled with vase upon vase of mum's favorite flowers. The scent is intoxicating. A deep sob wracks my body and shaking slightly, my knees buckle. Dad is at my side in a heartbeat, helping to hold me up and carry the greatest love of our lives to the small table which will soon lower her into the floor and away from us forever. We place her down gently, deep exhales are echoed around the room and tears are wiped away.

Donald arrives and stands at the head of my mother's coffin, his eyes red rimmed. He'd been fond of my mother so this day has taken its toll on him also. So much love laced with a deep sadness seeped from the walls of the chapel and here in this small space, you can feel it almost suffocating you.

My father's hand finds mine, as does Ally's and we take the few small steps between us and the coffin. Falling to my knees, my father mirrors my movements. Our heads bow onto the coffin, the white awash with colour from the flowers and the sweet smell taking us back to a time when it was the three of us. A time when we were happy and not broken with loss. Closing my eyes, my lips find the cool wood as a soft soothing instrumental melody plays out around us. Ally lowers to my other side, her hand lands on my thigh as my boys' hands find my shoulders. I reach for my father's hand to find it shaking violently. Holding it tight, I whisper in a broken voice, "You ready, Pops?"

I swallow around the lump in my throat and wait for him to respond. I suspect he is fighting a battle in his head as I am in mine. He blows out a shaky breath before answering.

"As ready as I'll ever be." His voice cracks on a sob.

I kiss mum one last time, the cool wood sending a chill sliding down my spine. I nod to Donald and close a hand over Ally's warm hand on my thigh. Beau and Justin grip my shoulders. I hear soft cries and gasping breaths which I suspect are from Erica and Cynthia on the other side of the room. I try to block out the sound, locking my eyes back on the glossy white coffin in front of me. The soothing music runs through me as my eyelids sit at half-mast. Silent tears spill down my cheeks and the coffin begins to slowly lower down into the floor taking fractured shards of my heart with it.

I'll miss you mum.

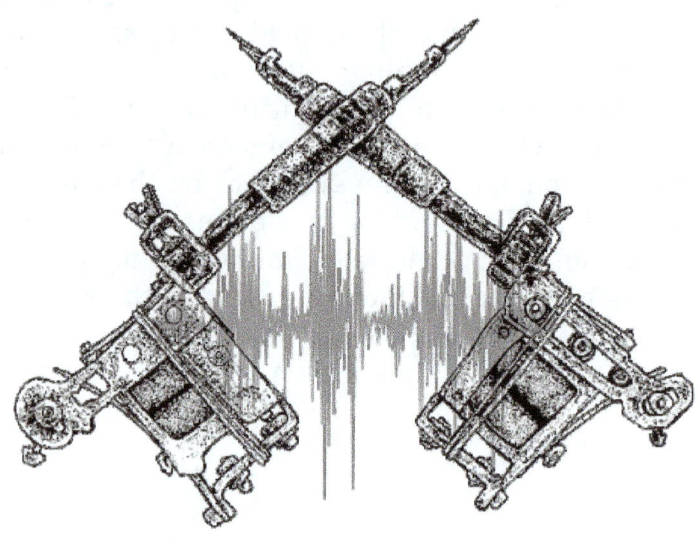

CHAPTER TWENTY-EIGHT

Ally

The drinks are flowing and music is blasting from the sound system which Justin has set up on Jim's - Xavier's dad's back verandah. Stories are being told, laughed and cried over, one after the other. My heart is still heavy for the man I love. That's the funny thing about grief, it comes in waves - one minute you can be fine, going about your normal day. Then, it can slam into you like a semi-truck knocking you to the ground and leaving you gasping for breath. Begging the earth to stand still, if only for a moment so, you can breathe again. I know this feeling well. For four years I have lived with it and each passing day the birds still sing, the wind still sways from left to right but nothing is ever the same again.

Today I watched my man bare his soul and crumble to his knees. I had no pretty words to tell him that it would all be okay, no false reassurances that his life will continue moving. Words are wasted in this particular instance, right now they mean nothing. They're another kick to the guts, reminding you over and over again that life will never be the same again.

The sun will be dimmer, the grass a little less green and you try to draw strength from everything and everyone around you just so you can open your eyes each morning. I look around the backyard, the late afternoon sun splashes golden rays of light around us, but I can't stop the gloomy feeling which settles deep in my belly.

Today brought back so many memories, it was hard to keep my tears in check. I didn't get to say a proper goodbye to my dad, my bitch of a mother made sure of that when she decided to have my father cremated while I was still in the hospital recovering. When I was finally released, she told me he was safe away from me where I couldn't hurt him anymore.

A muffled sob tears from my throat as tears ghost down my face. I place my plastic cup on the ground beside my chair and release Xavier's hand. Keeping my head bowed, I make my way towards the backdoor of the house, wringing my fingers so tight they begin to sting. Heading into the kitchen, I grab some paper towel from the roll on the wall near the fridge and wipe the tears from my face. My vision is blurred as I stare off into space. My breath hitches as more thick tears roll down my face. My chest tightens and shoulders heave as I sob. I need space. I need to breathe. I need air but I don't want to return to the backyard. Sucking down a shaky breath, I dash for the front door. I need a few moments alone to clear my head. Xavier has had enough to deal with today without me burdening him with my mini meltdown.

I push through the doorway; the sun has dropped lower in the sky and the moon has begun to appear. I watch as the sun's rays kiss the ocean and breathe in the salty air. X's parent's house is nothing like I expected, not that I'd really thought about it much. The home sits on top of a hill overlooking Merewether beach. It's a beautiful three bedroom, two storey home with glass walls facing the ocean. When we first pulled up to the front I was speechless. It's nothing like my mother's house which lies behind a false facade of happiness when what it really is, is a house of horrors.

Wrapping my arms around my waist, I take the few steps down to the path which leads to the road. Crossing the street, I stand at the top of the hill and stare down at the calming water, watching as small waves crash on the shore. Closing my eyes, I tilt my chin up to the sky, take in a deep breath and let it out slowly. Rolling my shoulders, I let the peaceful atmosphere soak into every cell of my body.

My tears slow until I have nothing left. My chest feels lighter just being out here. Exhaling another couple of breaths, I crack my eyes open to see the sun dip below the water, leaving nothing but the rising moon and a slight glow across the sky. Stars begin to spring free against the clear night sky and my eyes begin to make patterns with them like dot-to-dot. I smile as I remember doing this with my dad.

Heated breath brushes my neck as strong arms wrap around my waist. X places a soft kiss behind my ear sending heat rushing through me and making me hum. I bring my hands up to rest against his. Not a word is spoken. Only the pressure of his chin resting on my head reminds me he's with me and without even knowing it, he was exactly what I needed right now. Just being cocooned in his warm arms has me melting into him as we stand looking up at the stars dancing in the sky above. After what feels like forever, his deep whispered voice floats around me.

"We have this."

I nod my head against his chest.

"I just needed to breathe," I whisper.

His body tenses against mine for a moment before relaxing again.

"If you need to breathe, you come to me," he whispers.

"I didn't want to bother you." I lower my eyes to the ground, I really did want to go to him but didn't want to make tonight about me. Before I can explain, he swings me around in his hold and my breath catches in my throat as the moonlight catches the intensity of his ocean blue eyes.

"You need to fucking breathe, you find me."

There is so much emotion in his voice, it sucks the air from my lungs. All I can do after a silent standoff where his eyes flicker over every inch of my face, I nod. His face softens and leaning down, he brushes his lips over mine before turning me around so my back presses against his muscled chest.

"Right now, this moment with you in my arms, is all that matters,." he breathes into the top of my head. We stand for a little while longer and I notice a shooting star. Raising my hand, I point to it and watch as it fades into the inky black night.

"We should make a wish," I murmur, not wanting to break our moment.

"Nah, Babe." X sighs and waves his hand across the sky to indicate the rest of the stars.

My brows crease, wondering what he is trying to tell me. I don't have to wait long for an explanation and when it comes, I fall in love with him a little bit more.

"Why waste a wish on a dying star when there is a whole sky full of live ones. Pick one. Shit, pick each and every one of them, it won't matter. You could toss a penny in a well or blow on a dandelion. At the end of the day, they either fade, get lost or blow away. So, if you want to wish, wish upon the silver moon. Even though it eventually fades to allow for the daylight to come, it will always come back."

Those words, his whispered voice, heated breath against my ear, has goosebumps spreading across my skin like wildfire and tears spring to my eyes.

"I love you," I get out on a hitched breath.

"I love you too, Sweetness."

He kisses the side of my head and I burrow deeper into his hold, needing every part of me connected to him.

"If you wanna, let's do it, but I don't need to make a wish. I already have all I'll ever want and need in my arms."

Damn, this man. Soft tears ghost down the side of my face.

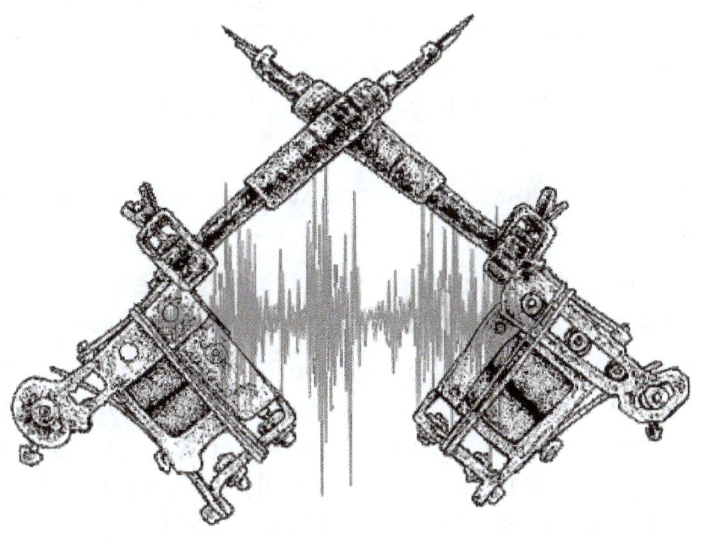

CHAPTER TWENTY-NINE

Xavier

Gazing up at the infinite stars blanketed by the night sky with Ally in my arms has to be one of the most peaceful moments of my life. I wasn't lying when I said I had everything I needed right here. Everything I've worked so hard for in my life -my business, my apartment, my truck, it could all be gone tomorrow, but as long as I have Ally in my arms it wouldn't matter. From the first moment I saw her I knew she was special but never in my life did I ever think I would get to be a part of her life. If Beau or Justin had told me months ago that this is where my life would lead me, I would have laughed in their faces and told them to fuck off. I never wanted to be tied down. I always thought I wasn't meant to feel this kind of love but now that I have it, I wouldn't trade it for the world.

Pushing a hand into my pants pocket I grab my phone and flick through the apps until I find what I'm looking for. With one arm still wrapped tight around my girl, I turn her to face me, click on my music app and hit 'play' on the song I want. The silence disappears around us as the first bars of *Say You Won't Let Go* by *James Arthur* breaks through the tranquility of the moment.

"What are you doing?" she whisper's, her eyes shining with unshed tears.

"Dance with me, under the stars." I shove my phone into the breast pocket of my dress shirt so we can still hear the music.

Wrapping my arms back around her waist, I pull her in tight, her body moulding into mine perfectly. Swaying from side to side, I bury my head into the top of her hair and breathe in her sweet apple scent. Her hands slowly slide up my chest and wrap around my neck. For three minutes and thirty seconds we were lost in each other, just feeling. We let everything go and stayed in the moment with each other. Feeling a wetness against my shirt, I pull back mesmerized as her glistening evergreen eyes gaze into mine. She blows out a choppy breath and it hits my neck as she fights the tears threatening to fall. A few seconds later, she loses the battle and soft tears flow down her heat blushed cheeks. Dropping her chin, she tries to shy away so I don't see, but I'm not having any of it. Reaching out, I place my fingers softly under her chin tilting her face up to mine.

"Don't hide your tears from me, Sweetness. They make you human. Each salty tear that trickles down your face makes you who you are and you're amazing. When you cry, I get to see a little bit more of you and I savor those moments. To me, you could never be anything but divine."

I tuck a loose tendril of hair behind her ear, her eyes glittering with an emotion so intense it shakes my soul. She rises up on her tiptoes and I lean down to brush my lips over hers before slowly moving her away. A look of confusion crosses her face but quickly vanishes when I twirl her around before bringing her back into my arms. Her chin rests on my chest and she peers up at me through her lashes, the glow from the moon making her gold hue shine like the sun. Sliding her hands around my neck, she gently strokes her nails up and down causing goosebumps to break out. When I plant a soft kiss to her nose, it scrunches under my touch because of my beard.

"You shine brighter than any star, Baby," I whisper once the song fades and the silence returns. "The first time I saw you, I had to catch my breath. The minute I touched you, I wanted to savor it - not knowing when the next time would come. You are everything I never knew I wanted and so much more. Now I can't breathe without you." I blow out a deep breath and two simple, but powerful, words slip from my lips as my heart echoes in my ears. "Marry me," I husk out.

This may not be the perfect time, I don't even have a ring, but something about this moment is so perfect. I don't think I could have planned anything more romantic than this, right here, right now, under the silver glow of the moon as the waves crash against the rocks below us. Staring into my eyes, I hear the hitch in her breath as she nods her head, but I need to hear the words. Running my hand down the side of her face, I rest my palm against her cheek. Her eyes flutter close at my touch. Seeming to snap her out of her head, she plants a small kiss into the palm of my hand. Her warm palm lays across my hand on her cheek, holding it there as her eyes stare into mine.

"Yes." Her voice cracks and after clearing her throat, her voice is stronger. "Yes. Yes. Yes."

Before she can say anything else, I slam my mouth down on hers, wanting to soak this moment into my body. Pulling back from the kiss, my chest warms as I watch her eyes flutter open and a shy smile curl her lips.

"I don't have a ring." Looking up to the sky, I husk out an embarrassed laugh.

I always knew I would ask her, but I'd planned to have it all set up properly when I did. Laughing, she cups my face and draws me down to her again. I'm only inches from her and my eyes lock onto the evergreen eyes which stole my soul.

"I don't need a ring, I just need you."

She leans forward, closing the gap between our mouths and kisses me with so much hunger my already hard cock pushes against the zipper of my suit pants. I pull back, needing to get my shit under control.

"We need to stop, before I fuck you into the ground," I grit out between clenched teeth.

Peeking over each of my shoulders, a mischievous smile takes over her mouth.

"I'm game." She reaches behind her and unzips her dress. "I always wanted to make love under the stars." She kicks her shoes off as she struggles to pull down her dress.

Fuck. "I don't want to hurt you and right now my control is pretty thin," I warn.

"You won't," she cocks a perfect brow, daring me to argue with her.

Fisting my hands at my sides, I open my mouth to object when she cuts me off with that sass I have missed so much in the past week.

"Either fuck me or stand there and watch me pleasure myself."

"Like fuck," I grunt, making her laugh. "You'd test the patience of a Saint, Babe." I pick her up by the waist, my control a thing of the past and I slam my mouth down on hers, not giving her a chance to say anything else. Falling to my knees I lay her out on the grass. Her auburn hair scatters around her, the black dress now hanging down near her waist leaving her spectacular bare tits on display, her fair milky skin glowing under the moonlight.

"Fuck it!" I don't bother to strip off.

Reaching down, I slide my zipper down, pop the button and push my boxer briefs down just enough that my hard as fuck cock springs free. The metal piercing surrounded by pre cum, glistens and I'm struggling to stay in control when she begins moaning with want and pinching her hard nipples between her fingers. Gripping her stockings, I rip them down her legs, hearing them tear as I go. Once off, I reach under her dress and snap her flimsy panties off in one quick movement, making her hiss at the action.

"Fuck, X, I need you now." She moans and arches her back, trying to get closer to me.

I run the tips of my fingers over her pussy to make sure she's ready for me. It's my turn to groan at how soft and wet she is. Gripping the base of my cock, I lean forward and grip her hair at the top of her head, firmly holding her to the ground. In one heated rush, I slam into her soaking pussy. Holding still for a moment, I soak in the feeling of her wrapped tight around me. My eyes roll back in my head as her moans bounce around me.

"This is going to be hard and fast, Sweetness."

I pull back before pushing back in on a groan.

"Oh God, yes," she moans.

She grips my shoulders and through the thin layer of my shirt, I feel her nails bite into the muscles of my back, making me grunt.

"What did I tell you to say when I'm inside you?" I ground out behind clenched teeth while slamming into her again and again.

Leaning down, my teeth latch onto her nipple, applying a little pressure. Her hips pick up speed, meeting me at every thrust.

"Xavier!" she screams before I cover her mouth with mine, not needing anyone to come out here and see my woman losing herself.

I growl into our kiss as her pussy contracts around my cock, coating it in her warm release. It's enough to have me losing my load. Tiny shocks shoot down my back as my balls draw up and I explode. Black dots swim across my vision as our panting breaths break through the otherwise silent night.

"I love you," I breathe out once I get my bearings back

"I love you, too," she gasps.

I roll over onto my back, taking her with me and we lie panting in an effort to recapture our breath.

Laying in the crook of my arm, her warm breath slides down my neck as we gaze up to the night sky. "We should go back." Ally's whisper disturbs the tranquility of the moment as she snuggles deeper into my side.

Pulling her closer, I lean down and kiss the crown of her head breathing in her sweet apple scent, not taking my eyes from the stars.

"In a minute," I murmur, not ready to move just yet. I feel content for the first time in what feels like weeks.

Laying her head back against my chest, her fingernails dance up and down my shirt covered abs, causing my muscles to jump and tense at the feather light touch. Angry voices from across the road penetrate the quiet and we sit up to look around. It's too dark to see anything, the only light is coming from the front of dad's house. I turn to Ally, making sure her clothes are back in order and chuckle when she holds up her torn panties. Reaching out, I grab them and stuff them into my pocket along with her stockings.

"Lucky it's not too cool tonight." She shrugs.

"I'll warm you up, Babe," I reassure her.

"I bet," she murmurs as she pushes to her feet and smooths her hands over her dress in an attempt to shift the dirt and grass. Standing above me, with the moon shining behind her in a halo effect, has my heart doing some funny shit inside my chest, knowing this woman is mine.

"You ready?" Her voice breaks into my thoughts, she stretches her hand out to help me up.

"Yeah, I guess." Gripping her small hand, in mine I push to my feet without allowing her to wear the brunt of my weight. Before she can walk away, I pull her into my chest. "We've got this," I murmur into her hair.

"We sure do," she whispers into my neck as the angry voices get louder.

"Shit, that sounds like Beau."

I take Ally's hand in mine and we hurry across the road as Erica's voice echoes off the side of the house. "I can't do this, Beau!"

"What the fuck is going on?"

Ally squeezes my hand when we come to a stop on the footpath in front of dad's house. Erica rushes past us with Beau hot on her heels but I reach out to stop him from following. It's obvious Erica is upset and doesn't want him near her. Thankfully, he doesn't fight me and stays by my side.

Letting go of my hand, Ally takes up the space between her and where Erica is standing next to her car which is parked across the road.

"STOP!" Beau shouts.

"There is nothing left to talk about, Beau." Tears stream over Erica's face.

"I beg to fucking differ!" Beau runs a frustrated hand through his hair.

"I'm sorry, Beau, but you don't know the real me. You think you do but you don't." Blowing out a deep breath, Erica locks eyes with me. There's so much sadness in her eyes. "Thank you for the job, X, but I quit"

"I don't fucking accept!" I'm getting pissed now.

"Ain't fucking happening," Beau spits out as his body tenses beside mine.

"Erica," Ally murmurs.

Erica turns into Ally and wraps her arms around her. They're too far away for me to hear what she whispers against Ally's ear but I see her nod into Erica's shoulder.

"I'll call you later," Erica says to Ally. She gives me a sad smile before turning and getting into her car.

Beau makes a start towards the car then, I hear the squeal of tyres and a set of headlights blind me.

"Fuck!" I shout as the sound of metal hitting metal echoes around the otherwise quiet cul de sac.

High pitched screams ring in my ears and the smell of fuel hits my nose. Erica screams and I can see her trying to get out of the car. I notice the driver's side door is crushed from the impact of hitting the other car which is now flipped over on its roof - half on the hood of Erica's car and half on the road. Smoke wafts around us, coating the cool air with petrol fumes. Not only can I smell the fuel, but also the tang of coolant from probably cracked radiators. Steam billows from under the crumpled hoods, curling into the air. The burnt-chemical smell from the deployed airbags, hits my nose causing my nostrils to flare. But, the most unnerving thing now is the strange silence. It's a piercing sound in my ears, so quiet but yet so loud. The crash was disorienting – loud, so loud. Now, my eyes dart around at all the chaos around me which seems to be happening in slow motion. The impact was severe, extreme and debris is scattered all over this once quite street.

Questions are running through my mind at a million miles an hour as I stand stunned with shock....

Erica?

Beau?

Ally?

Who?

What?

Where?

How?

For the life of me I can't think, is there anyone else? More questions, no answers......

Who was driving the vehicle which was so intent on slamming into us and why?

Is it revenge?

Why is it so dark all of a sudden?

I can't see, buzzing sounds in my ears. My feet are unable to move.

The smell of fuel leaking from the cars doesn't help the situation of me needing to think. I cover my nose in order to breathe properly. Everything is a fucking mess. Erica was screaming in pain, panic and red-hot fear. The blood curdling screams are too much for me to bear, ripping through my skin like a hot poker. With feet feeling like lead, I force myself to take a few steps. Steam mixed with cool air and the bite of chemicals hits me in the face. What causes my heart to thump erratically is the shocking sight of Erica – blood… too much blood. The sheer panic in her eyes. Her skin angry and coated with streaks of fresh blood. So much blood.

I look around for Beau. I know he's here somewhere. He was standing right beside me. Fuck. Scrubbing my hands over my face and up through my hair, I call out in panic. "Beau, where are you, brother?"

I spin around frantically and, in that moment, I see her. Flashbacks of her deathly still body in the hospital assault my mind and I race to where my woman is sitting on the road – all thoughts of leaden feet forgotten. I drop to my knees, the uneven surface of the asphalt biting into the skin and pain spears through me – I don't care. I pull Ally onto my lap and run my hands over her face, checking her features.

"Baby, fuck, where are you hurt? Sweetness, please, look at me."

Her eyes flicker open and I see the pain.

"Arghhhh," she mouths through dry lips.

"Fuck, where are you hurt?" My heart is pleading for her to be okay.

"No, um, no, I don't know?" She gazes at me, disorientated. "Beau? X where's Beau? He saved me, pushed me out of the way. Where is he?" Sheer fucking panic grips her and her eyes shift all around, frantically searching for him. Her fear hits me hard in the chest.

Scanning the area, I finally see him. He's lying on the cold road, as still as stone. My heartrate picks up speed, the thumping banging in my head. I need to go to him, but an internal battle is raging inside me, needing to know my woman is okay first.

"I'll go check on him." I try to hide the panic in my voice.

Sitting up in my lap, she looks around at the chaos around us and a sob tears through her throat.

"I'm okay," she whimpers before moving out of my arms to sit on the grass beside me. "Go, X, help him."

At her words, I snap into action and push up from the ground. As I rush towards Beau, I stumble. My palms hit the asphalt, small stones tearing the skin. I ignore it and move to his side, again dropping to my knees. He's so pale, unmoving. "Oh, fuck no he can't be....." My throat constricts and my attention is drawn to a fire which flickers to life under the hood of one of the mangled cars. At some point, dad's fire buddies have left the house and are shouting out rapid instructions.

Through a hazy blur of shock and disbelief, the faint sound of sirens in the distance causes me to look away from my brother. My eyes lock onto the driver of the other car. Anger rips through my body and my mind is hell bent on justice, I rise to my feet but before I can move towards the car, reach in and rip the person apart, I recognise the driver who has caused all the carnage..... Ally's mother.

"Fuck!" I collapse back to my knees not taking my eyes off her face which is smeared in crimson, her lips a deep shade of purple. A heavy hand hits my shoulder and I know without looking it's my dad. Erica falls to her knees beside me, tears flooding her blood-soaked face. Utter terror sounds in her words. "No. No. NO! Don't do this." She wails and shakes Beau by the shoulders. "Don't you dare leave me too!" she screams while running a shaky hand through his hair.

Her cries shred me like a knife.

"The ambulance is coming, Beau. Please, please, just hold on, damn it." She blows out a hard breath, wiping away the blood which is streaking down the side of her face. "Beau, cut this bullshit out. Please don't give up, Baby. I'm here and I'm not going anywhere, I promise. I'm so sorry I pushed you away."

I look up into my dad's eyes, tears roll from my burning eyes.

"No more death. Please, Pops, no more death," I choke out on a sob.

"Don't touch me!" Erica screams.

One of dad's mates, John, is trying to check the cut on her forehead.

Ally lowers to her knees beside Erica and wraps her arms around her. Erica falls into her embrace and deep wails wrack her body.

"I'm so sorry," Ally whispers while rocking her slightly.

I see her eyes scan the other car, the colour draining from her face when she recognises her mum slumped over the steering wheel.

"This is all my fault." Soft tears roll over Ally's cheeks.

"Fuck, that!" I grunt, pissed she feels the need to take the blame. None of this shit is her fault.

"If it wasn't for me...." she swallows hard. "....none of this would have happened."

"*She* did this, not you," Erica murmurs.

An ambulance screeches to a stop nearby and a flurry of activity surrounds us as paramedics race to where we are, another checks Ally's mother.

"She's dead," he says, sorrow coating his words.

"Good," Ally spits out.

My heart lurches, I'm so fucking happy we don't have to worry about that bitch anymore.

"We have a pulse," the female paramedic examining Beau says. "What's his name?"

"His name is, Beau and I'm going with him." Erica's tone brooks no argument. Dad helps her to her feet and I push to mine before helping Ally to stand.

"Miss, we need to look at your head," the male paramedic insists while he helps place Beau onto the stretcher.

"I'm fine," she murmurs as my father leads her towards the back of the ambulance.

Ally wraps her arms around me, weeping softly into my chest. I hold her tight as my arms begin to shake. Blowing out a rough breath, I savor her touch and close my eyes as the back doors of the ambulance close with a thud.

I open my eyes when a police car pulls in, one of the officer's steps out and hurries to the paramedic who is still with Ally's mum. The other makes his way over to us.

"Can someone fucking look at my girl now," I call out in anger to the paramedic who seems more worried about the dead bitch in the car than he does about Ally. I know I'm not thinking rationally.

"Sir, can you tell me what happened here?" The cop flips open a notebook as the paramedic finally comes over to us.

I grasp my woman tighter to my side and place a single kiss to her forehead while sending a silent prayer to whoever is listening, thanking them that my girl is okay. Now, I need my brother to wake up. If he dies because he chose to save my girl's life, that's a debt I will never be able to repay. Releasing my girl to the care of the paramedic, I turn back to the cop. I'm ready to get this shit done so I can get to the hospital and make sure my brother is alright.

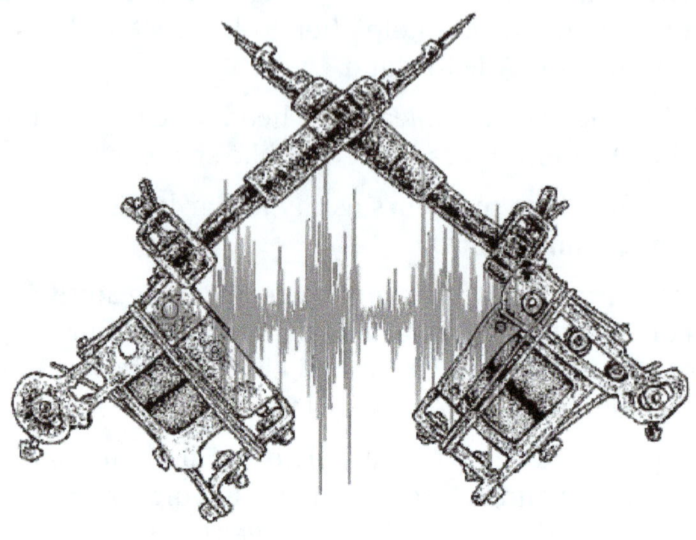

EPILOGUE

One month later...

Ally

"Are you going to tell what your tattoo means, Babe?" X whispers into my ear, his heated breath dulling the chill in the air. With my back moulded to his chest and his arms wrapped tight around my waist, I soak in his touch as the familiar feeling of home settles through me.

"About a week before all hell broke loose, I was at work. Anyways, my boss asked if I could stay back and I forgot to call my dad to let him know. When I finished work, I found a voicemail left by him, he was making sure I was okay. At the end of the message he said, *I love you Buttons.* I was in such a rush to call him back so he wouldn't worry that I completely forgot to delete the message like I usually did. When my dad passed away and I was allowed to go home from the hospital, I took everything I could from the house including my phone." I pause blowing air out through my lips. "The message had sat idle in my mailbox and I didn't have the courage to delete it. Whenever I had bad days, I would listen to it and it hearing his voice helped." I sniff as tears begin to ghost down my cheeks. "When Cynthia told me about her tattoos marking moments through her life that she never wanted to forget, I knew it was what I wanted." I run a hand under my nose. "I have a program on my phone which could show me the sound waves of his voice and when it got to the part I wanted, I took a screenshot and printed it out." I finish and lick my dry lips as X sways us from side to side to a silent melody only he can hear. Our eyes are on the cream coloured rendered wall in front of us where a small gold plaque with my father's name engraved across it is fixed.

After mum died, Xavier and I went to my parent's house and I found my father's ashes. Anger still flashes through me when I remember where I found him - buried at the back of the closet in my mother's room. A few deep breaths and the motion of Xavier swaying us, soothes me. I can focus again and push the anger away, knowing my father is finally at peace. As for anything else in that house, I took some of my father's belongings including his favorite jumper which I sleep in every night. X grumbled at first, stating I should be sleeping in nothing and insisting he was there to keep me warm. He understands that I feel closer to my dad when I wear it though. Along with the jumper, I also found some old photo albums filled with pictures of him and me together. The albums now sit on a huge new bookshelf X bought me, it takes up a whole wall in his apartment....I mean our apartment. Since the moment I was released from hospital, I have only returned to my place to pick up my stuff. Xavier insisted it was best for him to have me in his space and since I'd agreed to marry him, we should be living together. Honestly, who was I to argue with his logic if it meant I got to sleep in his arms every night?

As for my parent's house, X helped me put it on the market. It was a day of mixed emotions but the good memories I had from living there are overshadowed by all the bad ones and as X said, no matter what, I will always have those special memories with me.

When X's dad found out we were engaged he was so happy. I think it took away some of his pain and it was nice to see him smile a genuine smile. He gave X shit for not having a ring to give me and told me I could probably do better. X grumbled at his father's shit-stirring. I smile and glance down at my ring, it's absolutely breathtaking and it means everything to me. It's a beautiful gold band with a huge princess cut diamond in the center and two rows of encrusted diamonds flow down the sides. X surprised me with it three weeks ago. Just thinking about the morning he gave it to me sends heat rushing through my body

"Are you okay, Sweetness?" X asks, leaning his chin on my head.

"I'm perfect." I grip his hands with mine across my belly as butterflies swarm my stomach.

"Are you nearly ready to leave?" He plants a kiss to my temple, making me shiver.

"In a minute. Do you mind if we take a seat for a minute?" I point to a wooden bench seat near the small pond, smiling when I notice a couple of brown ducks diving down into the water.

"Are you still not feeling good?" Worry laces his tone as he takes my hand and leads me to the bench, but instead on letting me sit beside him, he pulls me onto his lap and wraps his arms around me.

"I'm okay." I rest my head on his shoulder as a deep rumble vibrates in my ear, he's not happy with my answer.

"X?"

"Yes, Sweetness?"

"I love you."

"I love you too, Babe."

"We've got this, haven't we?" I run my nails over his chest, loving the feel of his muscles jumping beneath my touch.

"What's going on, Babe?" I hear the concern in his words.

Lifting my head, I cup his cheeks in my hands, sidetracked a little when the sun catches my ring. I tilt my head, waiting for his answer.

"Yeah, Babe we've got this, now tell me what's wrong." He gives my hips a little squeeze which draws my attention and I lock my gaze with his ocean blue eyes, the same blue eyes which calm me and make me feel whole.

"I'm pregnant," I rush out before biting my lip as the silence lingers between us. After what feels like an eternity but was only mere seconds, his blue eyes seem to shine and he finally speaks.

"Fuck, yeah!" Gripping the sides of my face, his mouth slams down hard on mine, stealing my breath as we pour everything we have into the kiss. Our eyes stay locked on each other.

My story isn't a perfect one but it's mine. I no longer live with the guilt which once consumed me over a past I couldn't change. Pulling back from the kiss, I run my thumbs under his eyes and feel his thumbs doing the same to mine.

"You are my world, the reason I can breathe each day." He wraps me in his arms and his hands land protectively over my stomach as I burrow into his chest and rest my head against his shoulder again.

"You are my home, you brought me back to life," I murmur, resting my hands over his which are protecting the small miracle growing inside me. Closing my eyes, I vow to love our baby with everything that I am. I promise, when the time comes. I will share the story of when mummy found her wings and was finally able to breathe again.

...So, for now, this is The End, but it's also a brand New Beginning.

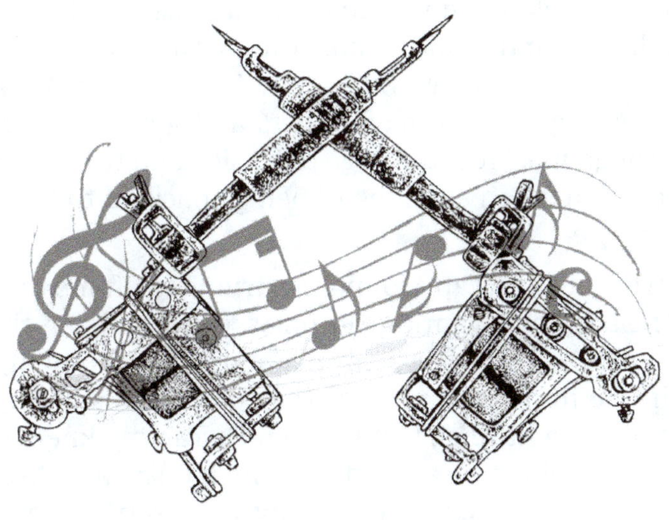

THE PAST

Bracing my palms down against the smooth wooden surface, I take a shaky breath as the words of *Little Wonders* by *Rob Thomas* plays above me. I try to drown it out, but I feel it right to my soul as my heart splits into pieces. I don't think the pieces will ever fit back together again.

"I will always love you," I choke out.

Bending forward, I graze my lips over the cool wooden casket. Breathing in deep through my nose, I try to take one last breath of him inside me, but all I smell are the roses surrounding me. A chill takes over my body and I'm left feeling as cold as stone. Closing my eyes, I try to block everything out. I'm hoping when I open my eyes that I'll find this has been a nightmare and everything will be back to the way they were a week ago. A time when we were happy and in love, excited about taking the next step into our life together.

Feeling my legs wobble, I try to lock my knees together so I don't crumple to the ground. It's no use and I feel myself start to fall. My hands slide against the wood, I have nothing left. I feel myself fading away and I allow it to happen. What's the point in fighting? My stomach twists and gut-wrenching sobs wrack through me. I feel the urge to be sick and try to ignore my bodies reaction when a feeling of being shackled to the ground comes over me.

Strong arms wrap around me, trying to lift me to my feet. I push them away, wanting no-one's touch. I hear the deep soothing voice of my father in my ear and after a moment, I allow him to lift me into his arms. He cradles me to his chest like he did when I was a little girl and I would scrap my knee. But this time I know he won't be able to take the pain away. I breathe in his familiar woodsy smell and allow it to settle deep inside, hoping it can reach into some of the cool places inside me to warm them. Even if it's a wasted effort, I'll try anything right now to feel something......anything rather than nothing at all.

"I've got you, Sweetheart," he whispers in my ear as he rubs his hand in soothing circles over my back.

I lift my arms and wrap them around his neck and cry hard. I know, no matter what anybody says or does, I will never be the same again.

Can someone so Perfect heal someone so Broken????

Inked Perfection

Coming in late 2018

KAY MAREE
INKED
Perfection
Inked Series Book Two